Undead Cheesehead
Monsters in the Midwest, Book Three

Scott Burtness

FREE Short Story

Get *Five Stars*, a FREE demonic horror comedy short story, when you sign up for **The Paranomedy Pint**, Scott's once-a-month email featuring a great book to read, a fun show to watch, something terrific to drink, and a little paranormal weirdness to enjoy!!

For Liz.

My love for you is undead. Dying. I meant undying.

Contents

It Had to Start Somewhere...

T HE *TABANUS SUDETICUS* FOLLOWED the scent of decaying flesh through an open window and into the confines of a box-shaped world. It had no thoughts, no plans, no aspirations. Those were the burdens of more evolved creatures. Only one desire occupied the tiny ganglion of nerves that served as the horsefly's brain. It was time to feed.

The densely packed olfactory nerves of its antennae twitched and sent it circling down until it landed on a patch of jaundiced skin. Serrated mandibles began to saw back and forth. When viscous blood welled up, the fly's labium extended to soak up the precious fluid.

Something in the blood aggravated the fly. After scrubbing at its eyes and mouth, it took to the air and buzzed angrily back and forth across the room. Again, it tried to feed. Again, the blood's strange taste pushed it back into the air. After a third attempt, the fly's wings froze mid-flap, and it dropped unceremoniously to the ground. Lying on a smooth, hard expanse, its legs twitched once, twice, and then were still.

· · · · ●· ●· · ·

Roland's head poked through an unmarked door. After confirming there was no one else around, he pushed harder and stepped into an unadorned hallway. A smooth, white floor was mirrored by a smooth, white ceiling supported by smooth, white walls. Light made its way from cleverly hidden fluorescent tubes to infuse the hallway with an even, unrelenting glow. Even if there had been an object to cast a shadow, the ubiquitous whiteness guaranteed that no shadows would be allowed. While Roland marveled at the strangeness of it, Carmen quietly shut the stairwell door behind them.

"Why do I feel like we just stepped into the future?" she whispered. "It's like a spaceship down here."

The other office temp nodded in agreement. "Remember the movie *Alien*? Looks like the medical bay on the Nostromo."

"And someone just broke the no-dork rule. That means I get the first hit."

Satisfied that they were alone, Carmen produced a small, tightly rolled joint. Grinning in response, Roland flourished a plastic lighter, flicked it, and held the small flame up. After his coworker had inhaled deeply, he took the joint, filled his lungs, and waited. When Carmen nodded, they exhaled in unison, creating a large cloud of sweet-smelling smoke. Carmen managed a second hit but coughed abruptly when she heard footsteps in the stairwell. With nowhere to run, she hid the joint behind her back and tried to look innocent.

"What are you doing down here?" the newcomer snapped as he stepped through the door.

While Carmen suppressed a giggle and tried to wave away the smoke, Roland stammered a response.

"Uh, we thought the conference room was down here," he quickly offered. "We're temps for accounting."

The stranger scowled, which was surprising. The expression was well-suited to the man's emaciated face, but it seemed out of place for a Get Wellies employee. The people Ronald had met so far had been a pretty jovial lot. It was hard not to be when your job was making stuffed animals with customized 'get well' messages embroidered on their plush little tummies. The man's lab coat and clipboard were also unexpected. Why would someone be dressed like a scientist in a stuffed animal factory?

Roland asked the question, but the man just scowled some more before saying, "The main conference room is on the second floor."

The pronouncement was so sharp, so severe, that the unfortunate temp automatically held up his hands in defense and took a nervous step backward.

"Sorry. We're new, and um. We got lost."

"You're not new anymore," the man in the lab coat snarled. "You're fired. Follow me."

Before Roland could think of a response, the man spun on his heel and strode down the all-white corridor. The newly unemployed office temp followed with a resigned shrug, trailed a few steps behind by an also unemployed but still-giggling Carmen.

· · · · ● · ● · · ·

A low croak pushed against the prevailing silence of the room, followed by the soft scrape of a fingernail along stainless steel. Nearby, but much harder to hear, one of six tiny fly legs twitched and mouthparts flexed. Another croak and scratch was answered by another twitch from the fly before silence returned.

· · · · ●· ●· ● · · ·

"Ahhhh. Aaaahhhh."

The faint sound echoed down the strange hallway, folding around itself and taking on a more ominous tone. A shiver squirmed down Roland's spine and set his arm hairs on end. The man they'd been following stopped abruptly at the sound, a look of confusion replacing his glower.

"Who else is down here?" he asked sharply.

Roland held up his hands. "I don't know. Look, we didn't mean to cause any trouble. Really."

"Shut up," the man responded brusquely. "Stay here. I'll be right back."

The lab coat billowed behind the man as long strides took him down the hallway. Suddenly, he turned and disappeared into the white wall. Roland blinked, wondering for a moment if the pot had been laced with something a little more interesting. Carmen started to clap.

"That was amazing!" she said. "We work with magicians."

"This is serious, Carmen. I told you we shouldn't have snuck off. Now we're gonna get fired." Roland slumped against the wall. "I hate getting fired."

Carmen responded with a devil-may-care grin. "Well, people should do what they're good at, right? We're good at being terrible employees. Now c'mon. I want to see where he went."

"He told us to stay here. We're in enough trouble already, so we should just stay here."

Carmen moved to stand directly in front of him, tiny roach to her lips and lighter flicking. After a short puff, she held it out. "We're blazed and fired. What else could happen?"

• • • ● • ● • ● • • •

The corpse sat up. Collapsed lungs filled with clean, pathogen-scrubbed air. The mouth that had previously been frozen in a rictus snarl began to work, opening and closing methodically. Fixed and clouded eyes twitched left, then right, the cloudiness dissipating as the irises expanded and contracted. An uncoordinated arm raised up and thumped a bony wrist against its forehead, its cheek, and finally, its nose. Halting, jerking movements pushed the wrist back and forth across the nostrils. Other senses started to return. Eyes registered light. Tongue tasted ozone and antiseptic. Nose smelled Lysol and a faint trace of decay. Ears heard a sharp gasp and a short burst of static, followed by a voice.

"This is Allen. We've got one. We've actually got one. Get down to morgue B-seven."

The corpse turned its head on creaking neck muscles. The light became more nuanced, revealing shapes and motion. Like flame for a moth, fresh blood for a shark, the movement and sounds drew the corpse forward. Shifting its weight, it slid on a hard, smooth surface.

Inch by slow inch, it scooted toward the irresistible movement. A moment later, it fell and landed on its face.

"Crap," the voice said, followed by another burst of static. "You have to get down here! It just fell off the table and is crawling, I repeat, crawling toward me right now. I'm going to try and get it back on the table."

The corpse didn't know what crawling was, or table. It only knew hunger, and that food was within reach.

The fly didn't know crawling or table, either. It, too, only knew hunger, and that food was within reach.

· · · ● · ● ● · ·

Roland almost didn't see the door, so perfectly did it blend in with the surrounding white wall. When he did spot the thin line of its edge, he stopped so suddenly that Carmen ran into him.

"Hey! Use your signal," she chastised. "Some people are walking here."

Once he noticed the door, he also saw the small plaque next to it. Printed on a white rectangle almost indecipherable from the wall were small, light grey letters.

Morgue B-7, Disposal Preparation

What the hell? he wondered. *Why would Get Wellies have a morgue?*

Before his weed-addled brain had time to consider the implications, a muffled voice reached his ears from beyond the closed door.

"Crap," the voice said. "You have to get down here! It just fell off the table and is crawling, I repeat, crawling toward me right now. I'm going to try and get it back on the table."

Carmen's eyes went wide as they met Roland's.

"Spooky," she said in a dramatic stage whisper, then opened the door.

The slight change in air pressure sent the smell of antiseptic and rot washing over Roland and a fly spiraling right at his face. He ducked the fly and looked up to see... two men dancing. The angry scientist guy in the lab coat was wrapped in the embrace of a mostly naked man, and the two swayed back and forth. Roland glanced over at Carmen and saw his own stunned confusion reflected on her face. When he returned his attention to the strangely dancing couple, he saw the naked man bring his mouth down to the scientist's neck. A geyser of red erupted and poured down the white lab coat. When the bleeding man started to scream, Roland's only lucid thought was to wonder what Get Wellies animal was best for someone that just had their throat ripped open by someone else's teeth.

• • • • • • • • • • •

Jerry shifted and squirmed in the reception area chair. Restless, he stood and walked over to a wall covered with framed articles about Get Wellies' work in the community. His eyes wandered across the accolades until they settled on a glossy photograph showcased in an expensive-looking picture frame. A quick inspection revealed that the photo was from a ribbon-cutting ceremony for a new hospital. Apparently, Get Wellies' CEO had made a sizeable donation.

"That's pretty impressive," he commented to the receptionist across the waiting room. "Five million? Guess I got into the wrong business. I should be selling stuffed animals, not paper," he quipped. A good-natured laugh started in Jerry's belly, but got stuck in his throat when the receptionist skewered him with a cool stare.

"The community is very proud of Get Wellies' contributions."

"Of course. Of course it is…" Jerry offered as an apology, although he wasn't sure what he was apologizing for.

The community in question was Fort Collins, Colorado. Normally, Jerry didn't cover that particular region, but a new sales manager at the paper mill was mixing things up. Jerry didn't mind. Travel was the only thing he liked about his job. It meant he had ample excuses to get out of Trappersville. The tiny, tick-infested town in northern Wisconsin was, in Jerry's opinion, not only the birthplace of boredom, but the place where boredom had been refined and perfected.

"Is that your CEO?" he asked, tapping the picture.

"Yes," the receptionist responded curtly.

"Who's that with him?"

Without looking up, the receptionist said, "President Bush, Donald Rumsfeld, and the Director-General of the World Health Organization."

Jerry was about to say, 'Wow!' but frowned quietly instead, suddenly unsure why a stuffed animal company CEO was bumping elbows with Bush and Rumsfeld. Fortunately, he didn't need to have answers to big questions. He just needed to meet his monthly paper stock sales quota.

Returning to the uncomfortable chair, Jerry sat and fidgeted, flipping the locks of the briefcase on his lap open and closed, open and closed. When he tired of that, he took to glancing at his watch. He'd glanced five times when he realized he was doing it in fifteen second intervals. A business magazine on the small table next to him held little appeal. The sports magazine held even less. Throwing decorum aside, he slid a horror novel from his briefcase and opened it to a dog-eared page. He was just getting back into the story when a small, yellow light began to flash.

Tucked up in a corner by the ceiling, the light hadn't drawn his attention earlier. Now that it was strobing, he realized that its placement ensured it would be visible from every corner of the room. His mouth formed a question, but the words froze on his tongue when he saw the look on the receptionist's face. Terror stretched her skin tight against her cheekbones, pulled her lips up her gums, and opened her eyes so wide that the whites showed in wide swaths around the irises.

"Please come with me, sir," she finally said, her tone brooking no argument.

"Um, you know..." Jerry hedged, "I think I left some samples in the car. I'll, ah... be right back."

He stood abruptly and spilled his briefcase to the reception area's floor. Stooping, he started to hastily scoop brochures and samples back inside.

"No, you can't leave," the receptionist said in a tight voice.

When Jerry looked up, he screamed. It wasn't because she was holding the door open to the inner offices with one hand. It wasn't even because she was pointing a pistol at him with her other hand. He screamed because a third hand was reaching through the open door and about to grab the woman's neck.

The receptionist echoed Jerry's scream and turned the gun on her assailant. Three shots rang out and then the hand's owner lurched forward. The man was gaunt and draped in a knee-length coat that must've been white before someone dumped a few gallons of gloppy red on it. His skin was an unhealthy shade of yellow-grey, and his eyes were bloodshot to such an extent that the irises were barely visible. As Jerry watched, the man's mouth stretched wide and bit down hard on the woman's cheek, sending a fresh spray of red across the front of his coat.

The paper salesman threw his zombie novel at the pair and ran for the exit. He hit the glass door at a full sprint but violently bounced back when it didn't open. Ignoring the throbbing pain in his shoulder, he shoved again and again, but the door wouldn't budge.

"Let me out!" he cried. "Let me out of here!"

Frantic, he grabbed his discarded briefcase, slammed it shut, and swung it hard at the glass. Over and over again, he assaulted the door, but the glass didn't even scratch. More shots rang out. Some struck the man in the bloody coat and spun him in a wild circle. Other missed their mark and hit the locked glass door. Cracks formed, radiating out from the center of each bullet hole. With a final desperate cry, Jerry threw himself at the door again and sobbed in relief as glass shattered around him. Rolling across the snow-dusted concrete apron, he came to his feet, briefcase in hand, and sprinted past the well-manicured evergreen shrubs framing the building's front walkway. Voices called out from behind him to stop, stop right now, but Jerry didn't listen. After climbing hastily into his rental car, he cranked the ignition, slammed on the gas, ricocheted off the bumper of another car as his tires fought for purchase on the slippery pavement, and sped for the exit.

"Screw the quota," he said in a shaky voice. "I quit."

Chapter 1

S TANLEY'S ALARM CLOCK WAS a thing of beauty. A reliable wonder of plastic and circuitry with a blue liquid crystal display. "It's time," it buzzed. "It's that time that you indicated was important. I'm so glad I was able to help wake you at this very important time."

Stanley wished he could come up with a truly wonderful way to thank his alarm clock. With its brown plastic casing cleverly colored to look like wood, a brightly glowing display, and more buttons, knobs, and dials than a jet's cockpit, it had served him without fail since he was in high school. He'd never been able to find a thank-you card for an electronic device, so he would just pat its snooze bar lovingly and said, "Th-th-thanks!"

Alarm clock attended to, Stanley reviewed the list of things he had planned to start the day. Pee, poop, shower. Brush and floss his teeth. Put on clothes, eat breakfast.

With a satisfied nod, he headed to the bathroom. A short time later, he'd crossed items one and two off his morning list and readied for the shower. The steaming hot water was nothing short of heavenly. After drying off with a thick towel, he wiped steam from the mirror.

"Lookin' g-good, buddy," he congratulated himself, and picked up his toothbrush.

Oral hygiene attended to, Stanley dressed his wiry frame in crisp 60/40 polyester-cotton blend underpants, well-matched tube socks with gold stripes around the tops, clean jeans, an undershirt, and a yellow and brown velour sweater with a warm collar buttoned all the way up. Winter had officially settled into northern Wisconsin. Buttoning up the collar would help to keep his neck warm.

Breakfast was a simple plate of fried eggs, buttered white toast, and a microwaved hotdog washed down with black coffee. Stanley sopped the remaining bits of egg yolk up with the final corner of his toast, took a last bite of hotdog, and swallowed the final gulp of coffee. A deep breath preceded a hearty belch that belied his slender frame.

After breakfast, Stanley settled into the next phase of his day. The blue Barca Lounger gave a satisfying creak as it accepted his weight, almost as if it too were anticipating the upcoming excitement. Stanley extended the footrest, placed his remote controls in their proper order on his lap, and powered up his entertainment center. First one VCR, then the main television, then the second VCR and second television, then the cable box and third television. The air around him hummed with electronics coming to life, and a variety of lights from the three screens danced across the living room. One of his favorite shows, *Judge Judy*, was about to start. Television number three was already tuned to the proper station. He'd be able to hear the case description and opening arguments while queuing up recordings of season two of *Veronica Mars* on the main T.V. and National Geographic on the third.

Soon, Stanley was happily absorbing a dispute over an electricity bill one neighbor incurred because another neighbor had plugged an extension cord into their outdoor outlet, episode thirteen of *Veronica*

Mars, one of his favorites, and a special on sheep cloning. When the phone rang, he already had the answer.

"Six. Six years, and that's a fact," he stated proudly into the receiver.

"Um, six years what, Stanley?" Lois asked politely.

"The sheep clone," he explained reasonably. "Them scientists made it in nineteen ninety-six, and it d-died about six years later."

"Oh, okay. Good to know. Thanks, Stanley. Say, I was wondering if you'd heard anything. You know, from Dallas."

Stanley didn't reply right away. He knew he hadn't heard from Dallas, but he was distracted by an itch in his nostril. Dallas always said he was picking his nose. That wasn't the case at all, or at least, not always. Sometimes a nose had an itch, and itches needed scratching.

"Allergies," he finally said. "Even w-with the antihistamines."

During the ensuing pause, Stanley returned his attention to *Judge Judy.* She was close to handing down a ruling, and he had a pretty good feeling that the plaintiff was going to make bank.

"But what about Dallas?" Lois finally asked. "Unless, are you, I mean. Are you talking about him being allergic to the full moon?"

Stanley's head started to bob excitedly. "Oh, Lois. That's a g-good idea. You bet'cha. Werewolves sure c-could be allergic to the moon. I bet they could. Like hives, but all over and hairy."

Lois asked again, "But you haven't heard from him?"

The up and down bobbing of Stanley's head shifted into a side-to-side shake.

"Nope. I'm really sorry, Lois. I ain't heard n-nothing. Don't you worry, though. Dallas, he's a t-tough guy, real tough. He's okay."

Stanley heard Lois sigh before saying, "I'm sure you're right, Stanley."

"Hey," he said with sudden inspiration. "You, me, and Herb should g-go bowling later."

"Tonight?" Lois asked. "I don't think tonight's going to work. Herb wants to get up early and cook me dinner. It's been four months since our first date. Can you believe that?"

Stanley almost dropped the phone with excitement.

"Really? G-gosh, Lois. That's pretty great. Really great. I'll get some b-beers. 'Waukee's Best. And, um." Stanley's mind churned as he tried to think of the best side dish for the occasion. "Fritos. That way, it won't m-matter what Herb makes for dinner. Fritos go with everything."

"But Stanley," Lois said with a laugh. "It's our anniversary."

"Oh. G-gosh. You're right, Lois. Absolutely right." The wiry man smacked his forehead with a palm. "What was I thinking? Snicker-doodles. Fritos are okay for lots of things, but this is sp-special. You t-tell Herby I'll still bring 'em, but I'll definitely get some snickerdoo-dles too. P-perfect for special occasions."

Another laugh tinkled through the receiver before Lois said, "No, Stanley. That wasn't what I meant. I meant that it's me and Herb's four month anniversary. That's something people usually spend with, you know. Each other."

A long silence filled the telephone line stretching through the Wis-consin trees. Stanley finally broke it by asking Lois if she thought Herb might want to stay up and watch football on Sunday.

"Sorry, but this weekend won't work," the witch apologized. "I have the weekend off, so we're going to drive down to Green Bay and spend a couple of nights."

"B-but, but it's football. Me and Herby and D-Dallas. We always. We used t-to. It's… Lois, it's the P-Packers! There's the j-jerky, and the beer, and the maple b-bacon donuts, and…"

Lois gently interrupted. "I know, Stanley. That's why we're going to Green Bay. We're going to the game."

"You and Herby are g-going to Lambeau? B-but, but Lois, it's outside. During the d-day. You're g-gonna burn Herby right up."

"I got him a big hooded Packers parka, tinted ski goggles, and one of those masks that covers up your nose and face. Not only will he be one-hundred percent sun-proof, but everyone's going to be dressed that way so he won't look weird. Oh, and that mask has a little hole for the mouth, so I got a big travel mug with a straw. Herb can even bring some blood to snack on," Lois added excitedly. "Don't say anything, though. It's all a surprise."

Stanley found his head nodding, but the gesture lacked enthusiasm. It felt more like the nod someone on the electric chair might give when asked if the wrist straps were comfortable. Ever since Dallas had run off into the night earlier that fall and hadn't returned, things had been different for Stanley. It hadn't been anything too obvious at first, so he didn't immediately notice. Like how you can skip showers for a few days or even a week and still feel normal. Maybe an itchy scalp or a little B.O., but nothing too off-putting. Now, though, it was getting hard not to notice how things had changed.

"B-but I took a shower today," he said, not fully realizing it had been out loud.

"Oh. Well, that's good, Stanley. Real good," Lois answered in a confused tone. "Um. Me too."

This time, the silence said more than words could.

"Well," Stanley finally managed. "You g-guys have a good time."

Lois wished him the same and hung up her end of the call. Stanley considered the phone in his hand. It felt heavier than when he'd picked it up, which was surprising given its sudden emptiness. Setting the phone carefully back in its cradle, Stanley returned his attention to the televisions vying for space on his credenza. At least they still had time for him.

As he'd hoped, a few hours of T.V. drove the blues away and left Stanley feeling better. He'd learned how important the nuclear transfer of DNA from adult somatic cells was when cloning mammals, and felt that if he ever needed to defend himself in court for stealing electricity, he'd be able to do so competently. Episode thirteen of *Veronica Mars* was so good that he decided to watch episodes fourteen and fifteen right after. By lunchtime, he was brimming with information and couldn't wait to share it.

Scooping up his winter coat and slipping on his favorite brown leather loafers, he trudged through the fresh layer of snow on his driveway and slid into his old Chevrolet Cavalier. The cold engine protested, but finally rewarded Stanley's pleading with a sputter-turned-rumble. He put the car in reverse and had almost backed all the way out to the main road when the realization hit home.

There was no one to tell.

It used to be that he could head to Steinknockers and talk while Dallas put back a daunting amount of beer, or regale Herb with any newfound knowledge over a game at Bay City Bowlers. Now, though, it was just him. Dallas had been gone for months, and Herb had a girlfriend. That meant Stanley had no one to talk to except Stanley.

"Crappers," he grumbled as he hit the brakes.

The Cavalier idled fitfully while Stanley tried to decide what to do. It was his stomach that finally offered a reasonable suggestion. Pressing on the accelerator, he backed onto the main road and shifted into drive.

Trappersville was a town in name, but to Stanley's knowledge, no one had ever successfully mapped its borders. It seemed like every time someone managed to say, 'Yep. That's it. That's the whole town,' some Sconnie would drop a trailer or pop up a little house deep in the trees and throw the whole notion of town limits into the dustbin. The one area that everyone agreed was definitely Trappersville was a small collection of paved roads and established businesses that were grouped together a few miles from Stanley's house. The First Lutheran Church anchored one end of Main Street, the Get'n'Gobble grocery sat at the other, and a collection of little storefronts filled the space between. The few blocks to one side of Main Street were filled with small houses in orderly lots. The few blocks on the other side held more of the same, but more importantly, held Bay City Bowlers. The town's only, and by default premiere, bowling and karaoke establishment had been a regular haunt of Stanley's for years.

He passed by it all and turned onto the main highway. A short while later, Ronnie's Famous Truck Stop, Diner, and Gift Emporium appeared on the horizon. Owned by a retired trucker, its diner was open 'round the clock and served up an impressive variety of Midwestern fare. Herb had been a cook there until Dallas had stabbed him with a broken pool cue, and Lois still worked there as a waitress. It was a go-to spot for lots of folks around town, which meant chances were good there'd be someone to talk to. Stanley turned into the parking lot and peered through the wide, plate-glass windows. He spied a few regulars and some guys he assumed were truckers packing in a good meal before getting back on the road. Perfect. After fitting his rusty Cavalier into a spot near the front door, he silenced the grumbling little engine, hopped out, and hurried through the cold to the welcoming warmth inside.

Taking a stool at the counter, Stanley grabbed a menu and flipped through its laminated pages. A few stools over, the truck stop's owner and namesake sat grumbling over a stack of papers.

"No, no, no," Ronnie muttered. "I swear, they're trying to ruin me. They're all trying to ruin me."

Stanley waved and offered a friendly hello, ignoring the sour look Ronnie sent his way in return.

"Who's ruining you, Ronnie? The IRS? I'll b-bet it's the IRS. Dallas always said them g-government types will take your last penny and send you a b-bill for a nickel."

Ronnie blew air out through his nose, producing a sound that reminded Stanley of the cloned sheep he'd been watching earlier.

"The electric co-op," he complained. "I don't know where in the hell they get these numbers from. Am I paying for everyone in town? Am I paying to keep the sun lit up all day?"

"Oooohhh, you should'a watched the *Judge Judy* today. Yes, sir. P-people say to me, 'Stanley, why do you watch that stuff?' And you know what. This is why. This exact moment is why. You wouldn't b-believe it, but today they had a c-case about someone stealing elec-tricity..." Stanley started, but found himself talking to empty air. Ronnie had grabbed up his papers and stomped away to his office.

Down but not out, Stanley waited patiently until Dee came round to take his order.

"What'll it be, Henry?"

"Oh, uh. Hi D-Dee. Stanley. I'm Stanley. You know. Dallas and Herb's friend."

"Sorry, sweetie. Of course you are. Dallas. Gosh. Where the heck has he been? Haven't seen that boy in months. And Herb? Lord knows where that psycho ended up."

"Right. Um," Stanley hedged, unsure of what to say.

It had been an eventful few months in the small town. Deaths, disappearances, even rumors of a vampire, but most people didn't know the half of it. Fortunately, Wisconsin folk weren't the type to make a fuss. When the dust had settled, they'd gone back to their daily lives. Even so, Herb and Dallas were still regular topics of idle conversation. Was Herb a serial killer? What happened to Dallas? Were vampires real? Thinking about it brought a scowl to Stanley's face. No one ever wanted to talk about what he wanted to talk about. It was always Herb or Dallas. Dallas or...

"Herbert Knudsen!" Ronnie spat. "I knew he was rotten. Rotten to the core."

The diner's owner had reappeared, face reddening at the mention of his former cook.

"I tried," he continued in a building rant. "Tried to instill a sense of responsibility in him. Tried to convey even the tiniest bit of under-standing of the importance of service," he lamented. "But you can't make pie of out rotten apples."

"You c-can make cider," Stanley offered. "I was watching this c-cooking show. You know, the one where they t-take leftovers and stuff you forgot you had in the p-pantry and show you how t-to whip up something delicious. This lady, she had all these b-bad apples. Did that stop her? No sir! She just g-got out the paring knife, cut-cut-cut," Stanley explained, hands pantomiming the graceful work of a kitchen cutlery master. "Stuck them b-bad apples right in the, oh. N-never mind."

Ronnie had vanished again, Dee had flitted away to take someone else's order, and Stanley was all by himself. With a heavy sigh, he propped an elbow on the counter and set his chin on his fist. A good sit'n'visit was a dwindling possibility and getting served seemed even less likely. He was about to call it quits when the door opened and a cold blast of air followed a familiar face into the diner.

Stanley watched Herb's old neighbor stomp snow off his boots, rub his hands briskly together, and make his way to an open booth a safe distance from the door. Jerry looked pretty rough. The hair sticking out from under his knit cap was lanky and disheveled. Dark circles weighed heavily under bloodshot, shifting eyes. When one of the cooks dropped something back in the kitchen, the resulting clang caused Jerry to flinch like a frightened animal.

That Jerry looks like he could use some company, Stanley decided.

Relocating from his counter stool, Stanley slid into the bench seat across from Jerry.

"Hey, J-Jerry!" he announced. "Sure is c-cold out there, huh. I heard on the weather that it's g-gonna be real chilly all week. It's because of the El Nino. That's a polar j-jet stream. Like a river, but with air, not water."

In response, Jerry looked everywhere but at Stanley. When Dee stopped over to take his order, he mumbled something about a burger and fries.

"Me too," Stanley added.

Jerry finally met Stanley's eyes. "Look, Stanley. It's nice to see you and all, but..."

"You too! Gosh, it's b-been, what? Months I guess. Folks j-just aren't out and about as much. Can't blame them. It's cold. Me, I usually keep to the c-couch. Lots of stuff on the T.V.s. You watch *Veronica Mars*, right?"

The paper salesman gave a slow shake of his head.

"Oh," Stanley said, a bit deflated. "You really should. That Veronica, boy oh boy. She's a sharp one. Like Jessica Fletcher. Some folks say you c-can't compare Veronica Mars and Jessica Fletcher. I say that's nonsense. I mean, sure. That Jessica's got all the looks, b-but they're both real smart. Always looking for the c-clues. Figuring out the tough stuff. You watch *Murder, She Wrote*, don'cha Jerry?"

Another slow shake of the head.

Stanley sighed and nervously drummed his fingers on the tabletop and asked, "*Columbo?*"

"Uh uh."

"But you watch *Judge Judy*, right? Everyone watches the *Judge Judy*. Or *Jeopardy?*"

"Um, no. Sorry."

Stanley hmph'd. He was about to scold Jerry for his disturbing lack of cultural development when he realized again just how rotten the man looked.

"You feeling alright, J-Jerry?" he asked.

Jerry let a slow breath out and focused intently on his hands for a moment.

"Do you," he started, and then furtively looked around before continuing in a lower voice. "Stanley, do you believe in... I mean, what do you think about..." he managed, and then blurted out. "I read horror books. That's what I like. Vampires. Werewolves. And zuh," he gulped before finally forcing out, "Zombies."

Dee arrived with two plates, each one weighed down with a heavy burger and enough fries to keep Idaho in the black for another month. Stanley grabbed up his burger and took a satisfying bite. While he chewed on the thick slab of ground beef, Jerry stared and swallowed and gagged a bit. A moment later, Jerry pushed his untouched burger to the side.

"You gonna puke, J-Jerry?" Stanley asked around mouthfuls. "If you're g-gonna puke, make sure you do it in the toilet. Me and Herb and Dallas c-came here once after drinking at Stein's. Herby puked in the sink, and Ronnie d-darn near had a heart attack."

The sage advice didn't seem to register. Instead, Jerry asked in a low whisper, "Stanley, do you think they could be real?"

"Heart attacks?" Stanley said. "G-gosh yeah. That's why they say, 'serious as a heart attack.' If they weren't real, p-people wouldn't say that. They'd say something else. Like maybe, 'serious as a flat t-tire.'"

"No. I mean monsters. You know. Like zombies. They're not real, are they?"

Stanley chewed thoughtfully and set down his burger. After careful consideration, he nodded his head.

"Yep. I mean, I haven't seen one myself. But vampires and werewolves and Bigfoot and b-boo hags and witches and stuff are all real. So p-probably zombies too."

Jerry's eyes widened, and he gulped loudly. He hurriedly fished a worn wallet out of his pants pocket and dropped a pile of crumpled bills on the counter. With a hasty apology about having to get home, he turned to grab his briefcase and slide out of the booth. The case caught the corner of the tabletop and popped open, sending brochures and paper samples spilling across the linoleum tiles. Jerry cursed and stooped to shovel the mess back into his briefcase, and Stanley bent down to lend a hand. Neither man noticed the small fly as it landed awkwardly on the ground, angrily twitched its desiccated wings, and crawled determinedly toward a brown leather loafer.

After Jerry had fled the diner, Stanley tried to spark up conversation with a few other patrons, but his efforts were consistently rebuked. Lonely and dejected, Stanley finally braved the drive back to his little house in the woods. After arriving home, he stomped loose snow off his worn, brown loafers, left them by the front door, and readied himself for another evening alone. Stanley had just tuned into the local news when a sound caught his attention. At first, it was so quiet he thought he'd imagined it. Silencing the television, he cocked his head and listened in earnest.

There. A soft buzz. The buzz of wings. Insect wings. He waited with uncharacteristic patience until he heard it again.

Bzzz. Bzzzzzz. Bzzz.

Taking halting, careful steps, he started to circle his living room. Every few steps, Stanley would pause and tilt his head from one side to the other and wait until he heard the telltale sound again.

Bzzz. Bzzzzzz.

The sound was definitely coming from the front of the room. He tip-toed closer to the door...

Bzzz.

Stanley swooped in and grabbed a loafer. Lifting it up for closer inspection, he saw what he'd hoped he would find. Stuck to a corner of duct tape that had peeled loose from the loafer's heel was a small fly.

"Woohoo!" he yelped with sudden excitement. "This m-might be it. You just be c-calm, Stanley. You j-just be quiet."

Taking three deep breaths, he let the final one out slowly through his nose. Stanley had been collecting various insects for years with the hope that he would discover a new species. After a mosquito had turned Herb into a vampire and a wood tick had turned Dallas into a werewolf, Stanley had devoted even more energy to his quest. He didn't doubt that he would discover a new bug. People discovered stuff all the time. For Stanley, it was really just a question of when.

Turning the loafer to allow himself a better look at the little bug, his forced calm started to crack.

"T-tabanus sudeticus," Stanley breathed. One of his favorites. He'd have to look closer at its mouthparts to see if it was male or female horse fly. Males had weak mouths suited to their primary diet of plant nectar. Females had more gruesome tastes: blood. Their mouthparts had serrated little blades perfect for cutting through skin and flesh.

"M-maybe you're a lady fly," Stanley wondered out loud. "You have some b-babies, and I'll know for sure."

A soft click accompanied the unfolding of a pocket magnifying glass. Stanley held it up and brought the loafer closer. He peered with first one eye, then the other, trying to get a look at the fly's mouth. Unfortunately, it had managed to get stuck in a position that obscured its proboscis. While disappointing, the magnifying lens did make it abundantly clear that the fly's coloring was odd. Horse flies usually had multi-colored compound eyes, brown-black hair on their thorax, and smooth, dark abdomens. Tilting his head for a better look, Stanley saw that this particular fly had eyes that were a uniform bloody red. The short hairs on its thorax were a bit wilted, and its abdomen was more of a jaundiced dark yellow than the usual grey or black. On top of that, its wings hardly seemed up to the task of flying. They looked dried up and useless and hung at odd angles between occasional twitches.

Excitement pushed Stanley to his feet, and he took off on a fresh lap around the living room. His tube socks tread rapidly across the carpet while his mind whirled off into the clouds. He'd done it. He'd found a new bug. Fame and fortune were sure to follow. Shaking hands with the President. A Nobel Prize. An appearance on *Oprah*.

"G-gotta be sure though, g-gotta be sure," he counseled himself as he paced.

Inspiration struck, and Stanley pivoted toward his modest kitchen. After quickly emptying a half-glass of Mr. Pibb into the sink, he set it on the table and carefully propped the loafer next to it fly-side up. A quick rummage produced a roll of duct-tape and a round coaster he'd taken from Steinknocker's Bar.

"G-good thing Stein let me borrow this," Stanley commented, delighted by his good fortune. He made a mental note to return it to the bar once he'd received his Nobel Prize.

Next, he ran upstairs and returned with his nose hair tweezers and a small notepad. With surgical care, he plucked the fly from the sticky loafer, dropped it in the empty glass, and secured the coaster on top with a strip of duct-tape. Once the fly was secure, he grabbed a pen and made some brief notes on the pad.

Stanley leaned back and exhaled. Phase one of his impromptu experiment was complete. Now he needed to move into phase two.

"Flowers, flowers," he muttered. "D-don't got none. Hmmm. What're you hungry for, little fly?" he asked rhetorically. "Would syrup t-taste good?"

A plastic bottle full of dark amber liquid appeared alongside the glass. Stanley peeled back the coaster and squeezed a few sticky drops inside. Raising the glass up close to his face, he watched intently to see how the fly would react. It completely ignored the maple syrup and instead lurched directly toward his eye.

"Okay. N-not syrup," Stanley announced with authority while adding more notes to the notepad. "I'm g-guessing you're a lady. Are you hungry, little lady?"

Stanley peeled back the coaster again and stuck a pointy finger into the glass. The fly reacted instantly and moved at a sideways stagger until it bumped his fingernail. Stanley obligingly turned his finger to offer up the meaty part, and the fly bit deep.

It *hurt*. Stanley had endured plenty of bug bites. It was par for the course when you lived in the Wisconsin Northwoods. This particular bite put all those others to shame. He resisted the urge to pull his finger back and forced himself to count to ten before flicking the little fly off. Once the coaster lid was taped back in place, Stanley stuck the finger in his mouth and made a few more notes in his notepad.

"D-definitely a lady fly. No doubt about th-that."

Enthused by his progress, Stanley decided it was time to celebrate. Still sucking on his finger, he pulled a can of Milwaukee's Best from the fridge, carried it back to his small dining room, and popped the tab. The cool lip of the can replaced his finger, and a long stream of alcoholic goodness washed the taste of blood away.

"Gonna b-be famous," he said with a smile, and then everything went dark.

Chapter 2

AWAKE. HAD HE BEEN sleeping? He must've been.

What woke him? Usually he'd be roused by an electronic beep signaling the start of a brand new day. He'd stretch his wiry frame and reach for the snooze bar of his favorite alarm clock. Not now, though. Not this time. It was quiet. Really quiet. So quiet you could hear a caterpillar fart.

He had probably just woken up early. That happened from time to time. When it did, he'd wait with barely contained anticipation for that beautiful beeping. He must've woken up early, so he waited, waited again, and waited some more.

Still quiet. Quieter than the crowd at Lambeau when the Packers were down by two at the end of the fourth and Crosby missed the field goal.

He tried to sit up, but someone had tied him down. Every time he tried to raise his back, he felt a distant tightness in his chest and something seemed to pull in his gut, but his torso wouldn't bend. A tiny memory sparked. Dallas. It was the kind of prank Dallas would play. Dallas was notorious for his pranks. For as long as Stanley had known Dallas, he had endured Dallas's sense of humor. Once, when Stanley had tried to own a cat, Dallas had crapped in its litter box. Stanley had come home to find the traumatized feline trying desperately to bury what Dallas had left behind.

Sure, Dallas was a prankster, but Dallas was gone, wasn't he? Was he back?

Stanley reached to pull at the cords restraining him. He tried to reach to pull at the cords restraining him. He tried to move his arm.

Dallas. He must've tied his arm down too.

Stanley closed and opened his eyelids, mostly to make sure Dallas hadn't done something really mean like glue them shut. They moved, but it required more effort than blinking should, like wipers pushing mud off a windshield. Another laborious blink, and someone turned a light on. No. Someone turned the knob on a dimmer, either up a little on a grey, diffuse light, or down on the dark. Whichever it was, more light or less dark, it relieved the complete and utter blackness of a moment before and let in shades of smoke and charcoal.

Inspiration struck. He couldn't move one of his arms, but maybe he could move the other. It seemed like a good idea, so he gave it a shot. A moment later, something passed in front of his face. That was interesting, so he tried moving his arm again. Yep. That blurry, hard to discern shape drifting slowly in front of him was likely an arm, and likelier his. The arm was apparently connected to his eyes, because the more he waved the one back and forth, the better the others registered shapes and tracked motion.

He returned his attention to the cords holding him Gulliver-like in place. It took a bit of convincing, but eventually he made the arm flop down on his torso. Fingers pulled, but he couldn't tell to what effect. They, like the rest of his arm, seemed numb.

Must've slept on it, he reasoned.

Stanley waited for the telltale tingling of blood returning to a sleeping limb. He waited again and waited some more. No tingling. Just the same sort of cool... nothing. He willed his fingers to bend and pull again. Something. Something soft. Pully. Stretchy. Velour? Velour. Like his favorite shirt.

That was weird. There should have been ropes crisscrossing his body. Suddenly suspicious, he tried to sit up again. His back raised up inch by slow inch, and he managed another couple of blinks at the same time. The flowing montage of shadows took on depth and color and became recognizable things. The blurry leg of a wooden table. An expanse of featureless brown carpet that stretched to a nearby blurry horizon. Closer were two skinny legs wrapped in denim and stretching down to a pair of tube socks.

Just like Stanley's, he thought.

He completed the thought at the same time he finished bending himself into a sitting position. Not having to concentrate on moving his reluctant muscles allowed him to more fully consider his last thought. Like a gummy tumbler in an old lock, the realization that he was Stanley fell into place.

Well, of course I am, he decided. That was easy enough to figure out. Why he was on the floor between his living room and dining room instead of upstairs in his bed was another mystery altogether.

A mystery. He liked mysteries. At least, he thought he did. Stanley sat on the floor for long minutes. During that time, he didn't feel much interest in solving a mystery. He didn't feel much interest in anything at all.

Stanley continued to sit until he decided he wasn't interested in just sitting, either. Bending his stiff limbs, he managed to awkwardly get to his feet. The new perspective did little to alleviate his lethargy, but it was a smidge more interesting than sitting. More minutes stretched away as Stanley simply stood and stared at nothing in particular. When he finally lost interest in nothing in particular, he decided he should try to take an interest in something. A foggy memory of watching television seeped into his consciousness. Stanley pivoted slowly toward the Barca Lounger and took a halting step. A second step followed, and a third.

Each halting step added a little kindling to the embers of his awareness. It was deep night. He was in his living room. He wanted to watch T.V., and he was trying to find the remote. The realization that he had a goal, a specific desire, pushed against the lethargy and felt almost fervent in comparison. Unfortunately, finding the remote was unexpectedly challenging. Heavy blinks had cleared some of the haze, but things still looked squishy and indistinct. Clumsy fingers fumbled around the seat of the Barca Lounger, but failed to find the remote control.

Crappers, his sluggish thoughts grumbled. *Need my glasses.*

Stanley kept a pair of readers in the house. Not because he really needed them, but because he liked the way Angela Lansbury would slip hers on when she needed to look intently at something. This seemed to be the perfect opportunity to slip on a pair of spectacles so he could look intently for the remote control. A lazy, uncoordinated turn pointed him back toward the dining room table. His feet dragged softly across the carpet until the edge of the table bumped against his waist. Hands waved back and forth while fingers twitched.

Gotcha, he thought with a vague sense of accomplishment. Raising up his hand, he felt the hard plastic frames hit the side of his mouth.

A second attempt overcompensated and poked him in the forehead. Third time paid for all. He felt a satisfying pressure against the bridge of his nose, only to realize that he'd forgotten to unfold the stems.

Some indeterminate amount of time later, Stanley realized he was staring through smudged lenses, and they were staying on his face without assistance. He experimented by turning his head left and right, each turn giving him a slow panoramic view of the main floor of his home. Things were still a little blurry, but they were bigger. Good enough.

When he finally found the remote, a spark of excitement flared, only to extinguish when his fingers refused to press the right buttons. Annoyance filled the space excitement had vacated, and Stanley let the remote drop from his hand to the floor below. Lurching steps took him to the credenza. Flailing arms bumped and knocked the various T.V.s, but he couldn't seem to hit the right buttons. He tried pushing harder, but instead of getting the tubes to light up, he only managed to send one television tumbling to the carpet below. Definitely annoying.

He stayed annoyed as long as he could, but even that emotion finally succumbed to the waiting listlessness. More of the night slipped away as Stanley simply stood and stared at the televisions he couldn't turn on.

Could read, he finally decided. *Reading's good.*

The plan held long enough for him to swipe a number of books from their shelves to the floor. When he finally accepted that holding a book and opening it to a page was a feat he wasn't capable of, Stanley tossed the plan and went back to the much easier task of standing in place and staring at nothing.

The hunger started somewhere indistinct. For all he knew, it might've started in his toe, or his shoulder, or his earlobe. Wherever it started, it didn't make much of an impression. It wasn't until the hunger found its way to his gut that Stanley took notice, and once he noticed it, he couldn't think of anything else. His feet moved of their own volition until the blurred, oversized door of his refrigerator filled his vision. After a few swipes, he managed to wedge his hand in the door handle. Leaning back, he let the weight of his body stretch his arm out until finally the door pulled open.

Stanley's hunger considered the contents of the fridge. There was meat. A hotdog. He grabbed it with hands that seemed as cold as the fridge and lifted the meat to his lips.

Plate. It should be on a plate, he realized.

The thought bothered him. Something was finally going the way he wanted. He was hungry, and he was about to eat. This was good. This was progress.

Should really use a plate, though, he thought again.

The little log of over-processed animal parts fell as he relaxed his fingers, producing a wet *thwap* when it landed on the kitchen linoleum. Waving his arms, Stanley managed to pull open a cupboard and reach for the dinner plates. The resulting cacophony of shattering dishes did little to improve his mood. Fortunately, there was still one unbroken plate. It was in the sink, and all he needed to do was give it a wash.

Moving like the unfortunate plaything of a drunken puppeteer, Stanley hit the faucet handle and produced a powerful stream of water. His attempt to grab the bottle of soap did little more than deposit the bottle in the bottom of the sink beside the plate. Rather than try to pick it up again, he pressed down and sent a stream of soap spraying. As the clear liquid hit the faucet's stream, bubbles formed.

So far, so good, he decided.

Now for the washing part. He moved his arms and dragged his numb hands back and forth through the sink, trusting that at least a few of the swipes were getting the plate. Satisfied that he'd done a decent job, he punched at the faucet again. The ice cold water turned scalding hot, but its flow didn't cease. A second jab was more successful. Water still trickled from the faucet, but it was better than the fire hose from a moment before. Concentrating fiercely, Stanley hooked his fingers under the plate's edges, lifted slowly, turned... and dropped it on the floor. The sound of another shattering dish was a stern reminder that he really shouldn't have nice things.

Crappers, he muttered to himself.

Eating from a plate was apparently about as doable as using the T.V. remote or reading a book. Sure, manners were important, but so was eating meat when hungry. With a mental shrug, Stanley started the awkward endeavor of bending over. His simple goal was to reach down, pick up the hotdog, and pop it into his waiting mouth. Easy peasy.

Not so easy. Bending was hard. He felt like someone had replaced his spine with rebar. The hunger drove him onward, but when his torso got to about a forty-five degree angle, he started to tip forward. Reversing the bend settled him back onto his heels and deep into thought.

Huh. Knees maybe?

Stanley slowly lowered his weight and heard his knees creak in protest. Inch by slow inch, he descended into a squat while holding his arms straight out in front of him for balance. When his elbows touched his knees, he decided he'd made it about as low as he could. Stiff fingers twitched and fidgeted, but the hotdog was too far away. The impatient hunger refused to let him stand. Instead, he set himself to rocking. Side to side, Stanley shifted his weight from one foot to the other. Once he felt he had enough momentum, he rocked left and scooted his right foot forward a smidge.

Alright! It was a little victory, but a victory none the less.

More rocking, and he managed to get the left foot to scoot forward. Rock, rock, right foot. Rock, rock, left foot. With each repetition, his eager fingers moved closer to the waiting hotdog. One more rock-scoot, and it would be his. Stanley's weight shifted left. His right foot moved the last few inches forward and settled in a small puddle of soapy water from the sink. The inertia that had previously been his ally turned coat and sent his foot shooting forward. He dropped heavily onto his rear, fell backward, and whacked his head against the kitchen cabinet. Along the way, he also managed to kick the hotdog and send it skittering across the floor.

Crappers, he grumbled again.

The hunger was still there, reminding him in no uncertain terms that its needs took precedence over any thoughts of wallowing in self-pity. Stanley began the slow process of getting back to his feet. It was obvious he wasn't up to the task of feeding himself. Fortunately, Ronnie's was open all night. Decision made, he shuffled to the front door, hooked a finger through his key ring, fought with the door handle for a few minutes, and made his way into the cold winter night.

Stanley's little Chevrolet Cavalier was dusted white with a fresh layer of fluffy snow. Already certain that operating a snow brush would only end like the rest of his recent endeavors, he used his forearm to move some of the white powder off the windshield. Satisfied he'd cleared a patch big enough to see through, he set himself to the challenge of pulling open the door and getting his reluctant body into the driver's seat. Raising a leg didn't work. Trying to go in head first didn't work. Finally, he settled on putting his rear end toward the open door, leaning back, and letting the door frame bend him forward while his butt inched toward the seat. Despite the slightly uncomfortable scraping of his shoulders and back of his head against the door frame, the method worked. Most of Stanley was inside the car.

Keys came next. After holding up a hand to confirm he still had them in his grasp, he slapped the side of the steering column. The resulting clank and jingle might've been funny if Stanley were capable of being amused. As it was, each unsuccessful *thwap* of his keys against the column just bumped the needle of his annoyance up a notch. The last straw came when he swung his arm and hit the column hard enough to knock the keys from his hand to the floor mat below.

Crappers, he grumbled one last time.

Using the car was out, and Ronnie's would be a long, long walk. The Get'n'Gobble was much closer. Stanley pulled himself from the Cavalier, pointed himself toward the road, and shuffled his feet forward. It was still going to be a long walk through a cold, dark night, but with luck, he'd get there right when the town's little grocery store opened.

Good thing, too, he thought as he began his slow trek through the ankle-deep snow. *I'm hungry.*

Chapter 3

S TANLEY'S ALARM CLOCK WAS a thing of beauty. A reliable wonder of plastic and circuitry with a blue liquid crystal display. "It's time," it buzzed. "It's that time that you indicated was important. I'm so glad I was able to help wake you at this very important time."

Stanley wished he could come up with a truly wonderful way to thank his alarm clock. He'd never been able to find a thank-you card for an electronic device, so he would just pat its snooze bar lovingly and said, "Th-thanks!"

Alarm clock attended to, Stanley reviewed the list of things he had planned to start the day. Pee, poop, shower. Brush and floss his teeth. Put on clothes, eat breakfast.

With a satisfied nod, he pulled his comforter aside, swung his legs off the mattress, and placed his feet on the floor. Feet that were already snug in a pair of tube socks and attached to legs that were covered in jeans.

"What the heck?" he wondered out loud.

Stanley was pretty particular about what he wore to sleep. In the summer, it was a light pair of nylon jogging shorts over his 60/40 polyester-cotton blend underpants and a 100-percent cotton tank top.

In the winter, he traded the shorts and tank for a set of flannel pajamas. But jeans and tube socks? Highly unusual.

The mystery didn't end there. Not only had someone dressed his bottom half, but his top half was ready to go, too. Someone had pulled him into an undershirt and covered that with his favorite yellow and brown velour long-sleeve shirt. They'd even taken the time to button the collar all the way up.

"K-keeps your neck warm," he whispered, the observation dusted with déjà vu.

He figured that whoever had dressed him hadn't gone so far as to make sure he was empty and had clean teeth,

Definitely would've woken up for that, he decided,

so he headed into the bathroom. After flushing the toilet, he briefly considered showering. A quick sniff of each pit later, he decided a shower wasn't really necessary and skipped right to cleaning his teeth. After a final rinse and spit, Stanley stood and considered himself in the mirror.

"Lookin' good, b-buddy!" he announced with a wink. The wiry, angular guy with a mop of brown hair pushed into a severe part and an Adam's apple sharp enough to cut cheese with winked back. "Let's get some breakfast and then figure out who came over last night and g-got you all dressed up."

There was definitely a mystery afoot, and Stanley did enjoy a good mystery. When he made it to the bottom of the stairs, the mystery deepened. More than that, it got a lot less enjoyable. Someone dressing him while he slept could easily be construed as an attempt to be helpful. An unconventional attempt, sure, but still. Stanley had never considered the advantages of getting dressed before going to sleep. He realized now that it was a darn good way to save time in the morning, unless you really did need to shower. If he had someplace important to be, he could easily shave twelve or even fifteen minutes off his morning routine. So sure, solving a mystery about why someone wanted to help him save time in the morning, and who would've had reason to be so considerate, was not a bad thing.

Figuring out why someone trashed his living and dining room? Not nearly as much fun.

Stanley took halting steps through the mayhem. His small, two-story home had a pretty common floorplan. The front door opened up to a small entryway. Turn left, and you'd find yourself in a modest laundry room that led to the back door. Go straight, and a flight of stairs headed up to the main bedroom and smaller guest room. To the right, a small living room and smaller dining room shared the same expanse of cushy brown carpet. Just past the dining room, a compact kitchen. All things considered, it wasn't a lot of space. Even so, Stanley was shocked to discover that pretty much the entire main floor was wrecked.

The living room's back wall was lined with bookshelves that had been full of books. Now, only a few tomes still occupied their intended places. The rest were strewn all over the floor, as if fleeing the toppled television that lay among them. The dining room table had held a collection of odds and ends. Newspapers from the past weeks, mail and bills, and other normal odds and ends. Just about everything that had been on the table had, like the books and T.V., been forcibly shoved to the floor. The only thing that was fortunately still in place was the glass containing his newly discovered horse fly. Stanley scooped it up with a relieved gasp and inspected the little bug inside.

"Oh, thank goodness," he breathed. "I'm g-glad you're okay, little lady."

A memory popped like a soap bubble, and Stanley looked at his finger. Where he expected to see an angry, red bite was just regular old finger-skin. He shrugged his acceptance at the apparent miracle. He did take a lot of vitamin supplements.

Worrying about whether someone had stolen his stuff, like a favorite book or maybe his monthly cable bill, he made his way into the kitchen. The sink's faucet was trickling. The fridge was wide open, compressor chugging away. The floor was a mix of broken dishes and soapy water. Right in the middle of it all was an uncooked hotdog. Whoever had decided to pay him a visit must've really hated plates and hotdogs.

"Holy c-crappers! Why would someone d-do this?" he asked with a hitch in his voice. "Why the heck would someone d-do this?"

Shaking his head at the sheer rottenness of it all, he picked up the phone and dialed Lois.

"Someone b-broke in!" he blurted out the second the call connected.

A long yawn stretched through the receiver, followed by the loud smacking of lips.

"What's that, hon?" Lois asked in a sleepy voice. "Someone's joking? Oh, Stanley. I'm sure whatever you heard was really funny, but maybe we can talk about it later. Herb kept me up all night, if you know what I mean."

Stanley shook his head. "B-broke in. Someone broke into my *house*. They dressed me up in j-jeans and socks and one of my favorite shirts and then made a great b-big mess outta my living room and maybe stole my c-cable bill and then they messed up my kitchen and they ruined my last hotdog," he gushed. Recounting the horrors out loud had him on the verge of tears.

Lois finally offered an appropriate gasp of sympathy. "Oh Stanley, that's terrible. Are you okay? Did you call the police?" she asked. Before Stanley had a chance to reply, she added, "Wait. They dressed you?"

Stanley's head bobbed in clear agitation. "Yep. You bet'cha. I woke up, and my j-jeans were on, and my undershirt and my velour shirt. You know the one. It's soft and has this nice c-collar that k-keeps your neck real warm. Socks, too. Tube socks, which makes sense, especially in the winter. No one's really ever seeing your socks when you're wearing the shoes, so it just makes sense to wear g-good, comfortable socks."

"And you didn't wake up?" Lois asked.

The bobbing turned back into a shake as he explained that no, he hadn't woken up.

"That's what m-makes the rest of it so weird," he said. "Why would someone be so g-gentle getting me into my clothes, and then be so rotten and make a mess out of things? I worry. I mean, little things b-bother me," he continued in his best Columbo voice. "I'm a worrier. I mean, little insignificant d-details... I lose my appetite. I c-can't eat. My wife, she says to me, 'You know, you can really be a pain.'"

"You're not married."

Stanley hmph'd. "I was doing Columbo. Columbo was married."

"Oh. Huh. I suppose he was," Lois conceded, before giving in to another long yawn. "Well, if you're okay, I think you should call the sheriff. They'll send over a deputy, someone real good, and get you all taken care of. Why don't you call us tomorrow and let us know how things worked out. Okay? Later, Stanley."

The call ended with a click. Stanley stared at the receiver in disbelief. The sheriff? He had a mystery to solve. What good would the sheriff be? Although the more he considered Lois's suggestion, the more he realized it probably would be a good idea. If the home invader did steal his cable bill, he'd need to have the official report to contest the late charges.

Stanley kept a pair of readers in the house. Not because he really needed them, but because he liked the way Angela Lansbury would slip hers on when she really needed to look intently at something. He figured a conversation with the sheriff's deputy would be the perfect occasion to slide them on. His hand reached toward where they'd normally be and came up empty.

"They got my g-glasses, too? No good no-gooders, and that's a fact."

Stanley pushed numbers on the keypad, listened impatiently to a few rings, and was finally rewarded with the raspy voice of Corliss Dunkel. She'd been working dispatch at the sheriff's department for as long as anyone could remember. Some folks even said she was there first, and they just built the county office building around her.

"What?" Corliss asked, the sound falling somewhere between a word and a cough.

"Um, hiya C-Corliss. It's Stanley Henkelmann. I had a home invader, and I need a d-deputy to file a report in case they stole stuff."

Phlegmy hacking filled the line and continued for a few moments, followed by the forceful clearing of an old throat long abused by two packs of cigarettes a day.

"Address?" Corliss finally asked.

Stanley prattled of his address and added a robust description of many of the trees that were viewable from the road to make sure the deputy didn't miss the turn. Corliss repeated the address, but neglected to confirm the description of the trees. She then inquired about the nature of the break in.

"Well," Stanley admitted. "I g-guess I didn't see a busted door or broken window."

Corliss followed up with a request for missing items.

"Hmmm," Stanley hedged, looking around the detritus of his living room. "I haven't looked too c-close, but they might've taken my c-cable bill. And they ruined a p-perfectly good hotdog." When a long silence followed, he repeated himself.

"Yeah, heard ya the first time," Corliss responded. "No forced entry, maybe a bill missing, ruined a hotdog. Got it."

After a few more questions about the nature of the disturbance, the ancient and ornery dispatcher explained that it would be awhile before someone responded.

"Sheriff's skiing in Utah. Deputy Farman's at the Get'n'Gobble. Someone's causin' a fuss," she offered, before indulging in a fresh wave of throaty coughs.

Stanley tried to get a quick 'thanks' in between coughs and finally just disconnected the call. With a determined grimace, he set himself to putting things right. By the time he'd muscled the television back onto the credenza, moved most of the books back on their shelves, swept up the broken dishes, and piled newspapers and mail back up on the table, he was famished. A hotdog would've hit the spot, but his had been thoroughly ruined by the mystery invader. There wasn't much sense waiting around for the deputy on an empty stomach, so he pulled on his boots and parka and reached for the key hook by the front door.

"Where the heck are my k-keys?" he asked when his hand swiped at air. "They took my keys?"

A quick glance outside added a fresh layer of weird to his already unusual morning. His keys were gone, but his Cavalier was still right where he'd left it, although the door was open. Running outside, he wondered why someone would take his keys but not take the car. He couldn't think of a single episode of *Columbo*, *Murder, She Wrote*, or *Veronica Mars* that even remotely paralleled the day he was having.

But I know what they'd do, he decided. *Look at the facts. Always got to start with the facts.*

Stanley dropped into the Cavalier's front seat, squinted, and scratched his chin. Someone broke into his house without actually breaking in, dressed him while he was sleeping, trashed his living room and kitchen, and wasted a perfectly good hotdog. Then they came outside, wiped off the car windshield and opened the door, but left the car where it was. It sure wasn't a prank. Even if Dallas was still around, his pranks never broke plates or wasted hotdogs.

"Enemies. Enemies. That's what th-they'd be asking me next. Like that Veronica Mars, she'd c-cut right to the chase, say something clever, and ask who I'd t-ticked off."

Stanley tried to think of who in town might want to do something like this. It was a depressing exercise. After lengthy consideration, he couldn't think of a single person that expended any mental energy on him, much less enough to be considered an enemy. Hungry and defeated, Stanley slumped forward and rested his forehead against the steering wheel.

And saw his keys.

The sudden elation lasted long enough for him to retrieve the keys from the car's floor and try to start the Cavalier. It ended when the car responded with nothing more than a *click*. Another few attempts confirmed what he already knew—the battery had died.

With a weary sigh, Stanley went back inside, traded his loafers for a sturdy pair of snow boots, pulled on his parka, grabbed his mittens, and trudged back out to his garage. Like any good Sconnie, he kept a jump kit ready all winter. After reviving the Cavalier, he let the old engine rumble and sputter for a bit before backing out of his drive and heading toward town. Stanley figured that while the day might not get better, he could at least face the rest of it on a full stomach.

Chapter 4

A FTER A LONG SLOG through the wintery night and into the wintery dawn, Stanley finally reached his destination. A gust of air brushed his face when the Get'n'Gobble's sliding doors whooshed open. He supposed it should've felt warm, a welcome respite from the frigid outdoors, but he wasn't all that cold. Hungry, sure. Cold, not so much. The realization was a little surprising. He'd slipped and fallen on the treacherous snow and ice more than a few times on his trek. Once, he even rolled down into a roadside ditch and had slide on his belly back up to the road. His shirt, jeans, and socks were muddy and soaked through with melted snow. A dusty corner of Stanley's brain knew he should've been freezing, but apparently the rest of him wasn't convinced.

Operating on instinct, his hands found the rail of a shopping cart and swerved into the first aisle. He bounced his way between the shelves like a bowling ball between bumper buddies, all the while wondering what he should get to eat. About halfway down the aisle, a display of granola bars caught his attention.

Fiber? he wondered. *Probably a good idea. Keeps the cholesterol down, helps you poop. Nothing better than a good poop.*

An arm swung out, and four or five boxes fell from the shelf. To Stanley's great delight, one even fell into his cart. A slow smile creased his face as he shifted his weight and sent the cart rattling forward again. Even though he had plenty of time to prepare, navigating the U-turn at the end of the aisle didn't work out too well. The sound of breaking glass echoed through the store as apple sauce jars fell from the end-cap.

Geez, he thought with a grimace. *They gotta stack those better.*

The next aisle held baking goods and international food. Stanley careened off the shelves and added a couple boxes of cake batter, a tub of frosting, birthday candles, a few taco kits with shells, seasoning, and salsa inside, a box of penne pasta, and two bottles of soy sauce to his cart.

"Wow," a voice said from somewhere behind him. "You must really hate the Get'n'Gobble."

Stanley made a slow pivot. His eyes followed a messy trail of boxes, bags, and jars that stretched back to the end of the aisle where a small crowd had gathered. At its front, a pimply faced teen regarded Stanley with a look of reverent awe.

"I always want to trash this place too, but I need the money," the teenager said. "Dude, you rock. There's a huge toilet paper display at the end of aisle seven. You should totally knock it over. That'd be rad."

Before Stanley could put together a response, another man shouldered his way to the front of the spectators.

Bellied his way, more like, Stanley decided as he watched the man swing his ample gut to force people aside. *Tasty looking belly, too.*

"That would not be 'rad,' Brandon. Get back to your register. Everyone, please move along. I apologize for this, but we'll have the aisles cleaned up in no time, no time at all," the heavyset man announced before turning back to Stanley. "Sir, we appreciate everyone's patronage, but please be a bit more careful."

Stanley gave a conciliatory wave and resumed his shopping. After crashing through two more aisles, he suddenly found himself at the meat case. His hunger looked down at the haphazard assortment of sundries in his cart, looked up at the meat case, looked down at his cart again, and shoved it to the side.

"Mmmaaaaahhhhtuh?" he asked the woman behind the case. She stared back, wide-eyed and speechless.

Thinking she hadn't heard him, Stanley tried again. "Mmmaaaahhhtuh," he said and tapped a hand on the case's glass front. "Ff-fooooorrrr. Mmmaaahhh," he added, thumping his chest with his wrist.

The woman continued to stare and added a quiet squeak. Stanley figured they were making progress, but before he had a chance to ask for some meat again, a new voice barked out from behind him.

"Turn around slowly, and keep your hands where I can see them!"

Since the meat case lady was the only other person around, Stanley decided the loud voice was talking to him. He wobbled from foot to foot and made a slow one-eighty. When he completed his turn, he saw a deputy from the sheriff's department. As if that wasn't surprising enough, one of the deputy's hands hovered anxiously over the butt of his holstered pistol.

"These fine folks don't want any trouble," he said, "so you just move along. Now, sir," he added when Stanley didn't move.

Stanley was flummoxed. He'd been shopping at the Get'n'Gobble since he was old enough to get a few dollars from his dad, ride his bike to the store, and bring back a six-pack of beer. Now everyone was acting like he was a stranger. And not just that. They were acting like he was a bad stranger. Unbidden, thoughts of Dallas and Herb surfaced. No one had ever treated him this way when he'd been out and about with them. As he looked at the very serious deputy and the unkind eyes of the shoppers gathering around him, Stanley felt himself deflate. He just wanted to eat, but had somehow run afoul of the law. His head drooped, and he contemplated the mud smudging his shirt and jeans and his dirty, soggy socks.

Ooooohhhhh, he thought with dawning realization. *No shirt, no shoes, no service.*

After a longing look back at the meat case, he waved an apology to the deputy and started a slow shuffle down the aisle toward the store's exit. The crowd took cautious steps back and gave him a wide berth, except for the pimply faced teen, who gave him a subtle thumbs up. The sliding doors whooshed, and Stanley was back in the cold, wintery air. The sun was still making its slow trek up through the morning sky. With a frustrated sigh, he pointed himself toward home and took slow, lurching steps across the snowy parking lot. The hunger complained loudly, but Stanley told it not to worry. He'd get some shoes, and then it'd be time for an all you can eat buffet.

Chapter 5

LITTLE TENDRILS OF SNOW blew off the hood and up the windshield as Stanley's Cavalier motored down the two-lane highway. He kept the speedometer a safe three miles per hour below the speed limit. After a lifetime of driving on Wisconsin's winter roads, he'd learned an ounce of caution was worth a pound of road salt.

Stanley turned onto Main Street and stomped on the brakes. Even at his safe speed, the car still slid a few feet and narrowly avoided hitting the unexpected jaywalker. Heart pounding, Stanley checked his rearview, both side views, and blind spots. When he returned his attention to the space in front of him, the man was gone. After whipping his head back and forth again, he discovered the man hadn't vanished after all. He'd just shuffled around the far side of the car while Stanley had been checking everywhere else. Craning his neck, Stanley watched the man continue his slow trek down the road.

Nice shirt, Stanley observed. *Those velour collars keep your neck real warm.*

He briefly considered offering the stranger a ride. The guy was obviously more than a few beers into his morning, but Stanley wasn't feeling too charitable. He'd had a rough start to his day and was really hungry.

Besides, at the rate he's moving, I'll bet I can catch up with him on the way back, he reasoned.

As he pulled away, the thought made him feel a smidge better. People always said be a Good Samaritan, but there was no need to be a Great Samaritan.

When Stanley walked into the Get'n'Gobble, he was greeted with a burst of warm air followed by an accusing, "Hey! You aren't supposed to be in here." A split-second later, a law enforcement officer roughly grabbed his arm and turned him back toward the door.

"I told you that you had to leave," the deputy barked. "I thought you'd be smart enough to know that also meant you had to stay away."

Stanley began to sputter and tried to ask why he was being detained. He'd never been in trouble with the law—not ever—and didn't have a clue what he'd done.

"I st-stopped at all the stop signs. I was d-driving under the speed limits. I even looked both ways b-before I walked across the p-parking lot," he pleaded with tears in his eyes. "I d-didn't do nothing. I swear!"

"Save it," the deputy growled. "You're a vandal and a no-gooder. You already cause a boatload of trouble here, and you're not doing it again. Not on my watch."

The Get'n'Gobble's doors whooshed open, and Stanley was about to be shoved forcibly out when another voice called out.

"Hold up, law dude!" a pimply faced teenager hollered from behind the register on lane two. "That's not the guy. C'mon. Look at him. The guy had glasses and was a whole lot. I dunno. Deader-lookin'."

The deputy yanked Stanley back from the threshold and turned him roughly around. He peered at Stanley, suspicion oozing from every stich in his polyester uniform.

"Ned?" the deputy asked.

In response, the oversized store manager lumbered over. "No, that's not him. That's just Stanley Henkelmann. Sorry," he offered to the shaken Stanley.

The deputy mumbled something that might've been an apology. He was about to turn away when Stanley grabbed his arm.

"S-sir, um. You said there was a no-gooder and a vandal. I had one'a those at my house. Somebody g-got in and made a real mess of my living room and k-kitchen. I called the station. I called, and that Corliss, she said a deputy would b-be coming over," Stanley managed. When the deputy didn't respond, Stanley pressed on. "Well, since you're here, and I'm here, and you're lookin' for a vandal, and I had a vandal..." he managed before the deputy silenced him with a dark look.

"Listen up, fella. They might think you're not the guy that messed up this store, but I'm not convinced. So do your shopping, but know this," the deputy warned, chest puffing up. "If you so much as put a can of beans back with the label in instead of out, I'll come down on you like the fist of God."

Stanley cringed. He searched the gathered crowd of onlookers. Besides the teenage cashier, there wasn't another pair of sympathetic eyes. Crestfallen, Stanley gave a brief nod of understanding. It was apparently enough to satisfy the deputy, because he shouldered Stanley aside and stomped off through the sliding doors.

As the gathered crowd realized the spectacle was over, they dispersed and returned to tracking down their individual lists of sundries. Stanley followed suit and freed a cart from the waiting rows. It was one with a bad wheel that dragged and squeaked; the noise putting him squarely back in the spotlight. As a growing number of disapproving glares focused on him, he decided it just wasn't worth it. Being passively ignored at Ronnie's was better than being actively disliked at the Get'n'Gobble. Leaving the cart, he turned and walked dejectedly from the store and back into the cold, wintery world outside.

Chapter 6

SOCKS DIDN'T PROVIDE THE best traction when walking on snowy sidewalks, so Stanley had veered into the main road that led away from the Get'n'Gobble. Bert "Two-shirt" Nesheim, the town's snow plow operator and a regular in the men's bowling league, had obviously passed through early in the morning, pushing snow aside and sprinkling a practical mix of salt and sand. The mid-morning sun was also warming the exposed asphalt and melting away the snowy remnants the plow had left behind. As Stanley trudged along, he welcomed the more stable footing the road provided. Not having to concentrate fully on keeping his balance freed up time to think about other things, namely his near-overwhelming hunger.

Shoes, he reminded himself, his thoughts keeping time with his shuffling steps. *Get some shoes. Get some food. Shoes, food. Shoes, food. Shoes, meat. Meat. Meat.*

That last thought caused him to stumble. He managed to catch himself a second before a rusted blue Cavalier skidded to a stop mere inches in front of him.

Nice car, he observed. *Those Cavaliers sure got the good brakes.*

Angling to the side, he made his way around the car and contin-ued on his journey. A distant part of his brain noticed the sounds of crunching tires and a fading engine, but he didn't pay it much attention. He'd already settled back into his slow, plodding pace.

Shoes. Meat. Meat. Meat. Meat. Meat.

The hunger was becoming unbearable. Each slogging step ratcheted it up from a persistent grumbling to an ear-splitting wail. It was even coloring his vision, sending angry flashes of searing blue and blood red before his eyes. He was so overwhelmed by the demands of his hunger that he walked directly into a parked car.

"You! I warned you," an angry voice yelled over the screaming sirens. "First, you're vandalizing private property. Now you're jaywalking, and you just hit an official sheriff's department vehicle. And don't you even think about running, or I'll get you for a hit and run to boot."

The sirens abruptly silenced, but Stanley's vision was still full of reds and blues. Squinting, he made out the shape of the car he'd just walked into. Standing beside it was the deputy from the Get'n'Gobble. The mean deputy that had yelled at him. At least, Stanley thought it was the same deputy. When he tried to peer more closely at the man's face, his mind conjured up some strange amalgam of all the people that'd been treating him so awfully. It wasn't fair. He hadn't hurt anyone. He just wanted something to eat. It wasn't his fault he broke all his plates and dropped his hotdog. It wasn't his fault he couldn't drive. Sure, he forgot to put on shoes, but that shouldn't be cause for all this fuss.

The hunger in his belly bucked and kicked and changed its shape, becoming a wholly new emotion. The newborn anger boiled and churned. It twisted Stanley's back and craned his neck. It clawed his fingers and stretched his jaw. When the deputy moved to grab his wrist, the anger shoved his head forward and clamped his teeth down on the deputy's cheek.

Blood sprayed like the physical expression of the man's surprised scream as Stanley brought all one hundred and fifty pounds of his hungry body to bear down on his victim. Unfortunately, Stanley's buck-fifty of hungry anger was no match for the deputy's two-hundred and twenty pounds of adrenaline-fueled reaction. Stanley felt himself sailing backward as the deputy lifted and tossed him like a beanbag. He felt the ground rush up to meet him and heard the audible whack of the back of his skull connecting solidly with the asphalt. As he lay on his back, arms and legs jutting up at odd angles, he didn't feel pain or even indignation. He felt a strange satisfaction. A feeling of accomplishing something important. Something right. Stanley licked his lips and felt the slickness of blood, tasted its warm coppery flavor. He worked his jaw and throat and swallowed little bits of flesh that had torn free from the deputy's face. The hunger that had been driving him absorbed the flesh, and while it wasn't satiated—not by any stretch of the imagination—it approved of Stanley's efforts.

Another emotion sat alongside the satisfaction and darkened its warmth with a cold shadow. Stanley tried to classify this other emotion, give it a shape to make it recognizable, edges he could hold. It felt like loneliness, like rejection. The realization that no matter what you did or how hard you tried, people just didn't get you, just didn't like you. It also felt about how someone would expect to feel if they just wanted to eat and were instead thrown bodily to the cold, hard ground.

Emotions are funny things. Some blend together perfectly, like strawberries and bananas in a milkshake. Others mix worse than oil and water. Stanley considered the strange blending of his emotions as he slowly worked his way back to his feet. The hunger, anger, and loneliness were mixing their way into a strawberry-banana rage. His friends had abandoned him. Everyone else he tried to connect with at best ignored him, and at worst accused him of being a no-good no-gooder and threw him to the ground.

He shuffled forward with the sole intention of letting this new-found rage pour out on the deputy, but the rage petered out as he drew closer to the other man. After throwing Stanley, the deputy had collapsed to the ground, moaning in agony and clawing at his face. He twitched and rolled and convulsed while Stanley watched, perplexed.

Geez, what a wimp, he thought. *I just bit his cheek.*

Remembering that delicious bite, Stanley angled closer and wondered if he could get a second nip in, but stopped when the deputy's convulsing abruptly ceased. He watched as the color drained from the man's face, leaving it an unhealthy yellow-grey. He continued to watch as the man's eyes fixed on an impossibly distant horizon and slowly clouded over. Stanley nudged his glasses and squinted as he tried to discern some sign of life, but no such signs were apparent.

Oh crappers...

All the emotions Stanley had been feeling dissolved. He wasn't hungry for a dead guy, and it didn't make much sense to be angry at a dead guy. He was still lonely, but dead guys weren't capable of being good company, and Stanley didn't think it'd be fair to hold a dead guy to unattainable standards. Suddenly empty, he slipped dejectedly back into the waiting lassitude and stared at nothing in particular.

"Aaaaaahhhhhhhh."

The moan caught Stanley's absent attention and reeled it back in. The deputy that had been quite dead apparently wasn't. He was waving an arm and making an effort to sit up. Stanley felt a weird déjà vu and stepped back to give him some space. After a few long moments, the man gained his feet and stared at nothing in particular.

Stanley contemplated the deputy. The angry, aggressive, derisive man was gone. In his place was a much more subdued man with grey skin, red eyes, and a flap of bloody cheek hanging from one side of his face. Stanley waited for the deputy to accost him again, threaten him again, or even grab and throw him again. When none of those things happened, he raised a hand and offered a tentative, "Haaaaaal-llooooo."

The deputy's chin lifted, and his blood-shot eyes focused on Stanley.

"Haaaaaaahhhhh," he responded as he lifted his own hand in an awkward wave.

"Ssstaaaaaannnn. Lllleeeee."

A moment passed, and the deputy responded, "Fffaaah. Fffaaaaar-rrr. Mmmmaaaaaaannn."

Stanley's heart wasn't capable of jumping, but he definitely felt something in his chest. Deputy Farman was talking to him. Was being nice to him. Emboldened, Stanley asked the next question that came to mind.

"Huuunnngaaahreee?"

"Yaaaaaahhhhh," Farman responded with a slow nod.

Stanley looked at his wet, dirty socks. He knew that there was no way he'd be allowed back into the Get'n'Gobble. He craned his neck and considered the sun shining weakly through the wintery clouds above. There were other places they could go, places that didn't have the same high standards as the local grocery store. Steinknockers came to mind. The bar had a modest kitchen that basically took stuff and deep fried it. Even better, Old Stein would let pretty much anyone in, provided they behaved themselves.

"Ssstuh," Stanley tried, the word surprisingly hard to say. "Sssteeeeinnnns," he managed, and waved an arm in the general direction of the local watering hole.

"Yaaahhhh," Farman agreed, and turned toward the still-open door of the squad car.

Stanley watched with no small measure of admiration as the deputy managed to get inside the cruiser and even slam the door. It took a few minutes, but it was still more than Stanley had been able to do with his Cavalier. Not wanting to miss an opportunity to get a bite with his friend, Stanley forced the passenger door open, shoved himself inside, and flashed his new buddy a bloody grin. The grin faltered when Farman dropped the car in reverse and stomped heavily on the gas, but returned in full force when the deputy found a gear that would allow them to go forward and sent them racing in a better direction. The car lurched and swerved like a two-ton version of Stanley's shopping cart. It careened from curb to curb, throwing the men first left then right as buildings, parked cars, and streetlights flashed by on either side. Stanley supposed it was only a matter of time before they collided with something. After they did, Stanley was rather impressed they'd made it as far as they had before the crash.

The other car was a sporty red Mazda Miata. A real looker of a car with a black convertible roof, shiny chrome rims, and a trim little spoiler off the back. The woman that got out was equally attractive and understandably upset. She'd been stopped at a stop sign when Farman drove straight into her rear bumper.

"What the hell, asshole?" the woman screamed as she wobbled out of the car.

Stanley supposed the wobbling was either the result of her nerves being a bit frayed because of the accident, or the difficulty of navigating snowy pavement in six-inch stiletto heels. While the woman surveyed the crumpled ruin of her rear bumper, Stanley let his eyes wander up her bare legs until they reached the hem of a garish coat that hung about halfway down the woman's thighs. The coat only partially concealed a voluptuous figure that he immediately decided would be darn tasty to snack on.

"Shit. I'm going to be late for my shift," he heard the woman say. "If I lose my job over this, I'm suing your ass. Nekked's is the only strip club for fifty miles."

Stanley moved to open his door, but Farman was faster. The deputy wobbled toward the woman while she showered him with derisive comments. Her tirade ended with a surprised squeal when she tried to slap him and he bit her wrist. Her free hand boxed his ear, and a knee shot up into his groin. The move was impressive, especially considering her footwear, and effective. Farman stumbled back, giving the woman the opening she needed to flee. After the brief altercation, Farman simply stood in place, his vacant stare watching the retreating taillights of the smashed up Miata's rear end.

"Aaaawwwww," Stanley commiserated after freeing himself from the squad car and making his way to Farman's side. "Waaaaaalllk nooooowww?"

His new friend bobbed his head, and the two began a halting, staggering, lurching journey that carried them further from the wrecked squad car and closer to an honest-to-goodness meal.

Chapter 7

E ATING AT RONNIE'S HAD left Stanley full but feeling empty. The waitress had taken his order, the cook had cooked his food, and he'd eaten a decent meal. If that had been his only goal, he'd have felt fine. Unfortunately, he had really wanted to talk to someone, but no one felt like talking back. Despite his best efforts not to, Stanley found himself wondering about Lois and Herb and Dallas. Who knew what they were up to? Whatever it was, it hurt to know they weren't doing it with him.

Lonely and alone, Stanley left the diner in a funk. While driving home, he was so caught up in his dark thoughts that he almost didn't notice the two men staggering down the side of the road. When he did, he couldn't help but roll his eyes. More drunks? Stanley was certainly not one to judge the drinking habits of others, but it did seem a little early in the day to be that far into their cups.

I suppose I could give them a lift, he considered briefly.

A glance at the Cavalier's clock put that idea to rest. He needed to get home before the sheriff's deputy showed up to investigate his home invasion. So he wasn't a Great Samaritan, or even a good one. He'd considered giving them a ride, which he decided made him an Okay Samaritan. That worked for Stanley.

When he arrived home, he made sure to park in the garage and lock it up tight. Stanley did some crosswords to pass the time and wondered idly when the deputy would arrive. After a couple of hours, he began to worry that the deputy might drive by, not see a car, and decide Stanley wasn't home. That wouldn't do, so he backed out of the garage and parked in the driveway. After another hour had passed without any sign of the deputy, he called the sheriff's department again.

"Yeah?" Corliss asked after a fresh round of coughs.

"Oh. Hi, Corliss. It's Stanley again. I mean, Stanley Henkelmann. C-calling again. You know, about the b-break in. No one's been here."

A smoky, mirthless laugh forced its way through the receiver, after which Corliss explained that no one had been there, either.

"We got a stack of calls. Jaywalker, litterbug, some lady parked in a handicap spot without a tag, even some guy walking around in a Viking's jersey and saying all kinds of nasty stuff about Vince Lombardi." Corliss paused after that one to let the significance settle in. "Anyway, Farman's going to have a busy afternoon when he finally gets around to answering my calls."

Stanley grumbled an insincere 'thanks' and set the phone back in its cradle. The day had officially settled into evening. He decided that he could either stay put and die of boredom while waiting for a deputy that wasn't likely to come or take in a few games at Bay City Bowlers. The town's bowling alley was a second home of sorts for most of Trappersville's menfolk. If Stanley wanted comradery, Bay City's was the place.

A short time later, his jeans hovered a few inches above a nice pair of suede bowling shoes instead of his usual leather loafers. Stanley carried his bowling bag to the counter, smiling and waving at all the familiar faces and trusting that they would've all waved back if they weren't so busy bowling. He asked for a lane, but the alley's owner, Slow Johnson, said everything was taken. He tried to join Stu, Dozer, and Wyatt on lane six, but the three giants said they weren't looking for a fourth. He tried to join a family on lane eleven, but the mom said she didn't want her kids bowling with a stranger. Lane after lane, he reached out in the spirit of friendship, and was rebuffed in the spirit of Midwestern passive-aggressive politesse.

Stanley finally asked Johnson to holler if a lane opened up and headed for the karaoke bar. Pushing through the bar's saloon style doors, he stepped up to the rail and waited for Rhoda, the omnipresent bartender, to notice him.

"Make it quick, hon. Busy tonight," she said after he finally caught her eye.

"Oh. Yep. You b-bet. Um. A 'Waukee's B-Best. That'll d-do," Stanley requested.

Rhonda deposited the beer, but before Stanley could ask if she'd seen the prior night's Final Jeopardy question, she was on to the next customer. After a long, contemplative swig, Stanley turned his attention to the karaoke stage. A couple were trying to do Sonny and Cher's *I Got You, Babe*, but it was apparent they didn't get each other at all. He drank his beer, endured the song, and waited with forced patience for a lane to open up. Seven songs later, he checked in with Slow Johnson.

"Oh, sorry 'bout that," the manager said. "Forgot you were waiting, and someone else got the lane. Want me to put you back on the list?"

Feeling worse than before he'd arrived, Stanley said no and finally called it quits on one of the worst days he'd had in a long time. The drive home from Bay City Bowlers was a glum one. He turned off the main road, threaded the trees lining his long driveway, and put the car in park. A twist of the key silenced the engine, and a familiar creak accompanied the door's opening.

"Rotten d-day," he complained to no one, "but I guess there's always t-tomorrow."

Ready to do nothing more than crawl back into bed and pull the covers up under his chin, Stanley stepped out of his car and onto a fresh dusting of powdery white snow. His foot shot out in front of him, and for a moment Stanley felt himself floating. When the back of his head connected with the car's doorjamb, his head snapped forward and jammed his chin down against his chest. At the same moment, the ground rushed up and pounded his back like a sledgehammer. A whimper slipped through his chipped teeth and blood-filled mouth before everything went dark.

Chapter 8

S TANLEY SURVEYED THE BLOODY slaughterhouse that used to be Steinknocker's Bar and gave a contented sigh. His gut protruded happily over the waistband of his blue jeans, and his jaw ached pleasantly from all the biting. Many of his new friends were still chewing on the gory remains of those patrons that weren't fortunate enough to turn before they were mostly eaten. A few paused mid-bite and looked his way. When they saw Stanley's red smile, they waved cordially in return.

It was nice, being around so many friendly people. It hadn't been that way when they had first arrived. Stanley had trudged through the snow, and Deputy Farman had followed. For a long while, that was all there was. Step after shuffling, lurching step through the ankle-deep snow. No significant thoughts besides the persistent desire to eat. When they'd arrived at Stein's, Stanley had leaned a shoulder against the door and pushed his way into a nearly full bar.

Drinking in Wisconsin wasn't just a pastime. It was a serious endeavor. Everyone had their own technique and spent most of their adult years perfecting it. There was the friendly drinker that would smile at newcomers and share good-natured jokes with whoever ended up beside him at the bar. The loudmouth, whose volume increased with each swig. The overworked drinker tended to sigh a lot and say things like, "TGIF, ya know?" There was the chuckler—or cackler, depending on the laugh—that found everything funny, and the grump that made sure everyone knew that no, it wasn't funny, and only a damn idiot would say so. Lots of different drinkers, but they all had one thing in common. Cold weekends at this time of year, when the holidays were in the rearview mirror and spring was still a distant hope, were the perfect time to come together and practice their craft.

Stanley and Farman had walked into a bar teeming with noise. Conversations, clinking glasses, old Stein's bark when someone bumped the jukebox or spilled beer on a pool table. It was the familiar din of a northwoods watering hole, and it filled the small bar like the smell of apple pie in a grandmother's kitchen. The noise had wrapped around Stanley and drawn him in, comforting in its embrace. Then someone noticed the two newcomers. Then a second person noticed them, and a third. As each new person laid eyes on the two men standing just inside the front door, they had fallen silent. The hush crept like a slow burn through a field, consuming each blade of grass and leaving a charred husk in its wake.

"The hell's wrong with you two?" someone had finally asked. Probably one of the grumps, but Stanley couldn't be sure. It was still early, so the guy could've been a loudmouth that was still getting warmed up.

"Yeah," a woman's voice said. "Halloween was months ago." The ensuing cackle let Stanley know exactly what type of drinker she was.

Stanley had shrugged off the cold looks and unkind comments and made his way to the bar. Farman followed and occupied a space beside him that another patron had quickly vacated. Stein, the bar's owner, made his cautious way over and tipped his chin in a polite, if guarded, nod.

"You boys look like death warmed over. Maybe you wanna head home, clean up a bit, and come back later?"

"Yeah," a fresh voice had added, seconding Stein's recommendation. "And get some shoes while you're at it. No shirt, no shoes, no Stein's."

Stanley had turned to look at the waitress, a new girl Stein must've hired to replace Helen after her mishap with Herb and the tanning booth the past summer. He figured all he needed to do was introduce himself and let her know that it was okay, he was a regular, and he and his new friend just wanted a bite.

"Haaaaaahhhh," he had started, and was roughly shoved aside.

Deputy Farman staggered past Stanley and charged the girl jaws first. When another patron had moved to intervene, Stanley grabbed at his arm with uncoordinated fingers. What happened after was a wholly new and rather exciting experience.

Stanley had never been in a bar fight. He'd been around plenty of them, drinking with Dallas guaranteed ringside seats to occasional brawls, but he'd never actually been one of the combatants. When a fist hit his face, his first thought was that someone must've mistaken him for Dallas. When the second fist hit his face, he realized that he actually was the target. The blows didn't hurt, but they did send him reeling and reminded him that he had no idea what to do in a fight. When someone made the mistake of catching him, Stanley did the only thing he could. He bit.

It was around that point in time that the small bar fight Farman had started by biting the waitress turned into a big bar fight, and it was one that the two men should have lost painfully and quickly. They had been woefully outnumbered. At least, they'd been woefully outnumbered until the waitress bit someone, and the fellow Stanley had chomped on bit someone else. Each person that had started by swinging at Stanley or Farman got bit, went down, and came back up on their side. The tide turned, one bloody, flesh-tearing bite at a time. Before Stanley knew it, he was shoulder to shoulder with the waitress that had accosted him and munching happily on a middle-aged local named Flo.

It was right about then that he realized they were zombies. It wasn't some big revelation, not like it was with Herb and Dallas. Herb had told him about the night he first figured out that he'd become a vampire. He'd collapsed onto his bathroom floor and cried bloody tears, denial finally succumbing to the unavoidable truth that he wasn't human anymore. Poor Dallas had had an even worse time of it when he learned that he was a werewolf. Stanley was there for that literal awakening. Dallas woke up on the floor of a rundown cabin in the woods covered in Fancy Dan's blood and full of Fancy Dan. Very dramatic. For Stanley, the notion that he wasn't human anymore and was, in fact, a zombie had just sort of dawned on him.

Wait a sec, he had thought as he was about to bite down on Flo's nose. *This ain't normal. No, sir.*

Relaxing his jaw, Stanley had thought back on the day he'd just had. Waking up on his living room floor and moving like a sloth on Quaaludes. Walking for miles with only a pair of tube socks between him and the snowy streets. The trouble at the Get'n'Gobble. Biting the deputy like the fly bit him.

Like the fly. The strange fly that bit his finger.

Oooohhh, he thought, nodding his head. *Yep. Must've been a zombie fly.*

With that realization, he had shrugged his acceptance, leaned back over Flo, and chomped down on her nose until the bones cracked like a chicken drummie.

Stanley shook himself out of his reverie. The commotion had all but ceased. The pained and terrified screams were gone, replaced with a collection of moans and groans. The recently turned and recently fed zombies shifted idly from foot to foot, bumping into one another and making small talk.

"Aaaaahhhh," one fellow said, his overalls marking him as the town's mechanic.

"Errrraaaaahhh," a lady responded, and then shared a gruesome chuckle with her companion.

Curious what was so funny, Stanley weaved his way across the bar, grateful for his slow pace. The floor was slick with blood and other fluids he couldn't identify, and keeping his balance was definitely tricky.

"Aaaahhhh?" he asked.

For a moment, he was sure he'd be rebuffed. Ignored. Told to move along. It was what always happened. Then the lady replied with a friendly, "Urrrrrgh. Aaaahhhh," and the man added, "Haaaarrrghuh."

Stanley couldn't help but chuckle. It really was funny. He was about to ask what had happened next when a scream erupted from somewhere outside. As one, the zombies all turned toward the sound and started shuffling. Their bodies pushed tables and chairs aside, and they piled up against the booths lining the bar's wall. Bloody palms slapped the paneling and knocked condiments to the floor. One of the sharper tools in the shed headed toward the bar's door. When the others remembered there was a way outside, they ceased their fruitless assault on the wall and lurched toward the exit.

Stanley was in the middle of the bumping, jostling crowd. Herded along by his friends and drawn by the continued screams, he made his way around the side of Steinknockers. A smaller clump of bodies was gathered near the far side of the parking lot. Drawing closer, he realized that the bodies were mostly women and mostly naked. Their tiny outfits covered a wide range of fashion trends with very little fabric. Stanley was impressed to realize how much a small swath of sequined lace or a few feathers could convey. They also revealed a significant amount of yellow-grey skin, the result making the strategically placed patches of sequins sparkle even brighter in the lot's sodium lights.

Those girls must be from Nekked's, he realized. The town's strip club wasn't a long drive from Stein's. When he spotted a voluptuous and scantily clad brunette still wearing a stiletto heel, his suspicion was confirmed. The girl he and Farman had crashed into must've made it to work after all.

The Steinknockers crowd converged on an unfortunate band of survivors that were in the process of being devoured by a bunch of undead strippers. Stanley didn't think he couldn't possibly eat another bite, but he'd been wrong before. Shoving and worming his way through the crush of bodies, he ended up next to the brunette. Together, they made short work of the remaining survivor and finished with a small intestine stretched between their mouths like a spaghetti noodle. Stanley let his end of the intestine drop, and the brunette hungrily slurped it up. As the last bit cleared her lips, she smiled, and Stanley lit up inside.

"Hiiiii," he said sheepishly.

"Haaaaaahhh," she replied with a coy wink. At least, he thought it was meant to be a wink, even though both eyelids drooped heavily and then pushed their way open again.

"Sssstaaaaannnwweeee."

After a long pause, she responded, "Laurraaaa."

Her hand, still coated in sticky blood and melting snow, slid forward and linked fingers with his. Stanley couldn't believe it. He'd started the day hungry and alone. Now, barely twelve hours later, he had a full belly, loads of friends, and a girlfriend to boot. A hot one, too. Laura's dark trusses were matted and clumped with sultry bits of gristle and blood, and her jaundiced skin practically glowed in the romantic glare of the parking lot lights. He couldn't wait to tell Dallas.

Except he couldn't tell Dallas. Dallas had left him. And he couldn't tell Herb either. Herb was off with Lois. Looking around at the collection of zombies, Stanley was surprised again by how nice everyone was being to each other. No one argued. No one fought. They clumped together in twos and threes and swayed idly in an invisible breeze. Some moaned, others moaned back. They were all really nice folks. So what if they weren't Herb or Dallas or Lois. He didn't need them. Not anymore.

Pushing himself awkwardly to his feet, Stanley surveyed his companions. Now that he had all these new friends, he wanted to do stuff friends did.

"Baaahhh. Liiiinnnng?" he asked. It seemed like a good idea. He'd always enjoyed bowling at Bay City's, and now he had enough people to start his own league.

The zombies shuffled and moaned. Some exchanged glances, but no one seemed too enthused.

"Eeeeeaaaaaat," Stanley added. Judging by how busy Stein's had been, chances were good there were plenty of folks to munch on at the bowling alley too.

As he hoped it would, that suggestion sparked a reaction. The zombies all turned toward him, ready to follow his lead. Still holding Laura's sticky hand in his own, Stanley pointed himself toward town and slid his foot across the pavement. When everyone else's feet did the same, a smile split his face from ear to ear.

Chapter 9

S TANLEY'S ALARM CLOCK WAS a thing of beauty. A reliable wonder of plastic and circuitry with a blue liquid crystal display. "It's time," it buzzed. "It's that time that you indicated was important. I'm so glad I was able to help wake you at this very important time."

Stanley wished he could come up with a truly wonderful way to thank his alarm clock. He'd never been able to find a thank-you card for an electronic device. Instead, he would pat its snooze bar lovingly and said, "Th-th-thanks!"

This morning was no exception. He pressed the snooze bar and opened his mouth to say thanks... and froze.

Wait a sec, his brain advised. Pulling back the covers, he discovered he was fully dressed. *Thought so. Felt a little warmer than usual.*

Stanley tried to remember what he'd done the previous night. Had there been drinking? After smacking his lips a few times and considering the absence of a headache, he decided not.

Why the heck am I all dressed? he wondered.

He was wearing jeans, a V-neck undershirt, and his favorite velour top. In addition, he was already bundled up in his parka and his feet were snug inside of his sturdy winter boots.

Getting dressed at night really is a time-saver in the morning, he conceded, *but I don't think I got any place special to be this morning.*

With a good-natured chuckle at how mixed-up he could be sometimes, Stanley reviewed the list of things he had planned to start the day. Pee, poop, shower. Brush and floss his teeth. Put on clothes, eat breakfast.

Stanley slid off the parka and tossed it on the bed, and pulled the boots free to reveal a nice pair of tube socks. A trip to the bathroom was next, where he crossed items one and two off his morning to-do list. After flushing, he briefly considered showering. A quick sniff of each pit later, he decided a shower wasn't really necessary and skipped right to cleaning his teeth. After a final rinse and spit, Stanley stood and considered himself in the mirror.

"Lookin' good, b-buddy!" he announced with a wink. Ready to start his day, he headed downstairs with a spring in his step.

The blue Barca Lounger gave a satisfying creak as it accepted his weight, almost as if it too was anticipating the upcoming excitement. Stanley extended the footrest, placed his remote controls in their proper order on his lap, and powered up his entertainment center. One of his favorite shows, *Judge Judy*, was about to start. As the curved glass came to life, Stanley daydreamed about what the case would be. *Judge Judy* always had the best cases. Once, a couple that had broken up went to court over flour poured into a gas tank. Another time, a photographer said a painter stole his camera. One of his favorites was a dispute over an electricity bill one neighbor incurred because another neighbor had stealthily plugged in an extension cord to their outdoor outlet.

Wait a sec, his brain advised for the second time that morning. *I haven't seen that one yet. That one's supposed to be on today.*

Perplexed, Stanley returned his attention to the T.V. and realized that *Judge Judy* wasn't on. He double-checked the channel and the time. Right place, right time, but no Judy. Instead, Pamela Anderson and David Hasselhoff were running across the beach as a rerun of *Baywatch* started.

That's a Saturday show. Why are they showing a Saturday show?

Usually, Stanley was up for *Baywatch*. The mysteries were never as good as Veronica Mars, but that Pamela Anderson sure was fun to watch run. As his eyes moved up and down while she bounced along the sand, a very peculiar feeling worked its way through Stanley. Something wasn't right. In fact, something was definitely wrong. The off feeling had started when he woke up and had made it perfectly clear it wasn't going away anytime soon.

When his stomach grumbled, he decided he was probably just suffering from low blood sugar. Tube socks padded silently across the living room carpet and carried him into his small kitchen. A quick yank swung the fridge door open, and Stanley realized he'd been robbed.

"Who stole my hotdog?"

Staring at the shelf in his fridge that he was certain had held at least one hotdog, Stanley again tried to remember what he'd done the previous day. He knew he'd gone to Ronnie's for a bite to eat. He bumped into Herb's old neighbor, Jerry. Later, he'd discovered a fly. When that particular memory surfaced, he closed the fridge and ran to the dining room table. Sure enough, there was the cup with a coaster taped across the top.

"Weird," he observed. He remembered catching the fly, remembered letting it bite him, but that was it. "Well, can't b-be solving mysteries on an empty stomach," he decided.

After retrieving his parka and boots from the bedroom, he trudged outside and found another unpleasant surprise. His car door was wide open and the battery was dead. Muttering a curse he learned from Dallas, Stanley dragged his jump kit from the garage, popped the Cavalier's hood, and got the engine to turn over. A weird déjà vu tugged again at the corners of his mind, but only for a moment. He would have plenty of time to ponder weird feelings after a cup of Ronnie's coffee and a plateful of eggs, bacon, hash browns, and white toast.

The drive to Ronnie's was surprisingly eventful. Usually, there wasn't much action on the roads around town. The occasional car in the ditch when someone dozed off at the wheel, or a slow procession of backed-up traffic if Old Mrs. Lowry was driving in a no-passing zone, tended to be the most interesting things you'd see. This morning, Stanley was passed by two fire trucks and an ambulance. All three had their lights blazing and sirens wailing. Always careful, he moved to the shoulder as they blew by, and wondered what the excitement was. It certainly didn't do much to dispel the odd feeling he'd been plagued with all morning.

"I'll b-bet somebody left their Christmas lights on the t-tree," he said to himself. "D-dangerous. Them trees, they get so dry. D-dry as tinder. Only takes a little spark and—whoosh!—the whole p-place'll go up like the Fourth of July."

Shaking his head at how irresponsible some folks could be, he turned onto the highway and pointed his Cavalier toward Ronnie's. The truck stop, diner, and gift emporium was one of his favorite place to go. When Herb used to work there, they had served up the most amazing French toast. Even after Herb had stopped cooking at Ronnie's, they still managed to put together a solid breakfast. After pulling into a mostly empty parking lot, Stanley walked in, fully expecting to be caught up in the familiar. Locals soaking up the morning newspaper while they soaked up egg yolks with toasted white bread. Long-haul truckers swapping stories about the times they'd avoided the highway patrol and made their runs in record time. Third-shifters from the paper mill finishing their day with dinner in the morning while first-shifters packed in a quick bite before heading into work. Instead, he walked into a near-empty diner. One person sat at the counter. The only other patrons shared a booth by the window. As Stanley hung his jacket on a coat tree, the sound of Ronnie in full-on rant mode reached his ears.

"No good. No damn good. Not a single one of 'em. They're trying to ruin me. And why? I'm just trying to serve. I got the higher calling. 'Open a truck stop,' it said. 'Best damn truck stop in Wisconsin,' it said. And what did I do?"

Unsure if the question had been directed at him, Stanley opened his mouth to answer. Before he could hazard a guess at what Ronnie had done, Ronnie answered for him.

"I opened the best damn truck stop in Wisconsin," the diner's owner said as he pushed through the swinging door that separated the kitchen from the dining area. Three plates of horribly burnt food were balanced precariously on top of each other. Ronnie wove between the tables and dropped the plates loudly at the booth by the window.

"Not my fault," Ronnie snapped defensively when one guy poked his blackened and shriveled strip of bacon with a fork. "They're trying to ruin me. The waitress didn't show up. The cook didn't show up. I called the backups, and no one answered their damn phone. I'm just trying to serve. Just trying to live up to my higher calling, but they're trying to ruin me," he muttered as he headed back toward the kitchen.

Stanley raised a hand in greeting as the harried owner stormed past.

"Morning, Ronnie. G-geez. You look stressed. You should try meditation. I saw this show on the T.V. where this g-guy was all sorts of stressed..." he started, but Ronnie had already disappeared into the kitchen.

When Ronnie didn't emerge after five long minutes, Stanley hesitantly called out and asked if he was alright.

"No," came a terse reply from somewhere behind the serve-through window. "They've ruined me. You want something to eat, cook it yourself."

Stanley chewed his lip in indecision for a moment and then shrugged. Pushing his way through the swinging door, he poured himself a cup of coffee and rummaged around for the ingredients needed to whip up a good breakfast. Carrying his meal in one hand and coffee in the other, Stanley settled onto a stool at the counter and shoved a forkful of hash browns into his mouth. They were good. Really good. So good that he wondered if he should ask Ronnie for a job. Before he'd even finished chewing the first bite, he took a second, and a third. Mouth still full of hash browns, he grabbed up a strip of bacon and took a bite. The bacon was good too. Really, really good, so he pushed the rest into his mouth. Belatedly, he realized he was in desperate need of air. He convulsively sucked in a sharp breath, and a lump of half-chewed breakfast lodged in his windpipe. He tried to cough, but the lump made that impossible. As the seconds ticked away, panic set in. He began to slap the counter and moan. He rocked back and forth faster and faster, desperate for air but unable to get any into his lungs. The edges of his vision blurred and shadows started to encroach from all around. Bits of shadow broke into floating spots that danced haphazardly before his eyes. He realized it was actually quite beautiful, and the panic subsided. In its place, a strange calm settled over him like a warm blanket. His chest still bucked and his back bent and twisted, but those were distant things. The only things that mattered were the floating, spinning, expanding dots erasing all the light.

The last thing he saw before the dark spots filled his world was Ronnie running from the kitchen. The last thing he felt was two arms wrap around him from behind and pull hard against his gut again and again. The last thing he heard before all faded to black was a nasally voice screaming, "No dying in my diner, damn you! No one will ever eat where someone died! It'll ruin me!"

Chapter 10

B AY CITY BOWLERS WAS hopping. Usually, the alley would close down by around midnight or one, but this was no ordinary night. The fun had lasted past midnight, well through the wee hours, and all the way into Saturday morning. Every lane was taken, the spaces behind the lanes were full, the loudly patterned carpet stretching from the registration desk to the bathrooms and beyond was packed, and even the karaoke bar was fit to burst. Loud moans echoed from paneled wall to paneled wall as the swollen mob of zombies prattled on about eating flesh, chewing on flesh, and other things, like swallowing chunks of flesh.

Like Steinknockers after he and Deputy Farman had paid a visit, Stanley was amazed at the transformation. When he and his fellow zombies had smashed through the bowling alley's glass double-doors, people had been so mean. Yelling, screaming, running around all panicked-like. As the zombies collided with the bowlers, people had started punching and kicking. One guy grabbed up a chair like a club. He would've bashed Stanley's forehead if Laura hadn't chomped down on the guy's neck mid-swing. Even Slow Johnson, the owner and manager of the bowling alley and someone Stanley considered a good acquaintance, had tried to kill him. He had produced a shotgun from beneath the front desk and started shooting—actually shoot-ing—at the zombies. The buckshot rocked them back on their heels or knocked them over and left them kicking like tipped cows. One of the strippers even lost her hand and lower arm to a blast, but shrugged off the flesh wound with resigned acceptance and kept biting. Like her, most of the zombies just took the bullets in stride. The unlucky ones that caught a blast full in the face went down and didn't get back up, but Johnson only managed a few head shots before he, too, was bitten. He was pulled down behind the bowling shoe counter by Jimmy Tibeaudeax, a sunken-chested, pimpled man who'd become a sunken-chested, pimpled zombie. When Johnson came back up, he moaned a greeting and officially joined Stanley's ever-expanding circle of friends.

As the zombies ripped their way through the busy crowd at Bay City Bowlers like lazy locusts through a ripening field, Stanley won-dered at the change enveloping his town. Before he'd been bitten by that fly, everyone had been separate from everyone else. Sure, people would say hi and trade wisdom about the best brand of snow tires or where to get furnace filters on sale. Parents whose kids were in the same class would make small talk when they crossed paths at the grocery store. People would go to their jobs and their favorite bars and the local library and small stores on Main Street and Sunday service at First Lutheran and talk about the Packers or the best places to fish or how that family trip to the Wisconsin Dells had been. Everyone knew everyone else. They intersected with each other in a hundred different ways every day of the week. Even so, Stanley knew from experience that they just skimmed through each other's lives without any real connection. He'd changed all of that. Him. Stanley Henkelmann.

Sure, the strange little fly got some credit, but it was Stanley that had chomped on Deputy Farman's cheek and set the real wheels in motion. After someone was bitten, assuming they didn't get completely eaten before they turned, they joined a community that was truly connected. There were no petty squabbles. No brawls in the karaoke bar when someone picked a song someone else wanted to sing. No kids pulling each other's hair or sticking boogers in their friends' bowling ball finger holes. No parents screaming at them to stop. The second someone was turned, all that stuff just melted away. Everyone went everywhere together, did everything together, and they all had so much in common.

Like me and Laura, he realized with a smile. *She's a zombie, and I'm a zombie. She loves biting people. I love biting people.*

Stanley never thought he'd find a soul mate, but life after death was full of surprises.

It was his turn to roll. Clumsy, blood-slicked fingers grasped at one of the balls on the return and finally found their grip. He wobbled up to the lane, stumbled across the foul line, and dropped the ball heavily on the wooden planks. Gravity helped it roll slowly forward until it connected with the pins with just enough force to knock one over.

"Yaaaaaaaahhhhhh," Stanley moaned happily. He was having one of the best games he could remember.

While Laura tried to carry her ball down the lane, a task complicated by the fact that one foot was bare and the other still had a stiletto heel strapped to it, Stanley looked again at all of his new friends. Some were dropping bowling balls on the lanes. Others just wandered down the pines and past the mid-lanes until they could kick over a few pins. Those that weren't bowling were engaged in other fun activities.

Clumps of zombies were eating leftover people, or making interesting patterns on the glass fronts of the vending machines with their bloody palms, or standing in place and staring at nothing in particular. No matter what they were doing, when another zombie stumbled and bumped into them, they'd moan a hello and wander off with the new zombie to do whatever they were doing. It was beautiful.

A zombie lady bumped his shoulder. Bowling game forgotten, he set off in the same direction. They stumbled up the short stairs that led up from the lanes to the main concourse and headed roughly in the direction of the main counter, where Slow Johnson waved his arms and hit various switches on the lane control board. Across the alley, lights flipped on an off, sweeps randomly cleared pins, and scoreboards reset, adding a level of excitement to the games that Stanley had never experienced when he was alive. When the zombie he was following bumped into the counter and came to a stop, Stanley bumped into her, rocked back on his heels, and found himself looking up through his blood-spattered spectacles at the leader board. Every summer, the men's bowling league had a big tournament. The winners were local celebrities for the next year until they had a chance to defend their title or fall to the next team of champions. Right up there at the top, a small placard proudly displayed the names Herbert Knudsen, Dallas Vinter, and Stanley Henkelmann.

I sure wish Herby and Lois and Dallas could be here, he thought. Despite having all these new friends and having a girlfriend for the first time ever, Stanley just couldn't shake that lingering twinge of loneliness.

He didn't like the loneliness. It felt like sadness and hunger, and he didn't like being sad and hungry. In an effort to raise his spirits, he turned to wave and moan at his zombie friends. Those closest to him moaned and waved back, and then those closest to them moaned and waved, and so on, the cordial gesture working its way through the alley like the wave at a Brewers' game.

So many nice people, Stanley thought. *So many friends.*

But none of them were Herb, or Dallas, or Lois.

Guess I just need more, he decided.

Stanley turned and shuffled toward the alley's exit. He bumped one zombie, then another. Soon, all the zombies bunched up at the double doors and spilled into the parking lot, each zombie following the ones that were following the ones that were following Stanley into the cold Wisconsin morning.

Just a few more friends, he thought again. *Just a few more, and I'll never be lonely again.*

Chapter 11

S TANLEY'S ALARM CLOCK WAS a thing of beauty. A reliable wonder of plastic and circuitry with a blue liquid crystal display. "It's time," it buzzed. "It's that time that you indicated was important. I'm so glad I was able to help wake you at this very important time."

Stanley wished he could come up with a truly wonderful way to thank his alarm clock. He sat up and stretched his bony arms, and froze with them in a wide 'Y' above his head. His arms should have been covered by his winter flannel pajama top, but instead were sleeved in warm velour. He flipped the covers back and saw that his legs, legs that also should have been pajama-clad, were sporting a nice pair of denim jeans. As if that wasn't strange enough, he'd also worn his winter boots to bed. As the alarm clock continued to announce the start of a new day, Stanley frowned and wondered why he was already dressed. He tried to remember what he'd done the previous night. Had there been drinking? He didn't remember drinking.

The furnace. I'll bet the furnace went out during the night, and I put on some clothes to stay warm, he reasoned as he finally switched off the alarm clock.

Stanley opened his mouth and huffed a few times, expecting to see his breath.

Huh. Must've come back on. The air in his bedroom certainly didn't feel cold. It felt like it was sixty-eight degrees, the temperature he always set the thermostat to.

Not in the mood to spend any more brain power on the problem, he reviewed the list of things he had planned to start the day. Pee, poop, shower. Brush and floss his teeth. Put on clothes, eat breakfast.

After crossing items one and two off his morning to-do list, he briefly considered showering. A quick sniff of each pit later, he decided a shower wasn't really necessary, so he skipped right to cleaning his teeth. Still smacking his minty fresh lips, he trotted downstairs and into his kitchen, eager to whip up some breakfast. He had a hankering for eggs and hotdog, one of his favorite breakfast treats. It was like eggs and sausage, but with a hotdog, which made it completely different. His excitement fell flat when he pulled open the fridge and didn't see any hotdogs.

"Hmmm. Guess I had a midnight snack when the furnace went out and I got up to get dressed," he reasoned, disappointed that he'd already eaten his leftover meat.

Since he was apparently stuck with dining out for breakfast, Stanley decided to have a slice of toast to hold him over. After dropping a slice of white bread in the toaster, he opened the cupboard for a plate.

"Where the heck are my p-plates?" he asked out loud. "What the heck happened to all my p-plates?"

Something close to a memory bumped around the back of his brain. He concentrated, focused, and thought real hard until he almost had it... and then the toaster dinged.

Crappers, he grumbled as the almost-memory slipped back beneath the surface of his conscious mind.

Grabbing the toast, he took a malcontent bite and headed toward the door to grab his parka. Out of habit, his hand swiped at the coat hook but came up empty. His parka was nowhere to be seen. Stanley started hunting around the house, flummoxed by where he might've left it. When he passed the front window, he noticed something even worse.

His car was gone.

Stanley grabbed the phone and dialed the sheriff's department. He was halfway through blurting out that he'd been robbed when he realized he was talking to a busy tone. Perplexed, he hung up and redialed and got a busy tone again.

"Sheriff's never b-busy," he commented. "What the heck's going on?"

He rang Lois, but no one picked up there, either. After leaving a long message on her answering machine about being robbed, he tried the sheriff again and finally got through.

"I've b-been robbed!" he exclaimed. "They got my plates and my hotdogs and my j-jacket and my car," he said before an angry cough cut him off.

"You think you got problems?" Corliss snapped in a gravelly voice. "I've been here damn near nonstop for three days, and the switchboard hasn't stopped. Whole town's gone crazy. Reports of assault, people biting people. It's mayhem, complete mayhem, and none of my deputies are answering their damn radios."

"B-but, b-but... I was robbed and I g-got no food and I g-got no car."

"And my give-a-damn's busted," Corliss replied, before disconnecting the call.

Tears welled up in Stanley's eyes and were just about to spill over when the phone rang. He snatched it up and started to let Corliss know that just because she was having a bad day didn't mean she could just hang up on folks. That was rude, really rude, and he...

"Stanley! Hush! It's Lois."

"Oh, hey Lois. Sorry about that. I j-just called the sheriff's and that Corliss, b-boy oh boy, was she rude."

"I'll bet," the witch agreed. "I guess you can't get to be her age and not find a few things to be crabby about. I just checked my messages. Oh, Stanley. I can't believe you were robbed. That's just terrible. The game starts at noon and should be done by three. We'll hurry back. Herb can always whammy the trooper if we get pulled over. I'll drop off Herb and head straight to your place after. Can you hold out until around four-thirty or five?"

Stanley's brow furrowed. Back from the game? What game? The Packers didn't play until Sunday. While he tried to fit the jumbled pieces of his recollections together in his mind, Lois reassured him that everything would be okay.

"You just stay put. I'll be there before you know it."

Stanley agreed and hung up the phone. There wasn't much else to do, so he settled into his Barca Lounger with a yawn. The stressful morning had taken its toll, and a nap was in order. Just a little cat nap to recharge.

A frantic pounding at the door jarred him awake. When he opened it, Lois exploded through the door and ran to his main T.V.

"What the h-heck, Lois? What's going on?"

Lois turned a panicked look on Stanley.

"Have you watched the news?" she asked. When Stanley shook his head, she flipped on the tube and started rifling through the channels.

"No, no, no. Crap. Is there news on Sundays?" she asked.

"Sunday? Lois, it ain't Sunday," Stanley responded, still trying to shake off the effects of his nap.

"Of course it is," the witch replied and then shushed him when an emergency newsbreak cut into a televangelist's sermon.

Lois knelt in front of the T.V., and Stanley returned to his Barca Lounger. Both stared quietly at the news anchor, a young, pretty woman named Robyn Larsen. She normally helmed the weeknight news segments, so it was a bit of a shock to see her on what Lois swore was a Sunday. The unexpected shift probably explained why Robyn didn't look nearly as polished as usual. Her normally puffy bangs were wilted, and her typically symmetrical makeup was lopsided. Her left cheek's rouge was about four shades darker than her right, and her eyebrows had a haphazard, scribbled-on quality.

"Please don't change the station," Robyn pleaded with her audience. "This is an emergency broadcast. If you're receiving this message, stay indoors. I repeat, stay indoors. Do not go outside. Stay away from people, even people you know. A large and growing mob of violent persons has been attacking area residents and," she managed before faltering and looking off camera. "This can't be right," she muttered. Whoever responded, what they said caused her eyes to widen in shock. "Um. A mob of violent persons have been attacking and *eating* people."

Lois switched off the television and let out a slow whistle. "I thought so," she said quietly. "I didn't want to believe it, but I thought so."

"Thought what, Lois?" Stanley asked in a scared voice. "What d-did you think?"

"Zombies, Stanley. Trappersville has been overrun by zombies. After I dropped Herb off, I passed a bunch driving here. They were shuffling along and moaning the most horrible moans. If there are cows in hell, that's probably how they sound."

Stanley's pulse quickened. His breath came in shorter and shorter gasps. He started to race in one direction after another, all the while looking frantically around the room.

"Um, Stanley," Lois asked with a frown. "What are you doing?"

"Hockey stick. Hockey stick. Gotta find a hockey stick!"

The witch stood and grabbed him as he raced by, dragging him to a sudden halt.

"Calm down! Why do you need a hockey stick?"

Stanley gaped at Lois for a long moment before realizing she'd never trained with the Society.

"Oh, right. You weren't there. You wouldn't know," he panted, out of breath from his harried running. "For the zombies, you g-gotta have a hockey stick. It's b-best if the end is pointy, but you can use the blade too and whack 'em in the neck. Randall said if you d-do it hard enough, you can take that head clean off. Especially if they've been d-decomposing for a bit. Makes the flesh softer so you j-just gotta get through the bone." When Lois stared at him in utter shock, he clarified. "The spine. You either c-cut that spine or you poke their b-brains out. Only way to kill a zombie."

"Randall... You're talking about the Society," Lois said with dawning comprehension.

Stanley rolled his eyes. "Who else would b-be telling me and Big D how to kill zombies? G-Glen from the library?"

"Crap. I forgot about the Society." The witch shook her head angrily. "Zombies, I can deal with. But trigger-happy monster hunters that have a bone to pick with a certain witch and her vampire boyfriend…"

Stanley chewed a fingernail. "So what do we d-do, Lois?"

"You have a second winter coat somewhere?"

Stanley gave Lois a look that conveyed in no uncertain terms how ridiculous the question was.

"Good," Lois continued. "Grab it. We've got to get back to my place and get Herb. After that?" she wondered, pushing a shaking hand through her golden locks. "I don't know, Stanley. I just don't know."

Stanley joined Lois in her mid-nineties Volvo. As he buckled in, he mentioned how he was always surprised when he saw her car. It wasn't what someone might expect. For a woman like Lois, you couldn't help but picture her in a fancy sports car, or maybe one of those new VW Beetles. Seeing her in an older, grey Volvo with the square headlights that had their own wiper blades was unexpected, and he said as much.

"B-but once you're inside, well," he continued with a gesture at the odd satchel dangling from the rearview, the arcane symbols scratched in the dashboard, the fat, dark candles in the cup holders, and the assortment of asymmetrical crystals pinned up above the windshield, "it's d-definitely your car."

"Don't poke fun. I love this car. Must be my Scandinavian roots. Let's just hope its reputation for safety holds up during a zombie apocalypse, too."

Lois was taking the long way home. In a town like Trappersville, that was more than just a saying. The long way usually meant actually having to drive a long, long way before another road appeared and offered a different direction of travel. When Stanley asked why she was driving halfway around Wisconsin instead of just driving back to her house, she politely reminded him that one, there was a zombie apocalypse that she was hoping to avoid, and two, that comments on her driving were a really effective way to end up walking.

Her plan didn't work out as intended. They'd turned onto a two-lane road and were only a mile or so from her house when they spotted a pickup on the shoulder. It was surrounded by a mob of undead, their grey and bloody hands slapping the side panels and windows. A few crumbled zombies sprawled behind the truck, evidence of the driver's failed attempt to drive through the bodies. Just visible through the truck's rear window was a man in a camouflage jacket and bright orange hunter's hat. He was rocking back and forth in what Stanley assumed was sheer panic.

"We have to help him," Lois said.

Stanley gulped loudly. "Oh, b-boy. I don't know about that, Lois. I mean, I know about them hockey sticks, b-but Dallas was the one that was supposed to swing 'em. I j-just did the, you know. The research and stuff."

Lois wasn't listening. She'd already pulled over the Volvo and had swung open her door.

"Just follow my lead. I'll throw a distraction spell and see if I can lead them away. When they move, you go get the guy and bring him back to the car. Ready?"

Stanley wanted to say no, but Lois was already on the move. She ran in a half crouch until she was a handful of yards away from the truck. Skidding to a stop, she twined her hands in an intricate pattern and then cast her arms toward the woods across the road. A loud clap sounded from deep in the trees. The zombies' heads all perked up at the sudden noise. One turned and took a few halting steps toward the trees. Lois wound her hands around again and made another throwing motion toward the trees. An instant later, a second loud clap sounded out from deeper into the woods. The zombie moved more confidently toward the sound, and the others turned to follow.

"Now, Stanley. Now!" she commanded in a loud whisper.

Stanley gulped again and did his best to imitate her crouched run. The final few zombies had crossed the road,

Oh boy. There's a joke in there for sure, he thought,

and the coast was clear. Stanley reached the truck, yanked on the driver's side door, and swung it open. Adrenaline thrumming, he realized that he actually liked being a man of action, a hero. If Dallas had seen Stanley in action, he would've definitely been impressed.

A realization blossomed clear as day when Stanley saw the man. He hadn't been rocking in panic. He'd been shoving shells into a shotgun. The same shotgun that was now pointed at Stanley's chest.

A second realization blossomed. Stanley really didn't want to be a man of action. He was perfectly content to be a man of non-action, watching his favorite T.V. shows and drinking and letting all the action happen far, far away.

A third realization blossomed, but this one was full of bright fire and a thunderous boom, and then everything went dark.

Chapter 12

*I*T'S LIKE *A*MWAY FOR *making friends,* Stanley realized. *I bite someone, and they bite two more, and each of them bites two more...*

When the zombies followed Stanley from Bay City Bowlers, there'd been a hundred or so, maybe even one-fifty. Now, Stanley couldn't even begin to guess. Like some vast amoeba, the swelling horde sent tendrils snaking down streets and through the woods. They piled up against fences until the fences collapsed. They pressed against barricaded doors until the barricades fell. They pounded against the windows of surrounded cars until the windows shattered. Over and over, a zombie would find its way into a place and more zombies would come out. Sure, they met resistance. It was Wisconsin, after all, so there were more guns than people in town, and folks weren't afraid to use them. Plenty of zombies took slug after slug, but only a shot to the head seemed to have any lasting effect. Otherwise, they'd just keep lurching along until their assailant ran out of bullets, and then there'd be another zombie.

Stanley stood with Laura near the north end of Main Street and surveyed the sprawling mob of undead with a sort of reverent awe. So many people just hanging out and getting along, and all it took was a bite.

"Wooorrrllllduh. Peeeaaace," he said.

"Yaaaaaahhhhhh," Laura replied and smiled.

Her lips were cracked and caked in gore. She'd lost a couple of teeth when an intended meal jabbed her in the face with the butt of a rifle, and her left eye lazed to the side like it was trying to contemplate the dent a baseball bat had left in her cheek. She was, in a word, beautiful.

World peace *and* a girlfriend. Stanley could hardly believe his luck and couldn't wait to tell Herb and Lois, and Dallas too if he ever came back. They were going to be so jealous. Mind made up, Stanley nudged Laura's arm, shuffled feet that were still clad in the ragged remnants of his tube stocks, and set off in the direction of his house. Once he got home, he'd give Herb and Lois a call and invite them over. Then it would just take a few quick bites, and everything would be perfect.

Chapter 13

S TANLEY'S ALARM CLOCK WAS a thing of beauty. A reliable wonder of plastic and circuitry with a blue liquid crystal display. "It's time," it buzzed. "It's that time that you indicated was important. I'm so glad I was able to help wake you at this very important time."

Stanley wished he could come up with a truly wonderful way to thank his alarm clock. He sat up and stretched his bony arms, and froze with them in a wide 'Y' above his head. He was wearing an older winter coat, one he usually only wore for shoveling. Once upon a time, it had been a jaunty red with bright yellow bands around the arms. Years of use had dulled the red to more of a rust, and the armbands had turned the color of Dijon mustard that was way past the expiration date. A mosaic of duct tape sealed holes in the nylon shell and kept its polyester stuffing inside, and the zip-off hood's jammed zipper guaranteed that hood's zip-offing days were done. It was an old coat, well past its prime, but it was also a good coat, one that had served Stanley well and would continue to do so without complaint for many seasons to come.

"A lot of memories in this here c-coat," he said fondly, the memories distracting him from the inexplicable fact that he'd been wearing it in his sleep.

Still wearing his coat, he made his way downstairs and rummaged in the fridge. He'd been pretty sure there was a hotdog, but there wasn't one now. Had he been robbed? He made a quick inspection of the windows and doors. Nothing seemed out of the ordinary, but someone had definitely gotten a hold of his hotdog. It was a mystery, plain and simple, and Stanley did enjoy a good mystery. He decided a quick run to the Get'n'Gobble was in order so his brain wouldn't have to run on an empty stomach. Fortunately, he already had his coat on and even his boots.

"G-gosh, you sure planned this one right," he congratulated himself as he walked outside. "Saved a bunch of time not having to g-get dressed."

The winter air on his face was crisp and invigorating, but nothing compared to the shock of realizing his car was gone.

"Shoot. This is a mystery, and that's a f-fact," he muttered forlornly. A missing hotdog was one thing. Someone taking his Cavalier? That was something else altogether.

"B-better call the sheriff," he decided and headed back inside to make the call.

Stanley rang the sheriff's department nine times. Each time, the line buzzed with a disconnected tone. Perplexed, he decided to call Lois. If he didn't have food or a car, he'd need someone to take him shopping and drop him by the station after so he could file a report.

"Oh, hey there, Lois," he said when she picked up. "Say, d-darndest thing. Someone stole my last hotdog and my car. C-could you maybe bring over some food? I'm starving."

When Lois didn't respond, he figured maybe she hadn't heard.

"Lois? You there? Geez, these phones. I'll tell ya. Did you g-get that one they had on sale at the hardware store? B-boy oh boy, I hope not. I heard that they got them so cheap because that no-good B-Bundy that owns the place bought 'em from the back of some g-guy's truck that was passing through on his way to Oconomowoc. Can't be trusting stuff that c-comes off the back of some guy's truck, no sir. Except maybe jerky," he amended.

When Lois still didn't respond, he listened hard. He could hear someone breathing, so he asked again, "Lois? You there?"

"Don't. Move. I'm coming over," the witch said, and then disconnected the line.

Stanley pulled out a chair at his small dining table and rested his chin on his hand. A plastic cup with a coaster taped on top sat off to one side.

"G-good morning, weird little fly," he said with a smile. "At least whoever nabbed my hotdogs d-didn't get you, too. Tell ya what, after Lois helps me get some b-breakfast, we'll do some more tests and see if we can figure out what you are."

Stanley passed the time by sliding the little fly's impromptu enclosure back and forth from hand to hand, all the while wondering what experiments to try next. He'd given it a good look-see with his magnifying glass the night before, and even let it bite his finger, but was still no closer to determining if it was just a weird looking fly, or a brand new fly.

The sound of skidding tires crunching on snow-covered gravel caused him to raise his head and look out the front window. Lois was running to his door, followed more slowly by someone bundled up from toes to top in boots, jeans, and an oversized Packers parka. The hood was pulled up, and a ski mask and goggles completely covered the person's face.

"Herby!" Stanley guessed, overjoyed at the unexpected visitor. He hurried to his front door and pulled it open. Instead of a warm reception from Lois and her swaddled vampire boyfriend, he found himself staggering backward as some unseen force pressed hard against his chest.

"*Nustro lindum, baleck tull!* Dark imposter, demon's game, return you now to whence you came!" the witch shouted. At the same time, she made a series of sharp, quick gestures with her hands and ended the motion by thrusting her palms forward.

Stanley loved watching Lois cast spells. It was always so exciting. When the strange pressure on his chest relented, he started to clap.

"Wow! N-nice spell, Lois. What did it d-do?"

Rather than answering, Lois glared at him and stomped forward. Without invitation, she grabbed his cheeks and pinched, pulled at his ears, poked him sternly in the chest, and again in the belly.

"Hey! Why are you p-poking me?" he complained, swatting ineffectually at the witch's hands.

Before she could answer, the bundled-up vampire pushed her aside and wrapped Stanley up in a bear hug.

"It's you! You're alive!" Herb cried. "It worked. Lois did it. And you aren't even in a beer can."

Stanley endured the unexpected gush of emotion from his friend. When the vampire finally released him, he asked, "Why would I b-be in a beer can?"

Lois poked him again in the chest, earning another pained, "Hey!" from Stanley.

"You are supposed to be dead. You got shot. You died," she said, accentuating each 'you' with another poke. "I tried to bring you back like I did with Herb, but it didn't work. It should've worked, but it didn't. So I was a wreck. I was sobbing all night, Herb too, and then," she continued, voice rising, "you called me. And when I went back to check on your body, you... Stanley, you dissolved."

Uncomfortable feelings stirred deep in Stanley's chest, and it wasn't from the repeated poking. Murky memories crept up. Confusing, overlapping, contradicting memories. Waking up. Falling. Waking up. Choking. Waking up. Getting shot. The cascading memories were terrifying. If déjà vu was a feeling of tedious familiarity, Stanley figured he was having some déjà boo.

"Lois, you're starting to sc-scare me. I'm starting to sc-scare me."

The witch's face softened. "Is it really you, then? But how?"

For the next half an hour, Lois tried a number of different spells. She apologetically explained they were to suss out demons and shapeshifters and the like. When she finished, a confused look marred her beautiful face.

"You aren't a demon, or a shapeshifter, or a boo hag, or anything else I know how to check for. But Stanley," she said, and then chewed her lip in thought. "You aren't exactly human either."

The witch held out a small pendant, one of many that hung from her neck. To Stanley, it looked like a clear glass marble struck through with fine lines of red and grey.

"With the right incantation, this glows in the presence of a human. Glows, mind you. Now watch."

She'd already done it once, but Stanley and Herb both paid better attention the second time. Lois uttered some odd-sounding words and passed the marble back and forth in front of Stanley. It glowed... and then flickered. Glowed and flickered.

"Maybe its batteries are getting old?" Herb asked. When Lois gave him a look, he added, "What? How am I supposed to know how these things work?"

Lois chewed her lip again, deep in thought. "What do you remember?" she asked softly.

Stanley moved to his Barca Lounger before answering, eager for its familiar comfort.

"Um. I went to Ronnie's for breakfast. I bumped into J-Jerry. You know, your old neighbor," he added, looking at Herb. "I g-got home, and there was this buzzing. I found this little lady stuck to some d-duct tape on my loafer," he explained, holding up the cup. "I don't usually wear the loafers in the winter, b-but it hasn't been too bad out and the snow wasn't so deep, and b-boy oh boy, those loafers are sure comfy. Do you got the loafers, Herb? You should really g-get some."

Lois sternly redirected him back to his recollections.

"Oh, sorry. So, I was experimenting with the fly, you know? Ch-checking to see if maybe it was a new kind of fly. You know I've b-been collecting all sorts of insects. One of these d-days, I'm going to find a new one, j-just you wait. And when I do..."

Lois cleared her throat.

"Oh. Okay. Right. So anyway, I let it b-bite me."

Lois and Herb gasped in unison.

"You let it bite you?" Lois asked, incredulous. "Stanley, if I hadn't already watched you die, I'd kill you. After what happened to Herb and Dallas, you seriously tried to get bit by a strange bug?"

"No complaints here," Herb offered. "Have you seen me bowl?" the vampire said with a smile, but quickly stowed his good humor when Lois skewered him with a dark look.

Stanley shrugged apologetically and tried to explain that he wanted a Nobel Prize and to meet the president and maybe be a guest on *Oprah*.

The witch shook her head, causing her blond hair to wave gently around a face gone sad. "Oh Stanley, I don't think it works that way," she sighed. "Well, what's done is done. Who knows what that fly is, and who knows what you are now?"

"You think maybe it really was a sp-special bug? You think I'm like Herb now, or Big-D?" Stanley asked as his eyes lit up with possibility.

"Like I said, who knows?" Lois repeated. "But let's look at the bright side. At least you aren't a,"

"Zombie," Herb finished.

"Right," Lois agreed. "It'd be terrible if you were turned into a,"

"Zombie," Herb finished again, stressing the word.

Lois raised an eyebrow. "Sweetie, I can finish my own,"

"Zombie!" Herb said again, this time pointing at the front window.

Stanley turned to follow Herb's finger and screamed. There, right outside his window, was a grey, haggard face with disheveled brown hair and blood-splattered glasses. Glasses that looked a lot like Stanley's favorite readers. The angular face turned from side to side, pivoting above a velour shirt collar. Red teeth flashes as the zombie worked its jaw, and a sharp Adam's apple bobbed up and down. While Stanley stared in speechless shock, a second zombie face pushed up against the glass. This one had clearly been an attractive woman before she died, lost a few teeth, and got hit in the head by something hard enough to leave a noticeable dent in her face. A third and fourth zombie had joined their undead companions before Lois finally recovered from the shock and yelled that they had to go. She turned and ran for the back of the house, followed closely by Herb and Stanley.

"That one," Stanley huffed as he was dragged along by the vampire. "There was one in g-glasses that..." he tried again, but whatever he was about to say was forgotten when he saw that more zombies had piled up against the back door.

"Upstairs!" Lois commanded.

"What?" Stanley asked, shocked. "B-but there's nowhere to g-go from up there."

"Just get us to a room with a big window." Lois said, urging him up the stairs.

Curiosity warred with concern as Stanley led his friends up to his bedroom. Lois went straight to the window that looked out over the trees behind his house.

"Okay. This is good. It looks like there aren't that many in back. If we can clear the yard, we can sneak through the trees and circle around to my car. Herb? You up for this?"

The vampire was squinting and hissing softly. He was trying to stay in the relative shadows, but the mid-morning sun didn't leave much of the room untouched.

"Yeah, yeah, but I hate being up during the day. Let me bundle back up," the vampire complained. He pulled his facemask up and goggles down, and finished by pulling his Packers parka green hood up over his head.

"Ugh," he said in a muffled voice. "I'm exhausted. Can I get a quick sip?"

Lois responded by pushing up her sleeve and holding her arm in front of Herb's face. Herb pulled his facemask down, gently bit down on the inside of Lois's wrist, and wrapped his lips around the puncture wounds. He sucked for a short moment and then leaned back with a long sigh. Lois cleared her throat and looked pointedly at her still-bleeding wrist.

"Oh! Gosh. Sorry," Herb apologized. He pressed his index finger against one of his long incisors until a bright red pearl welled up, and rubbed the tip of his finger over the wound on Lois's wrist.

Stanley watched in awe as the wounds closed before his eyes. "That sure is something," he breathed, earning a smile from Herb before the vampire replaced his ski mask and gave a thumbs up.

Lois placed her hands on Stanley's bony shoulders. "Herb is going to carry you down. You just have to hold on tight. Can you do that?"

A loud crash sounded from downstairs. The zombies had broken a pane of glass, probably the front window from the sound of it.

"D-don't got much of a choice, huh," Stanley commented, trying to keep his voice from betraying his fright.

Herb swept him up in his arms while Lois pushed open the double-hung window and pulled out the screen. Once the opening was clear, Herb frog-hopped up to the sill.

"B-but what about you, Lois?" Stanley asked over Herb's shoulder. "Who's gonna c-carry you?"

Lois just smiled and asked if Stanley was ready.

"Um, yes?" Stanley lied.

"Good. Don't scream."

Before Stanley could ask what he shouldn't scream about, the vampire crouched down, extended his legs, and leapt from the window.

Stanley figured that jumping out of the second-story window is what he wasn't supposed to scream about, but he screamed anyway. Fortunately, he retained just enough good sense to bite down on Herb's parka-shrouded shoulder so it didn't make much noise. The two men sailed through the air in a gentle arc and landed near the far end of the backyard. Herb set the shaking Stanley on his feet and helped to hold him up while the skinny man caught his breath. Pressing a hand to his chest in an attempt to calm his pounding heart, he looked up to the window they'd just jumped from.

Lois has stepped through the window and stood with her heels on the sill and her back pressed up against the house. Her breath came in small puffs as her lips moved, and her dark coat swayed dramatically in the light breeze as she slowly spread her arms. Stanley gasped as Lois stepped away from the window... and didn't fall. A second step, and both feet literally stood on thin air. A third step took her slightly lower than the previous one, and a fourth took her lower still. It looked for all the world like she was calmly walking down a set of stairs. Her arms were still spread gracefully to either side, reminding Stanley of a grand dame descending to the ballroom. The zombies crowded around the back door, pounded and moaned, completely unaware that their intended meal was walking over their heads. The magic stairway led Lois on a gentle descent across Stanley's back yard and ended just before the tree line. The witch stepped lightly to the snow covered ground and dipped in a short curtsy.

"Wow!" Stanley exclaimed and immediately realized his mistake. The zombies pressed up against his back door turned and started shuffling in their direction.

"Oops," he apologized, and the three friends turned and ran.

Despite Stanley's gaffe, luck was on their side. The zombies in the backyard were slow, and the zombies that had been out front had all managed to get inside, their dark shapes moving like shadow puppets in the broken window. The trio made it to the car without further incident, and Lois quickly sped them down Stanley's long drive to the road.

"Where we g-going?" Stanley asked from the back seat between gasps for breath.

"Maybe Michigan. Or Canada," the witch replied. "If we could drive to Iceland, I'd say Iceland."

Stanley gaped. "We're leaving? Leaving Trappersville?" he asked in shock. Trappersville was his home. The thought of leaving caused Stanley to tear up. No more breakfast at Ronnie's or beer at Steinknockers. No more games at Bay City Bowlers. "Do they even know how to b-bowl in Iceland?" he asked, forlorn.

"I don't know what else to do," Lois said, clearly frustrated.

"Hey," Herb said through his ski mask while placing a mitten-covered hand on her thigh and giving it a gentle squeeze. "We're going to be okay. You'll think of something. You always do."

"And if I don't?" she replied tersely. "What then?"

The vampire yawned hugely. "We'll take a nap, and then figure it out together. All of us," he added with a nod to the rearview mirror. "You're incredible, and Stanley's the smartest guy I've ever met. Have you seen him program a universal remote? It's awesome."

Stanley's head bobbed in assent. "And you t-too, Herby. You're like a superhero."

"See?" Herb said in a reassuring tone. "You're amazing, he's smart, and I'm a superhero. A really sleepy superhero, but still, we've got this, right?"

Lois drove for a moment in silence, lips pressed tightly together. Finally, she gave a determined nod and took the next left.

"So, where we g-going, Lois?" Stanley asked again.

"My place," the witch responded. "I need to grab a few things, and then we'll find a place outside of town to hole up and figure out our next move."

The rest of the trip passed in silence, each friend lost in their own worried thoughts. When Lois made the turn into her driveway, she instantly slammed on the brakes.

"What's up?" Herb asked groggily, the abrupt stop rousing him from his nap.

"Someone's at my house."

Herb peered through the windshield. "Oh, yep. Who do you think it is?"

Lois shrugged, making it clear that she wasn't expecting anyone. She asked Herb what he could see. The vampire had unnaturally good eyesight, even when he was looking through the heavily tinted glass of his ski goggles. He leaned forward and peered through the windshield while Stanley and Lois held their breath.

"Two, no... three people. A couple of guys, for sure. One's real big. Like, wow. I didn't know they could make guys that big. He's like Stu and Wyatt and Dozer combined big," Herb said by way of comparison.

Stu, Wyatt, and Dozer were one of the teams on the men's bowling league. The three men worked together at the paper mill. Each one looked capable of pulling a full-grown tree out of the ground with their bare hands. Stanley tried to imagine someone as big as the three of them combined.

"Whadaya mean, Herb? Like, as t-tall as all of them standing on each other's shoulders? Or do you mean like as b-big as they'd b-be if they was standing right in front of each other? Or side-by-side? G-gosh, that'd be a person like ten feet wide."

Herb just sighed and shook his head, earning a small smile from Lois.

"What?" Stanley asked. "What's so funny?"

Instead of responding, Herb gave a slow whistle. "Oh boy. Aletia's in there."

Stanley echoed Herb's slow whistle. Aletia was Dallas's girlfriend. Or had been until she learned he was a werewolf and he killed her friends. If Aletia was there, that meant the Society was there. And if the Society was there, Lois and Herb were in big trouble.

"Let's g-go," Stanley urged. "Let's just g-go."

Lois shook her head. "Can't," she said. "If we're going to stand a chance of surviving, there's some stuff I should get." The witch pursed her full lips in thought. "I'll need help carrying things. I can sneak two of us in, and the other will be the get-away driver."

"Okay," Herb said, doing his best Dallas impression. "Let's do this. Stanley, you're driving. We're gonna be coming out of there hot and heavy, so the second we get in the car, you burn rubber."

Stanley nodded, but Lois shook her head.

"Sorry, but that won't work. What I have in mind means we're going to have to be really quiet. That parka of yours sounds like someone walking through a pile of dry leaves, and you can't take it off."

Turning to look at Stanley, she said, "I can't make us invisible, but I can make us really hard to see. If we're quiet, we can slip in, grab what I need, and slip out. Think you can do that?"

Stanley's mouth went dry and his pulse pounded. The last time he'd seen the Society, they'd tied him up and tried to stab Dallas and burn Lois. Not exactly the kind of experience that left you feeling good about another encounter. He was about to say as much, but Lois and Herb were both looking at him expectantly. Well, he assumed Herb looked expectant. It was hard to tell with the goggles and facemask. Stanley sagged, resigned to his fate. His friends had saved him time and again. The least he could do was be really quiet and help Lois carry some stuff.

"Okey doke," he said with more confidence than he felt. "G-get in, g-get out, g-get drunk, g-get laid."

"What?" Lois asked, shocked.

"J-just something Dallas used to say," he explained. "Boy oh b-boy, do I wish he was here."

Lois and Stanley stepped quietly from the car, and Herb slipped into the driver's seat. The witch closed her eyes and took a deep breath. As she slowly released it, her fingers started to twist and twine.

"*Urbenz fontila, byrachen ull wanthra.* Shadows, heed my dire request to move unseen among the rest."

Stanley thought he was getting to be a bit of an expert on strange. He'd seen things that most folks would agree were well outside the realm of normal. Vampires, werewolves, 'squatches, and now zombies. He'd chatted with Herb when Herb was nothing more than a disembodied soul in an empty Milwaukee's Best can, and had a front-row seat when Lois put that soul into the body of a dead monster hunter named Randall. It was no wonder that Stanley considered himself well-versed in weird, but he quickly discovered that weird could always get weirder.

Even with the wintery sun shrouded in cold, grey clouds, everything around them cast a shadow. It was a simple fact that wherever there was light and stuff for that light to hit, there were shadows. Shadows gave things their shape, texture, and depth. The underside of tree branches. The backside of leaves on the bushes between the trees. The car door handle and the wheel wells and the snowy ground beneath the car. Shadows were everywhere, and they did what shadows were supposed to do.

At least they did what shadows were supposed to do until Lois finished casting her spell. As the last syllable left her lips, all of those shadows stopped behaving like they were supposed to and started flowing into a single, growing shadow. The effect was unsettling. Stanley had never realized how important shadows were to making things look normal. As the trees and bushes and leaves and car all slowly lost their shadows, they seemed to flatten, expand, and get noticeably brighter. All the movement that had been so perceptible just a moment before was getting harder and harder to discern. And all the while, the one remaining shadow grew and took on a life of its own. Stanley's eyes stung and watered, but he couldn't make himself blink. Instead, they continued to stare at the shadow as it began creeping steadily in their direction.

"L-Lois?" he asked worriedly.

The witch reached for his hand. As their fingers intertwined, she gave a reassuring squeeze.

"Just wait," she counseled.

The shadow reached their toes, pooled up at their feet, and began to fill a shapeless space around them. Stanley squeaked nervously when his boots vanished from view, then his legs, his narrow waist, his chest.

"L-Lois?" he asked again, stretching his neck to raise his chin.

"Nothing to worry about. It's just about done."

The pool of shadow slipped up over his neck. He felt a cool, dry sensation as it crept up his chin. It tickled his lips and nostrils, almost causing him to sneeze, and then it was over his eyes. The disturbingly bright panorama before him darkened like he was seeing everything through heavily tinted glass.

"Let's go," a voice whispered. He turned his head to see who had spoken, and saw Lois's face and hair floating in a dark, translucent sea.

"Okay," he replied. At least, he thought he'd replied. He knew he hadn't whispered, but even so, his voice sounded impossibly soft.

Hand in hand, Stanley and Lois crept toward the house. The hunters had left the front door open, but they still had to pass through the screen door. Lois stood quietly and waited while Stanley kept squishing down his rising panic. After what felt like an eternity, Lois nodded, gently pulled the screen door open, and tiptoed inside.

The first thing Stanley saw was the man Herb had mentioned earlier, and Herb had been right. The man was ginormous. His neck alone looked as thick as Stanley's torso. A dark shirt stretched against a broad chest and heavily muscled arms, and black track pants with white stripes down the seams strained across quadriceps that looked borrowed from a mountain gorilla. His bald head served to accentuate wide-set eyes and a broad nose. The lower half of his face was covered in a beard a shade darker than the surrounding skin. As Stanley gaped, the man smiled and spoke to someone just out of sight, his teeth flashing pearly white. The words sounded impossibly far away, preventing Stanley from discerning what the man was saying. A softly accented female voice answered, faint as the ghost of an echo, and Aletia stepped into the room.

When Stanley saw the deadly hunter, he focused intently on controlling his bladder. Before it had a chance to empty, he felt Lois gently tug his sleeve. She held a finger to her lips for silence and walked further into her living room. The shadow that enclosed them stretched and then separated. The part that went with Lois encased her completely, undulating like a giant soap bubble. She paused and then took a careful step directly between the giant and Aletia. When neither hunter registered her presence, she gave Stanley a subtle thumbs' up and walked to a table beside the sofa. With a quick glance at Aletia and the giant, she reached out a hand and grasped a black felt sack that was about the same size as a bowling ball bag. When her fingers touched the fabric, the shadow extended from Lois's hand and stretched over the bag.

Stanley stared in amazement as the witch walked back to his side, each step careful as a cat in a room of sleeping dogs. When she was close enough, their shadows rejoined, and she handed the bag to him.

"I'll show you what to put in the bag," she said quietly, her voice so soft that Stanley took most of her meaning from reading her lips.

Frightened, but resolved to do his part, Stanley gave a quick nod. Lois smiled reassuringly and worked her way back around the giant and toward a bookcase that stretched along the room's wall. As she walked, she pointed at items and looked meaningfully at Stanley. Taking the hint, he followed in her footsteps. As he passed each item she'd indicated, he'd check to make sure that the hunters weren't looking his way, slip it into his own concealing shadow, and deposit it in the bag. The sack gained weight as a variety of books and strange objects slowly disappeared into its mouth, but somehow always had room for each new object she pointed at.

Stanley's meager arms were starting to shake. It felt like he was carrying half of the town's library. He gasped quietly in relief when the witch turned and gave him the 'OK' sign. As one, they retraced their steps across the room. With a final glance back at the Society hunters, Lois pushed open the screen door, stepped through, and held it open for Stanley to follow. He took one last look at Aletia and suddenly found himself thinking of Dallas. The poor guy had really fallen for the woman, and Stanley had thought they were a cute couple. Too bad she wasn't willing to overlook the whole werewolf thing. Small-minded, in his opinion. Folks came in lots of shapes and sizes, and had all sorts of quirks. Being a hungry, oversized wolf that walked on two legs a few nights a month shouldn't come between two people that were in love. Just didn't make any sense.

Stanley was still contemplating Aletia and thinking about Dallas when the third hunter appeared from Lois's bedroom. One look, and Stanley knew the guy was bad news. If he had walked into the roughest biker bar in the county, the other guys would look like Boy Scouts next to this one. The mental image fit, seeing as how the hunter was dressed in motorcycle boots, black jeans, and a well-worn leather motorcycle jacket. A chain connected a wallet to the man's black belt, and a crossbow rested with easy familiarity on his shoulder. The dangerous man said something to his companions, and they all shared a laugh while he fished a cigarette from the breast pocket of his jacket. Stanley was still quivering when the man started walking directly toward him.

"Stanley," Lois whispered. "Let's go!"

He wanted to go. He really did, but someone had swapped out his legs for pillars of ice when he wasn't paying attention.

"Stanley!" the witch said again.

The urgency in her voice melted the ice from his joints. Lois ran ahead, but Stanley was forced to follow more slowly, burdened by the weight of the sack he carried. He was almost halfway to the car when he made the mistake of looking back. When he did, he saw the dangerous man step onto the front stoop of Lois's house. A Zippo clicked. The man raised the lighter up to his cigarette, but stopped just short of the rolled tube of tobacco's tip. Flame reflected in his eyes as they traced their way along a set of dragging footprints that led to... nothing. With unexpected grace, the hunter flipped his Zippo shut, slipped it into a pocket, brought the crossbow down and released a bolt.

Stanley had just enough time to yell, "Crappers!" and then all went dark.

Chapter 14

S TANLEY'S ALARM CLOCK WAS a thing of beauty. A reliable wonder of plastic and circuitry with a blue liquid crystal display. "It's time," it buzzed. "It's that time that you indicated was important. I'm so glad I was able to help wake you at this very important time."

Stanley wished he could come up with a truly wonderful way to thank his alarm clock. Before he had a chance to express his meager gratitude, a familiar voice said, "Oh, bother. I forgot to switch off the alarm."

Stanley opened his eyes and saw a man in his bedroom. A man holding his alarm clock. A man wearing a strange, colorless single-suit whose fabric looked almost liquid in texture, like it had been poured onto the wiry and angular body. A man with a mop of brown hair pushed into a severe part and an Adam's apple sharp enough to cut cheese with. A man that looked exactly like him.

"Oh, this is awkward," the man that looked like Stanley said in Stanley's voice. "We weren't supposed to meet, and most certainly weren't supposed to meet like this."

Stanley silently agreed. As near as he could tell, no one was ever supposed to meet an identical twin they never knew they had by waking up to them. He tried to put that observation into actual words, but his words had apparently left the building.

"I imagine you have some questions," the Stanley said as he carefully set the alarm clock back on Stanley's bedside table.

Stanley considered the Stanley. He decided to think of it as 'the Stanley' because that was like thinking of any number of inanimate objects. The refrigerator. The T.V. remote. The foot cream in his medicine cabinet. The Stanley. All very normal, very non-threatening things.

"Yep," he squeaked.

"Right. Hmmm. Where to begin? As they said about the Big Bang, might as well begin at the beginning. That seems like a reasonable proposition, don't you agree?"

Stanley found himself nodding. Obviously pleased, the Stanley sat at the foot of Stanley's bed, eloquently crossed his legs, and rested his hands on a knee.

"I do apologize for the shock. Before I begin to quite literally talk to myself, did you need anything? Perhaps a glass of water? Or a cup of coffee? I know that's one of your favorite things in the morning. I'd offer to make you breakfast, but that would take more time than I have to spare, I'm afraid."

Stanley considered the offer. "Water. G-gotta stay hydrated," he managed to say through an incredibly dry throat.

"Excellent," the Stanley replied. "Just a moment."

The Stanley left the room. Stanley was about to convince himself that he'd just had an incredibly odd waking dream when he heard the kitchen sink squeak on.

Not a dream, then, he decided.

The Stanley returned a moment later with two glasses and handed one to Stanley.

"How very interesting. The glasses were exactly where I would have put them. That said, you should really invest in some dinner plates," the Stanley commented with a measured look at Stanley. Returning to his place at the foot of the bed, he took a delicate sip of water. "Now, to explain things. I, as I am certain you've discerned, am Stanley."

"The Stanley," Stanley clarified.

"Quite," the Stanley agreed. "I am the original. The alpha. Stanley Prime, as it were. I was abducted by aliens when I was walking home from school. They had been studying and cataloguing Wisconsin's life forms. Quite a tall order, I'm sure you'll agree. Concerned about staying on schedule, they opted to enlist a human specimen to assist with their work. I was that specimen. After a brief negotiation, I found their proposed terms amenable and chose to remain with them. Are you following?"

Stanley blinked. He was most certainly not following, but didn't want to embarrass himself in front of himself, so he forced a hesitant nod. When the Stanley arced an eyebrow, he added a thumbs' up and smiled for good measure.

"Hmmm. As I was saying, I negotiated terms with the aliens. One of the conditions for my staying was that I would be able to return to my original life whenever I chose. However, how was I to explain my absence? What would people think if I disappeared for months or years and then suddenly reappeared? I certainly couldn't say I'd been abducted by aliens. They would think I'd lost my mind."

"Not if you k-kept the umbrella," Stanley offered. "You c-could show them it wasn't lightning. No, sir. If it was lightning, it w-would've ruined the umbrella."

The Stanley blinked and then continued his story. "The aliens offered to create a clone, a temporary Stanley that would occupy my place in my life until I saw fit to return. They also provided that," he added, pointing at the alarm clock. "In the event that my clone died, that would create a new clone and ensure my continued presence in my life."

The Stanley frowned and considered his doppelgänger. "They neglected to inform me that the cloning device was a prototype with a few, um, glitches. You may recall that after you were abducted, you had no recollection of the event, but all of your clothes were on backward. If only that had been the full extent of the problems… but no matter. The clone—you—served its purpose. You have occupied my life and ensured that all of my former associates still think I am alive and well and living among them. It is unfortunate that they don't realize the full extent of my intellectual prowess," he mused. "Also, I must admit that I am not overly fond of your life choices. Bowling? How crude."

Stanley's face flushed. He began to sputter a defense, but stopped when the other waved his objections aside.

"Again, no matter," the Stanley continued after a drink of water. "As I mentioned, the device is glitchy. The aliens promised to fix it, but they've been so busy. Also, no one expected you to die, and we certainly didn't expect you to die repeatedly. To the outside observer, it would appear that dying is the only thing you're truly adept at."

The Stanley stood and crossed to the bedside table. He set his glass next to the alarm clock and squatted down to peer more closely at the little plastic box.

"I was about to finally fix it when you died again and triggered the cloning function. Which brings us to the present," the Stanley said in a tone that indicated story time was over. "Now, that should cover all of your questions. I'll just need a moment, and this whole ordeal will be resolved."

The Stanley reached for the alarm clock. Stanley leaned in with interest to watch, but was distracted by the slamming of the door downstairs and the heavy pounding of footsteps. A moment later, Lois and Herb burst into his room.

"You're alive! I knew it!" Lois exclaimed, followed by a suspicious, "Hey, wait a second..." from Herb.

The Stanley startled and jumped a clear two feet away from the bed. "Oh my. This certainly couldn't get much worse, could it?" he gasped. In the moment before he disappeared in a flash of yellow light, he added, "No one was ever supposed to see both of us."

"Were there just two Stanleys here?" Herb asked through his face mask, breaking the long silence that followed the vanishing of the second Stanley.

"P-pretty much," Stanley affirmed.

The vampire pulled his mask down and slid his goggles off his head. "Lois? Was that, you know, witchy stuff?"

Lois was still looking at the empty spot that had held a second Stanley a moment before.

"No witchy stuff," she said slowly.

Stanley flipped the covers off of him, revealing that he was already dressed. After he climbed out of bed, he went straight to his alarm clock. Examining it from every possible angle, he explained that Lois was right, it wasn't witchy stuff.

"Aliens," he said. "I always t-told you there was aliens, and I was right. There sure was some aliens."

Stanley filled his friends in on his strange encounter, ending with, "And then you t-two showed up and that Stanley Prime j-just up and disappeared."

"Unbelievable," Lois gasped.

"That bit about the glitch explains a few things, though," Herb said thoughtfully.

Lois glowered at her boyfriend and then turned back to Stanley. "So, you think he was telling the truth?" Lois asked. "You think he was the original Stanley, and he's been living with aliens all this time?"

"I guess," Stanley mumbled, looking deflated. "He must b-be the real thing. And me... j-just some guy with a g-glitch."

Lois wrapped Stanley up in an unexpected hug.

"You poor dear!" she exclaimed. "I don't know if that other Stanley was telling the truth or not, but as far as I'm concerned, *you're* the real Stanley."

"But which one, Lois?" Stanley asked. "The one that walked out of that soccer field in high school? Or the one that showed up the first time I," he gulped, "I d-died? Or the s-second time? Or the third? When that Stanley P-Prime was talking, I was remembering. All of it, Lois."

Herb stepped around a stray beam of sunlight and picked up the alarm clock. "Look on the bright side. If he was right, as long as this little thing is close to an outlet, you're immortal. That's something, right?"

Stanley looked from Lois's genuine concern to Herb's effervescent optimism. The vampire was definitely on to something. He might not be sexy like a vampire, or totally badass like a werewolf, but he was something.

"Gee, I g-guess you're right, Herby," Stanley acknowledged with a growing sense of wonder. "Although if it's all the same with you, I'd k-kinda rather not keep dying so much."

Herb laughed and clapped his friend on the shoulder, and Lois pulled him in for another quick hug.

"Speaking of dying," she said, her voice dropping to a more somber note, "I'm honestly not sure who's left in town that hasn't. After you got killed last night, we managed to get away, but had to spend the night in the car. Too dangerous to stay put. There are zombies everywhere."

Herb nodded. "We had a hunch you'd show up again. Couldn't be sure, but we had to check. And it gets worse."

Stanley frowned. "Worse? G-geez, Herb. What could be worse than everyone turning into zombies?"

"The Society," the vampire answered. "We got a glimpse of them on the way over. Aletia was there, spinning around a group of zombies with a couple of knives and stabbing them all in the head. That one that got you with the crossbow? Well, I guess you were just target practice. I saw him take out five zombies, every single one a head shot. And the big one?" Herb whistled and pushed a hand through his unruly red hair. "He's got some kind of club that's gotta be as tall as me. Swinging it like Babe Ruth and clearing four or five at a time.

Their heads were exploding like overripe melons. It was gross. Like, really, really gross."

"It's horrible," Lois added, on the verge of tears. "They're slaughtering our neighbors, our friends. Even," she faltered for a moment, and Herb reached out to squeeze her shoulder. "Even kids. They aren't trying to help. They're just killing everyone. We have to stop them."

Stanley shared their horror. He knew from very personal experience how much it sucked to die.

"But how?" he asked. "I mean, Herb, you're real fast and strong, and Lois, you can do some p-pretty incredible stuff. But me... Dallas always said I'd b-be worth less than a wet fart in a fight."

"Dallas," Herb repeated mournfully. "If only he were here. No one fights like Dallas. He'd put those Society jerks in their place, sure as Sheboygan."

The three sat quietly for a minute, each lost in their own dark thoughts. Finally, Lois broke the silence.

"Maybe I can find him."

Stanley and Herb started to clamor over each other, asking how and how soon and what could they do to help.

"Astral projection," she said. When she was met with blank stares, she tried again.

"I've read about it. It's like a spirit walk. I leave my body and search for Dallas from the astral plane. From what I've read, space and time are a little different there. I should be able to cover a lot of ground really quickly. If I have something of his, I can use as a lodestone, a compass of sorts, I can probably find him."

Herb frowned and asked, "Probably?"

Lois laughed nervously. "Or get lost trying."

Herb's frown deepened. "And… what happens if you get lost?"

This time, Lois didn't laugh. She looked down at her feet and said quietly, "I don't know."

While Herb immediately started telling her that it was too risky and that she'd only be doing any astro-stuff over his twice-dead body, Stanley set himself to thinking. He'd been lost plenty of times, but only when he'd been by himself. He couldn't recall a single time that he'd been lost when he was with somebody else.

"We'll g-go with," he announced. "Me and Herby. We c-can help you find your way back."

The vampire agreed. "Good idea. We'll go too. In the… plane. The astro one. We can do that, right?"

"Well," Lois finally said. "I guess if I had to get lost in a different plane of existence, it'd be nice to be lost with my two favorite fellas."

A plan started to take shape. They knew they couldn't stay in town. All the zombies and a roving trio of monster hunters made that prospect too dangerous. Stanley suggested heading up into the Nicolet forest. He figured it'd be quiet, being winter and all. Plus, it was far enough out that the zombies wouldn't be anywhere near it. Lois and Herb agreed it sounded perfect.

"Okay. I just need something of Dallas's that he had a really strong connection to. Something he really, really loved," Lois said. "Any ideas?"

Stanley and Herb shared a look.

"I th-think I got an idea," Stanley said.

Chapter 15

S TANLEY WAS HUNGRY AGAIN. He and a large group of friends had roamed back and forth through the entire town. With each pass, they'd added a few more zombies to their ranks, but no one got much to eat. He had voiced his frustration and was answered with hundreds of commiserating moans. Everyone enjoyed a good standing around or walking in the same direction, but even those exciting pastimes had started to lose their appeal. What everyone really wanted was more people to chew on.

Maybe we need to hit the road. Green Bay? he wondered with sudden inspiration. It was the third largest city in Wisconsin, so there'd be plenty of people. Plus, there was always the chance he'd get to eat a Packer. If he got to bite a Packer, especially one of the starters, Dallas and Herb would be so jealous.

Mind made up, he wobbled in a circle until he figured he was pointing roughly southeast and started shuffling while Laura limped along at his side. The horde of zombies sprawling around him bumped and staggered into one another and slowly fell in line. Stragglers that had wandered off on their own realized that something exciting was amiss and shuffled to join the mass of undead filling the road from curb to curb. Soon, Stanley was confident he had the entire town of Trappersville following him on his slow, optimistic trek to Green Bay.

Things were going just fine until they weren't. It started when a zombie a few yards to his left went down. Then two more a ways off to his right disappeared. A moment later, a loud whoosh was followed by a mighty splattering. Gooey chunks of skull and brains rained down on the zombies around him as the heads of four more zombies nearby exploded.

"Hhheeeeeyyyy," he grumbled. They were clearly under attack, but he didn't know by whom.

He didn't have to wonder for long. A dark silhouette streaked in front of him. Bright flashes followed, and two more zombies went down. When Stanley turned to look, he saw their skulls had been expertly sliced open. The silhouette streaked back, and he finally registered a woman. She was dressed all in black. Black, knee-high boots, black leggings, and a form-fitting, black turtleneck. As she ran, black hair streamed behind her. The smooth, dark skin of her beautiful face framed white teeth that shone in a ferocious grin as she thrust with a long knife and sent another of Stanley's zombie friends to the ground.

Aletia, he realized with a shock. *Where did she come from?*

The Society hunter wasn't alone. To one side, a biker-looking dude shot and reloaded a crossbow over and over, slowing only to pull bolts from the skulls of downed zombies. When Stanley looked in the other direction, he found an explanation for the earlier explosion of zombie heads. A giant of a man swung a large club in wide arcs. When it connected, it pulverized the skulls of all the poor undead in its path.

Stanley noted these details and felt a twinge at the loss of his new friends, but it was a distant and vague feeling of loss. He had lots and lots and lots of friends now. Losing a few probably wasn't so bad. What was of greater import was the fact that three fresh, juicy humans were within reach.

"Huuuunnnnngrryyyy," he announced, and the zombies responded with a throaty roar.

Their shuffling took on a renewed sense of purpose. Stanley felt himself pushed forward from behind by the growing surge. The hunters noticed, too. Stanley heard the giant bark out a warning, his voice splitting the air like a cannon. He and the biker guy fell back, putting more and more distance between themselves and the zombie horde. Only Aletia remained, dancing in and darting away, her blade cleaving skulls like they were butter.

Stanley tried to follow her movements, but she was too fast. He always seemed to end up looking at where she'd just been a moment before, and then suddenly she was right in front of him.

"Dios mio!" she exclaimed, the tip of a long knife mere inches from his forehead. "Stanley?"

"Hhhiiiiii, Tiiiiaaaa," he moaned.

Before she could respond, Laura lurched forward and tried to bite the hunter's arm. Aletia turned and dodged gracefully away before returning her shocked stare to Stanley.

"Laaauuurrraaa. Aaaaallleeesshhaa," he said, gesturing from one beautiful woman to the other.

"Huuunnngry," Laura said, her bruised and battered face glowering.

She had a good point. Seeing Aletia appear virtually out of thin air had been a bit of a surprise, and it was always nice to catch up with old acquaintances, but Stanley sorted his priorities out quickly enough. He took an uneven step forward and stretched his jaws wide. The hunter took a step back, then another as Stanley and Laura and a growing number of zombies advanced. She held out the wickedly sharp blade of a knife and kept it trained on Stanley's head, but she didn't lunge. She just kept walking backward, a conflicted look darkening her eyes. When the loud giant yelled again, she turned and sprinted away.

"Aaaawwww," Stanley complained. A snack on the way to Green Bay would've hit the spot, but there'd be plenty of people to eat soon enough. Stomach rumbling, the zombie settled back into his slow trod, the excitement of a few moments before already forgotten.

Chapter 16

Lois EASED THE VOLVO slowly up the drive to Dallas's house. It had been a depressing trip. They'd passed the horde, making sure to stay far away from its edges. After they'd passed its tail end, the only zombies they'd seen were immobile ones whose legs had been twisted or crushed or severed. Those that still had working arms dragged themselves forward, attempting to follow the others. The snow was smeared with gore like snail trails in their wake. The other bodies they had seen were dead dead, their uneaten remains in various states of gruesome repose. When the sun finally set and darkness settled over the Wisconsin town, it was a blessing. The only horrors they saw were the ones that briefly appeared in the light cast by the car's square headlamps before disappearing into the night.

Lois killed the engine and asked Herb if he could take a quick look around, just to be safe. The vampire kissed her on the cheek and stepped out onto the snowy drive.

"Brrr," he complained. "It's cold out here, even for a vampire."

The door slammed shut and a red-headed blur in a green Packers parka streaked into the shadows. Stanley had just gotten out the words, "Holy c-camoly, that Herb sure is fast," when the vampire returned.

"Coast is clear," he said as he opened Lois's door.

The witch stepped out to join her boyfriend. Stanley followed, and the three approached their friend's house in quiet anticipation.

"What do you think we should look for?" Lois asked. "When searching for someone from the astral plane, you need something that person is really attached to. Something they love more than life itself. If it's a strong enough bond, it can also help make you visible to them."

"How the h-heck do you know all this stuff, Lois?" Stanley asked. "Last summer, you were j-just waiting tables at Ronnie's. No offense," he stammered when Lois skewered him with a dark look. "It's impressive. B-but how'd you end up knowing so much?"

Herb smiled proudly, and Lois's features softened.

"You know quite a bit yourself, Stanley," she said. "How'd you get to know all of those Final Jeopardy answers?"

Stanley rubbed his chin in thought. "I d-dunno. I mean, I do know. First, you g-gotta understand that the answer is a question. That t-took some getting used to, let me tell you. I think th-that's why people love *Jeopardy* so much. Turns all your expectations right on their head. Sure d-does."

While Stanley paused to let everyone take a moment and appreciate how innovative the game show's creators were, Herb twisted the handle on Dallas's front door and broke the lock. The three friends hurried into the relative warmth the dark house offered and huddled in the entryway.

"After you g-got that part down," Stanley continued, "it's not so t-tough. You just gotta record 'em on the VCR and watch 'em a bunch of t-times."

"So you study," Lois prompted.

Stanley blinked in thought. "Yeah, I g-guess so. Yep."

Lois nodded. "Me too. Lots."

"It's like dating a college girl," Herb stated. "I never got to date a college girl, but I imagine if I had, she'd have been studying all the time too." His voice dropped as he added for Stanley's ears, "She's a hot college girl, too."

"I heard that," Lois said playfully as she batted Herb's arm. "Now come on. We need to find something Dallas was really attached to."

As Lois headed into the main floor's living room, flipping on lights along the way and rubbing her hands together to warm them, Stanley and Herb shared a secret smile.

"How long do we let her look?" Herb asked.

Stanley made a face. "I d-dunno. Maybe ten minutes?"

"You're terrible," the vampire replied. "And she'd kill me. I think the most we can get away with is five," he advised sagely while Lois worked her way through the detritus of Dallas's bachelor lifestyle.

"Maybe this?" she asked, holding up a football trophy from Dallas's high school days.

When Stanley and Herb shook their heads, Lois headed upstairs. A few minutes later, she returned, gingerly holding a magazine.

"This particular issue of *Penthouse* seems well used," she said in a more than disgusted tone. "Potential?"

Again, Stanley and Herb shook their heads, but this time, the two men couldn't suppress a shared chuckle.

"What?" she demanded. "What's so funny?"

Herb stifled another laugh and asked, "Oh. Nothing. You're doing great. I'm sure you'll find something."

Lois walked over to Herb, grabbed his ear, and pulled him further into the room. "If you want to have sex again, you'll tell me what's so funny."

"Okay okay okay!" the vampire cried out. "It was Stanley's idea."

"Hey!" Stanley protested. "We had it at the same t-time. Don't you go believing him, Lois. Same t-time, that's a fact."

Lois glared at the two overgrown children. "So? What is it?"

"You wanted something Big D really loved, right?" Stanley asked. "Something he loved more th-than life itself?"

With a dramatic flourish, Stanley pointed outside at the raised up, four-wheel drive, V8 Dodge Ram pickup truck that sat like a brooding beast in front of the garage. Even under a heavy dusting of snow, the lovingly waxed, custom electric blue paint still shone, and the chrome fenders, running boards, bed rails and exhaust glinted like hidden treasure.

"I think that'll d-do," Stanley proclaimed proudly. "I think that Deloris will d-definitely do."

Lois face-palmed, incredulous that she'd forgotten just how much Dallas cared about his truck. When they'd been on a date, he'd drunkenly flipped the truck and nearly killed them both. In the days after, Dallas had worried more about Deloris than Lois. It was the final nail in the very small coffin of their brief fling.

"Keys?" she asked, and Herb obliged by grabbing Dallas's spare set from a small table near the door.

After they unlocked Deloris, the vampire slid into the driver's seat, eyes wide. He cleared his throat as he slid the key into the ignition.

"Just gonna warm her up, Dal," he said to the ether. "I swear I'm not trying to take your girl. It's cold, so we're gonna run the heater for a bit. That's okay, right?"

All three held their breath, suddenly convinced that Dallas was going to explode from the shadows and shove Herb back inside a beer can for daring to sit at Deloris's wheel. After a tense moment, they all exhaled and shared a nervous laugh, only to flinch again when Herb turned the key. The engine tugged stubbornly after sitting for months in the winter air, but then grabbed and roared to life. Like some old world leviathan waking from a century-long sleep, the truck rumbled and set their teeth vibrating. A minute passed, and warm, dry air flowed from the vents.

"Okay, this shouldn't be too complicated," Lois said, drawing some odd curios from her bag. "According to the books, it's not unlike going into a trance. I just need to weave the spell, meditate, and give myself over to the separation of me from myself," Lois explained in a reasonable, if slightly worried, tone.

Stanley raised a hand.

"Yes?" Lois asked.

"What about me?"

Lois said she had been considering that on the drive to Dallas's house. She figured that a mild sleeping spell could work, since the sleeping mind was already accustomed to walking that fine boundary between one's physical self and their actual self. She would just need to find him and draw him out.

"Oh, sure. Makes sense," Stanley agreed. "Like hypnosis. I hypnotized Herby once. We were bowling and he g-got sick all over his shoes."

The vampire frowned. "Uh, Stan, I don't think. I mean, I'm pretty sure you never actually hypnotized me. You told me to pretend I was curled up on my bathroom floor when I wasn't feeling good at the bowling alley," Herb clarified. "I don't know if that counts."

Before Stanley could object, Lois shushed them both and started to prepare for the casting. She had gathered a few ingredients from her satchel into her lap and started to softly speak some strange-sounding words when Stanley raised his hand again.

"Yes, Stanley?" she asked patiently.

"What about Herby?"

Lois sighed. "Same as you, Stanley."

"Oh. Okay. I Th-thought so, but figured I'd better check. Never hurts to check. Measure tw-twice, cut once. An ounce of p-prevention is worth a p-pound of cure. Look before you,"

"You're right, Stanley," Lois interjected. "You're very right. Now... hush."

"Wake up Stanley," a voice said, so he did.

"Oh, hey Lois. Hi, Herb," Stanley said lazily. "Must've d-dozed off for a second. Anyway, I was just making sure me and Herb both knew what to d-do. I think we g-got it. Right, Herb? So you j-just go ahead and do that spell, Lois. I'm all set."

Herb smiled. "Look down."

Stanley frowned, suddenly self-conscious. Did he forget to zip his fly again? He turned his back to his friends and looked down. And down. And down.

Far, far beneath him, he could just make out the bird's-eye silhouettes of a Swedish sedan, an all-American monster truck, and the roof of a house. Tree branches encroached from all sides, their shapes viewable in stark relief against the snowy ground below.

"Lois?" Stanley asked worriedly, while squeezing his eyes shut. He'd never been real fond of heights. An unbidden desire to just be home overcame him. Home in his Barca Lounger instead of floating a mile above the ground. Home in his Barca Lounger instead of worrying about zombies and monster hunters and aliens. He just wanted to be home.

When Stanley cracked open first one, then a second eye, he felt his last meal heave in his stomach. Dallas's house was still there, nestled in the trees below, but he could also see his house, so close he could practically reach down and touch it. As if that wasn't disorienting enough, he could also see everything occupying every square inch between the two homes. Stanley squeezed his eyes shut again and valiantly choked back the urge to vomit. He forced himself to take slow, calming breaths. As his heart rate slowed and his stomach settled, he risked opening his eyes again. This time, the strange, twisted view of the world that had made him suddenly and violently ill had resolved into familiar surroundings. His living room, seem from the vantage of his favorite chair.

That's more like it, he thought, breathing a mental sigh of relief.

"Stanley!" Lois yelled, and suddenly he was floating a half-mile above Dallas's truck again.

"Oh, hi Lois," he said, trying not to sound annoyed, and simultaneously trying not to be perturbed by the fact that his two friends were literally standing on air in front of him.

The witch grabbed his hand and laced her fingers tightly with his.

"Well, first lesson learned," she sighed. "We have to keep looking at each other or stay connected. You're supposed to help make sure I don't get lost, remember? I swear, keeping track of you two is like herding cats."

"I was at Bay City Bowlers," Herb confessed.

"I still can't believe your sense of self is strongest in a bowling alley," Lois grumbled, earning a chagrined look from her boyfriend.

"Me neither. I for sure would've thought it'd be Petro Patterson's. I love convenience stores."

After a final warning from Lois to keep holding hands or, so help her God, she'd leave them in the astral plane for a week while dressing up their physical bodies in Vikings jerseys and posting pictures on the internet, she started to look for Dallas.

As Stanley was dragged along, he realized that 'look for' wasn't really the best description. The astral plane was a funny place indeed. Distances didn't seem to matter at all. It was like every possible place existed all at once. All it took was a subtle shift of your attention, and you could be in Sheboygan, Wisconsin or Beijing, China, or both places at once. And the people. All of the people. Stanley knew there were seven billion people, give or take, on the planet. He'd never imaged what that would look like if you could see them all at once.

"Holy c-cow," he whispered. "How we gonna find Dallas in all of this?"

Herb didn't seem as worried as Stanley, and actually seemed to be enjoying himself. He kept asking Lois if they could go to Wisconsin Dells, or Lambeau Field, or Wausau, for some fried pickles. He'd heard from one of the guys he used to bowl with that there was this great place for fried pickles in Wausau, and even if he couldn't eat them because he was a vampire, it'd still be cool to check it out.

Every time Herb thought of a new place, the three would be there. Then Lois would tell him to focus and they'd be here again. Then a new idea would pop into Herb's head and they'd be there, and Lois would grumble and they'd be here.

"Are we there yet?" Stanley asked. "All this jumping around is m-making me sick. What happens if you yack in the astral p-plane?"

Suddenly, the three were floating above an unbroken expanse of forest. Trees stretched to the horizon in every direction, dappled in the light of a trillion stars and a waxing moon.

"I think we're close," Lois said. She looked down, and they were among the trees.

"Dallas?" she asked softly. "Dallas, is that you?"

A short distance away, a man sat comfortably in the snow between the tree trunks. His legs were drawn up, allowing him to lean forward and rest his elbows on his knees. Since the man had his back to them, Stanley couldn't tell what his hands were doing.

"You did it!" Herb hollered, kissing Lois's hand. "Hey Dallas! Lois did it! She found you!"

The man's head cocked to one side, and Stanley saw it was true. It was Dallas. Even in the half-light of a moon soaked night, he was unmistakable. Emotions Stanley didn't realize had been bottled up broke free, and heavy tears poured down his face.

"You're okay," he cried. "I kn-knew it. T-toughest guy I know. Of c-course you'd be okay."

Stanley dragged Lois and Herb behind him as he moved toward his friend.

"You are okay, aren't ya?" he asked when Dallas still didn't respond.

When they came around the front of their sitting friend, Dallas's hands came into view. Whatever Stanley had been expecting those hands to be doing, it was a far cry from what he actually saw. Delicately balanced in each was a knitting needle. Piled in front of him was a skein of pink—pink!—yarn. As Stanley, Herb, and Lois all tried to pull their respective jaws up from the ground, Dallas resumed knitting what looked suspiciously like little booties.

"Oh D-Dallas," Stanley said, tears still streaming, but for an entirely different reason. "You are not okay."

Even though they were standing directly in front of him, Dallas gave no indication that he was aware of their presence. Needles clicked in a slow rhythm, pausing only when Dallas dropped a stitch. When that happened, he'd curse softly, back out a few pulls, and start again.

"What's wrong with him?" Herb asked.

Lois responded by closing her eyes, her beautiful features pulled into a mask of concentration.

"Deloris," she said quietly, and then repeated it more loudly. "De-loris."

"Baby?" Dallas asked, ears pricking and eyes searching the woods.

"Lois, Herb, and Stanley are in Deloris," Lois announced.

The knitting needles and yarn fell from Dallas's hands as he pushed himself to his feet. He looked restlessly around, pivoting in a wary circle and sniffing the air.

"Who's messing with me?" he asked in a challenging tone. "Dwight? Amber? C'mon you guys. Stop screwing around."

Lois stepped up to Dallas and raised herself up on her toes until she was practically nose to nose with the taller man. Stanley and Herb were at her sides, hands still linked with hers.

"Dallas," Lois said again. "Open your eyes, you dolt. Think about Deloris and see us."

The werewolf blinked, yelped, and jumped back a good three feet.

"Sonofabitch!" he cursed. "Where the hell did you three come from?"

"Nice to see you, too," Herb remarked.

Dallas had the good grace to look embarrassed. He offered a gruff apology followed by a, "Come here, you." He stepped forward to give Herb a manly hug, but his arms whooshed right through the vampire. Perplexed, he swiped at Lois and Stanley, but with the same result. Horrified, Dallas clapped a hand to his mouth and spoke through his fingers.

"Oh god, you're dead. You're all dead. How'd you die? What happened?"

"We're not d-dead, Dallas," Stanley corrected. "We're astral projecting with Lois. Our b-bodies are back in your truck. Pretty neat, right? Lois made me and Herby g-go to sleep, and then we woke up and we were everywhere all at once, and then we were here, and now we're t-talking with you even though we're b-back home. Hey, j-just curious. Where are we, Big D? Or I guess, where are you?"

Dallas exhaled, his look making it clear that he hadn't appreciated the scare one bit. After taking a moment to compose himself, he swept his hands out. "Home," he said serenely. "Northeastern Ontario, about halfway between Mammamattawa and Smoky Falls."

Stanley frowned. "So your hotel's close by, then?"

"No hotel, Stanley."

"Wow. You g-gotta house already? How many b-bedrooms? You g-gots the walk-in kitchen, or one of them open floor plans, you know, where the d-dining room and living room and k-kitchen are all sort of the same room? Those are nice. Makes it feel nice and open. How about a hockey rink? I figured maybe them C-Canadians would have that instead of a pool."

Dallas chuckled. "No house, Stanley. Just this. Just what you see."

The werewolf explained that after he ran off into the night, he'd hiked up through Michigan's northern peninsula, alone with the sun and stars and, of course, the moon. He didn't want to hurt anyone else, so he tried to get as far from civilization as possible.

"I snuck across the border, which those Canadians should really do something about. Maybe build a wall or something. Anyway, I just kept heading north. The nice thing about not really having somewhere to go is that you can end up pretty much anywhere, and it's okay."

What Dallas hadn't realized was that he'd been followed. For the better part of a month, he had the sneaking suspicion that he was being watched, but he didn't give it much thought. He was too busy being depressed about being a werewolf and killing an innocent person and that kind of stuff. Instead of trying to figure out if he was being followed, or by whom and why, Dallas had just kept sleeping and waking up and eating when he was hungry and sleeping again. The next full moon, he got quite a surprise.

"It was a pack. A whole bunch of werewolves. I'd turned and was chasing a deer. Suddenly, there was a howl nearby, then another. They came out of nowhere, but not to get me. They helped me hunt. We herded that deer and ran it down. When I finally caught it, the others all came in to feed with me. It was awesome," their friend exclaimed. "I shit you not. You ain't lived until you've hunted with a pack."

"Who were they?" Stanley asked, caught up in the story. "Were they Canadian? They must've b-been. Canadians are so nice. J-just makes sense that Canadian werewolves would be p-pretty nice, too."

Dallas smiled at his friend. "Yeah, they're pretty nice. We ran and hunted and howled the whole night away. When the moon set, we got introduced formal-like. Dwight, he's the pack leader, is from Ontario. Like me, when he turned, he decided the best thing he could do was put as many miles between him and people as possible. That's easy to do up here. Over the years, he found others and brought them into the fold. Now the pack's got a solid twelve werewolves, plus a handful of folks that pass through from time to time."

In the ensuing months, Dallas learned a lot. He'd always considered himself outdoorsy. He could pitch a tent and build a fire and whip up some decent grub, provided the grub came out of a can. Dwight made Dallas see how little he actually knew about living off the land. He didn't need anything besides what nature had to offer. He had started a little commune deep in the woods, and everyone that joined the pack did their part to make it work. It had a few long, low row houses they used for sleeping and social activities. When they were human, they'd spend their days making or mending little necessities and doing the countless chores needed to survive.

"We even have a little farm. You know, tomatoes, cucumbers, carrots, lettuce, that sort of stuff. I guess they tried to keep a few goats and chickens, but that didn't work so good," Dallas admitted. "They had to keep replacing them after every full moon."

Nights were spent sharing stories. Dallas learned a lot about his new pack mates, and they learned a good deal about him. There was no judgement, just acceptance. That was also when he learned about the Great Wolf.

"That's the best part," he said earnestly. "See, all this is happening for a reason. There's a big wolf, so big that when you think you're looking at stars, you're actually just seeing little flecks of ice on his coat. So big that all you can ever really see is his eye when it opens up all the way. That's only once a month because he's so big, he blinks really slow-like," Dallas explained. "Anyway, everything that happens is because the Great Wolf wants it to. All you gotta do is just give yourself over to the Wolf."

"So that's it?" Lois asked in a caustic tone. "You just traded in your old friends for new ones, huh? Just left us all to wonder and worry night after night for months, while you've been up here all the while playing cult and knitting... What is that, anyway?"

Dallas looked down at his craftwork. "Oh, they're booties. Sonya's having a baby. Everyone thinks it'll be a girl. We can smell it, you know."

"Knitting pink booties," Lois continued. "You abandoned your friends to knit baby booties in the woods of Ontario. Dallas, that's just... That's just awful."

Dallas responded to Lois's attack with a calm nod. "I know it seems that way, but it was never my choice. The Great Wolf brought me here, and once I got here, well... there aren't exactly phone booths, so I couldn't call."

"I'm glad for you, Dallas," Herb said earnestly. "I mean, you always liked the outdoors, and now you, um. Well, you're outdoors all the time. So that's good. But here's the thing. We need you to come home."

"I am home, Herby."

"No, like Trappersville home. Your house home. There's some really bad stuff going on, Dallas. The whole town's turned into zombies, and the Society is there killing 'em all. We need your help."

Dallas returned to sitting on the ground. A moment later, the needles started to click.

"Society, huh?" he asked, too nonchalantly. "You mean, like Tia?"

Herb nodded and explained that it was Aletia and two other guys. Both real tough.

Dallas pursed his lips in thought and then shook his head. "Can't do it, buddy. I've found my place, and besides, whatever's going on, it'll be okay. The Great Wolf's got a plan, and you're all part of it. Even if you aren't wolves," he added. "At least, I think so. I guess I never asked Dwight if non-wolf people get to be part of the plan." Dallas shrugged. "Anyway, if you see Tia again, maybe. I dunno. Maybe tell her I said hi."

The needles started to click again, looping and pulling the yarn in calm monotony. The witch dropped Herb's hand and swatted angrily at the knitting needles, but her hand passed right through. She cursed in frustration and cursed again when she realized Herb had vanished.

"Oh great," she complained. "Now I have to go find Herb again. I hope he's back in the truck."

The clicking stopped.

"Deloris? You said you're in Deloris," Dallas remembered. "How… You know. How is she?"

Lois gasped in shock. "Seriously? You haven't changed. Not one bit. Herb tells you the whole town is overrun by zombies, and you ask about your stupid truck?" she yelled.

"She's not stupid," Dallas retorted.

"D-Deloris is fine, just fine," Stanley soothed, eager to head off an argument. "But, but we really d-do need you, Dallas. Those Society folks are real tough. We c-can't figure out a cure for the zombies if they're around trying to k-kill us. You gotta beat 'em up. Beat 'em up real g-good so we can help everyone else."

Dallas shrugged apologetically. "I don't fight anymore. Dwight says that kind of violence just isn't what the Great Wolf wants. You never see wolves going around pummeling each other, do you?" When neither Stanley nor Lois had a ready answer for that, he nodded authoritatively. "See? All part of the plan, and right now, the plan for old Dallas is to stay put and finish these here booties."

Lois was about to say something else, and from her expression, it was going to be some pretty choice words. Before she could utter the first syllable, a faint voice echoed in the still night air around them.

"Lois? Stanley? Where are you guys? Can you hear me?"

Stanley kept a firm grasp on Lois's hand while his head spun from side to side.

"Herby? We're here. Where'd you g-go?" he asked, still searching the nearby trees for some sign of the red-headed vampire.

"Deloris," the faint voice said, echoing eerily in the space around them. "I'm awake. You two are still conked out. But, um. Well, you should probably get back here."

Lois looked worried. "What's going on, Herb? Are you okay?"

For a long moment, there was silence as the witch, werewolf, and alien clone held their breath. They all exhaled when Herb's distant voice finally replied that yes, he was okay, but there were zombies.

"I thought they were gone. You know, the big group heading out of town. But I guess there are still some stragglers. Anyway, they've circled the truck and they're trying to get in. I think we need to go."

Dallas squinted at his slightly translucent friends. "What does he mean, 'they've circled the truck?' Whose truck? My truck?" The werewolf jumped to his feet, pink yarn forgotten. "Are they messing with my baby? You'd better tell me they aren't messing with my girl!"

Another long pause followed, during which Lois and Stanley hovered a few inches from the ground that Dallas paced. When Herb's voice flittered down through the ether, it didn't carry good news. The number of zombies was increasing, and they were starting to shove and rock the big V8 pickup.

"Vikings in the playoffs!" Dallas swore loudly. "Don't you let them scratch her, Herb!"

Lois's mouth was pressed into a tight line. Her lips barely parted as she growled, "Gee, Dallas. I thought this was all part of the Great Wolf's plan."

"Well, there's that, sure," Dallas agreed, "and then there's Big-D's plan, and I've decided I like mine better. You two get back there and make sure they don't mess up my baby. I'll be there soon."

"There where, D-Dallas?" Stanley asked.

Dallas squinted. "Hey, where'd you go?"

Things were taking on that 'everywhere at once' quality again. Stanley repeated his question, but the other man clearly couldn't hear or see them anymore.

"Shit," he heard Lois say. Opening his eyes, Stanley saw that he was once again in the back of Dallas's truck. The fact that they'd lost their astral connection to Dallas before they could decide on a place to meet was only part of why Lois had cursed. She was more concerned about the thirty or so zombies that were smooshed up against the side windows, red eyes staring and bloody teeth gnashing.

Herb gave her a fierce hug and then reached into the back seat to slap Stanley on the shoulder. "How'd it go?" he asked.

"I'll fill you in on the road," the witch replied. "Let's get out of here."

Herb's eyes widened in disbelief. "In... you mean, in Deloris?"

Stanley gulped and added, "No, sir. No way, Lois. Not nobody d-drives Dallas's truck except Dallas. That's a rule. Unless he's real drunk, and you're driving him home. But even then, it's only okay b-because he's in the truck."

Lois smiled a mirthless smile and asked if it was a rule worth dying for. Without another word, Herb put the giant truck in drive and started to idle forward. The zombies in front of the truck parted like a gory curtain, stumbling and shuffling to either side. Their nails screeched along the side panels, causing Herb to grimace, but eventually, they were free of the mob. Even though the coast was clear, it was still slow-going for the first few miles. Herb was convinced that Dallas was going to kill him again if anything happened to Deloris. He came to complete stops at every stop sign, and only proceeded after checking and rechecking for cars. When he did press on the accelerator, it was with such hesitation that the truck crawled forward slower than an overweight turtle.

"Where should we go?" he asked, still white-knuckling the steering wheel.

Stanley still thought losing themselves in the Nicolet Forest was the best option. Herb started to turn the truck north, but Lois stopped him.

"We need to check on the zombies," she said. When Herb and Stanley asked if she'd lost her marbles, the witch explained. "As far as we can tell, most of the town's already been turned, and now they're on the move. If we're going to try to help them, we need to know where they are."

Stanley rubbed his chin and squinted an eye. Where would he go if he were a zombie?

"Society said z-zombies are always hungry," he recalled. "If there's no one left in t-town, they're probably looking for more people to eat. Only small towns up in this p-part of the state. If I was a hungry zombie, I'd head down to Shawano, hang a left, and t-take Highway 29 right into Green Bay. Yes, sir. Lots of folks to eat in Green Bay."

Lois agreed, but said they had to know for sure. Herb obliged and circled the truck back toward town, a town that used to be one they'd known and loved, but was now a strange and hostile land.

Chapter 17

WORLD PEACE. THE IDEA was stuck in his brain like the torn flesh between his teeth. Stanley sucked at both and savored the paired flavors. Having friends was great. Having more friends was better. But being friends with every single person in the world? The slow-moving cogs in his mind shuddered with excitement. That would be a lot of friends.

Where should I go for more friends after Green Bay? Michigan or Illinois?

It was an important question, since it would determine if he turned left or right when he finally ate his way to Lake Michigan. He was still pondering it when a pickup truck pulled out from an intersection a short ways up the road. The truck was instantly recognizable, bringing a smile to Stanley's gore-streaked face.

"Daaaaaallllaaaassss," he moaned.

He shuffled forward with renewed vigor. He hadn't seen Dallas in months. Suddenly, the hundreds of friends trailing into the distance behind him ceased to matter. He wanted his *friend.* The truck slowed to a stop, driver's side perpendicular to the advancing horde. Stanley scrubbed at his bloodied glasses with a bloody wrist. It didn't clean the lens, but it moved enough sticky streaks around until he had a clearer view. The tinted driver's window was rolling down, revealing an unexpected but still familiar round face capped in red, disheveled hair.

Herb? Stanley realized. *Driving Deloris? Oooohhhh, Dallas is gonna be mad.*

Stanley chewed on the incongruity for a minute and decided Dallas must be drunk in the other seat. It was so Dallas that Stanley couldn't help but smile even wider. The smile was also fueled by the realization that he was about to be reunited with his two best friends. Just when he thought he was having the best night ever, Lois leaned forward and peered past Herb.

Lois too! he thought. *Geez, who should I bite first?*

Before he had a chance to make that important decision, the rear window rolled down and revealed another face. Was that Dallas? Stanley rubbed a dirty finger across his glasses and tried to get a better look. While he squinted, the guy in Deloris's back seat began to scream. The windows rolled up, and the truck accelerated away.

Stanley slowed, confused why his friends would drive away like that. What were they doing?

"Ooooohhhhh," he moaned with dawning understanding. He wasn't supposed to know Dallas was back. They were probably going to surprise him. That meant they were going to a surprise party. Parties meant people.

People means people to eat, he thought.

Stanley veered left to follow the truck's receding taillights. He cut across the front of the horde that was inching its way toward Green Bay, Laura following in his wake. They bumped their way across the zombies, each bump causing another zombie to literally follow in their footsteps. Like a giant ship correcting course, the massive mob of undead turned their backs on Green Bay and started to head north.

161

Chapter 18

"**N**o wonder he loves this truck," Herb observed as Deloris hurtled down the road at just shy of a hundred miles per hour. "Oh my god, this is awesome! My Pinto can barely clear fifty."

Stanley and Lois weren't having as much fun. Lois clung to the passenger side's 'oh shit' handle like it was a life preserver and she was lost at sea. Stanley was buckled in tight in the back seat, legs pressed up against the back of Lois's seat and hands pressed against the roof. Only his trust in Herb's preternatural reflexes kept him from bawling like a baby as the giant pickup roared down the road.

One upside to Herb driving like a bat out of hell was that it provided a distraction from the shock of seeing his undead twin. The distraction didn't last long, though. Too soon, Herb had to slow down and navigate his way off Highway 55 and down a trail just wide enough to accommodate Deloris. After a few long minutes, they emerged in a clearing near what could either be described as a small lake or a large pond. The second that Stanley's brain wasn't completely suffused with panic, it started thinking about the other Stanley.

"That was a z-zombie me," he cried. "Why was there a z-zombie me? Do you think that was the Prime? Do you think he g-got bit?"

Lois reached around her seat to squeeze Stanley's hand. "I don't think so," she said. "He was wearing normal clothes, not that weird jumpsuit. Plus, Prime can teleport, right? So I doubt he'd be easy to catch, much less bite."

Stanley nodded, impressed by the witch's deductions. "So if he's n-not the first me, he's g-gotta be a clone, too, right? And if he's a clone, too, how many of me are there?"

No one had a ready answer, so they sat in silence while Herb parked Deloris. As Stanley had predicted, the untouched wilderness around them was completely deserted. Even so, Herb decided to situate the big truck as far from the rutted path as possible.

Even in the depths of winter, the countryside was beautiful. It was part of why Stanley loved Wisconsin. There were so many places throughout the state where you could slip away and completely forget about civilization. The three friends sat quietly in the truck's cab and soaked in the stillness of the winter night. When Herb killed the headlights, the resulting darkness was pure and complete. Craning his neck to look up from his window, Stanley saw that a light breeze had cleared all the clouds and laid a sparkling blanket of stars across the sky.

"Sure is p-pretty," he commented, earning nods of agreement from Herb and Lois. "So, now what?"

When no one offered a suggestion, Herb recommended that Lois and Stanley try to get a little sleep before sunrise. Lois was exhausted, physically and emotionally, so Stanley offered her the back seat so she could stretch out a bit. Within minutes of closing her eyes, soft snores floated up to the front of the truck.

"You should try to get some sleep too, Stanley. Lord knows you probably need it," Herb advised. "After the day you've had, you've gotta be spent."

Stanley contemplated the stars for a moment before answering. He had definitely had a confusing day. That morning, he'd learned that he was actually a clone of the real Stanley, and that the real Stanley had been living somewhere in the Wisconsin countryside with aliens. That evening, he'd discovered that there was another clone, an undead clone that was leading a horde of zombies on a path of destruction. Stanley had always felt that journeys of self-discovery were important, but had never thought they could be so literal.

"I g-guess I'm not too tired, Herby," he finally answered. "I'd rather stay awake. Seems like every time I w-wake up, my life gets weirder."

Both men sat quietly for a long stretch, lit only by the dashboard lights and wrapped in the quiet rumble of Deloris's engine. When Stanley spoke again, he spoke very softly, so he didn't disturb the sleeping witch behind him.

"Sure was nice seeing D-Dallas today," he commented. "G-glad he's been doing good."

The vampire nodded. "Can you believe he was knitting?" he asked, earning a soft snort and quickly suppressed chuckle from Stanley. "I've never heard of a knitting werewolf."

Another stretch of quiet ensued, but it was a little more comfortable than the one before.

"Sure was nice seeing you too, Herby," Stanley said quietly. "I mean, really, you know, seeing you. And Lois," he added. "B-been awhile, you know?"

The vampire frowned and searched his friend's face. "Has it?" he asked. "I mean, we just, you know. We... we were bowling."

"You whammied folks at Bay City's so you, me, and Lois could get a game in," Stanley remembered.

"Right! That was a good time, wasn't it?"

Stanley nodded sadly. "That was weeks ago, Herby."

Herb rubbed his chin. "Was it?"

"And that's kinda b-been it. I mean, I see you g-guys here and there, but we haven't, I mean, it hasn't," Stanley tried, and then exhaled slowly. "Herby, it just ain't b-been like it was. Dallas left, and you and Lois do a lot of you-and-Lois stuff, you know? I guess I understand, though. I mean, why hang out with me when I'm not even really me?"

Herb scowled. "Stanley, what are you talking about? Of course you're you. And we do like hanging out with you, but, gosh, I dunno. Me and Lois... There was so much happening, so much crazy stuff right up until that night with the Society. We just didn't have time to even begin to, you know. Be a couple."

"I know, Herby. I know. And I'm happy for you t-two, I really am. I just. I mean, you and me haven't watched a single P-Packers game all year. And I know they're usually on d-during the day, but I taped all of them."

Herb wiped an unexpectedly wet eye. "You've been taping all the Packers games? Stanley, I don't know what to say."

"I thought, I j-just thought that maybe when Dallas was b-back that we could watch 'em," Stanley explained with a shrug. "Get some food and some b-beers and maybe some blood and just, you know, watch football. Like we used to."

"I'd like that," Herb said. "I'd like that quite a bit."

"Me t-too, Herb," Stanley said solemnly. "Me too."

As he said the words, Stanley felt an uncoiling, followed by the release of a pent-up exhaustion. An unexpected yawn popped his jaw.

"You really should get some sleep," Herb advised, eyes glinting.

Stanley slept.

Sometime later, when the sky was stretched between the fading night and coming day, Stanley woke to find Lois switching places with Herb. The vampire hunkered down in the back seat, careful to ensure that no patches of skin would be accidentally touched by the rising sun. Once he was covered, Lois stepped outside the truck and snuck off into the woods to relieve herself. When she came back, it dawned on Stanley that he really needed to go, too. He found a secluded spot a few yards into the trees and melted a pocket of snow with a warm stream.

Does Herby pee? he wondered idly. In the past months, he tried to recall if he'd ever seen the vampire go to the bathroom. When nothing came to mind, he shrugged, zipped, and hopped back through the snow toward Deloris.

Lois was leaning against the side of the truck, a steaming mug in her hands. Stanley's nostrils instantly recognized coffee.

"Where'd you g-get that from?" he asked, incredulous.

In response, the witch emptied the mug into the snow, causing Stanley to squeal in protest. Before he could ask why she'd waste perfectly good coffee, Lois leaned over the mug, whispered a few words, and held the mug out toward him. As he watched, dark brown liquid spiraled up from the bottom of the mug until it reached the top.

"One coffee, black. Sorry, the spell doesn't include cream or sugar," she said with a smile. "Careful though. It's hot."

Stanley eagerly accepted the mug and proceeded to burn his mouth on the first sip. After squeaking in pain, he *mmmmmm'd* contentedly. Coffee burns on the roof of your mouth meant you'd just had coffee, and he felt that was a fine thing indeed.

"C-can you do beer, too?" Stanley asked. "Or potato ch-chowder? Geez, if you can, we'd c-could live out here for months."

Lois laughed, the musical sound doing more to sooth his worry than a night of Herb's whammy-induced sleep. His world was upside down, but being with Herb and Lois, and knowing that Dallas was on his way home, was slowly putting things right. When he said as much to Lois, the witch agreed.

"Seems like the past year has been one crisis after the next," she observed. "I just wish things could be normal again."

"B-but what's normal?" Stanley challenged. "Who's normal? Lois, what the heck am I? Who the heck am I?"

Lois took the bottomless mug of coffee from Stanley's shaking hands and set it on the truck's hood. Coaxing him into the trees, she started to gather small branches and sticks. Stanley followed along and helped, the simple task of gathering firewood a welcome respite from the whirling of his thoughts. When they each had a respectable armful, they returned to Deloris and started arranging them in a carved-out hollow in the snow.

"Change is a funny thing," she started. "Sometimes, it takes a big change to find out who you really are."

"Like g-getting snatched up by aliens?" Stanley asked.

"Well, I wasn't thinking about that, exactly," Lois hedged.

Stanley crossed his arms stubbornly while Lois cast a small spell. Flames flickered deep within the pile of sticks, and soon a warm fire sent a small tendril of smoke into the morning sky.

"But that's what happened to me," Stanley challenged. "The real me. And who am I? J-just a glitchy clone, an imposter. Just holding a spot until the real me wants his old life b-back." He kicked angrily at the snow. "Like at Lambeau, when p-people will leave empty brat t-trays and beer cups on their seats when they go to the b-bathroom, so no one takes their seats. They use g-garbage to hold their spots, Lois."

The realization that he wasn't anything more than an empty beer cup holding a seat crushed down on him, the pressure squeezing tears from his eyes.

"I'm a beer cup, Lois! He's super smart and doing stuff with aliens, and I'm just a no-good piece of t-trash."

Lois shook her head angrily, the woman's temper burning up hotter than the fire by their side. She stomped over to Stanley, gripped his bony shoulders, and gave him a good shake.

"No. You. Are. Not. I don't believe that. Herb doesn't believe that. Dallas doesn't believe that. And you'd better not believe that, either," she said with a threatening glare, "or so help me, I'll turn you into an empty beer cup so you can tell the difference."

Stanley cowered before the unexpected outburst, his tears going from a trickle to Niagara Falls in an instant. Apparently satisfied that she'd made an impression, the witch let go of his shoulders and gripped his cold hands instead.

"Listen to me. Who knows more Final Jeopardy answers than you?"

Stanley choked back a sob and gave a weak shrug.

"No one," Lois said. "Who knows more about *Columbo,* or *Veronica Mars* than you?"

The sobs diminished to loud sniffles, and Stanley shrugged again.

"No one," the witch repeated. "Not a single person on this green earth. Who in Wisconsin has a bigger collection of bugs than you? Who figured out all of those riddles the Society left for Dallas?"

"Nobody," he sniffed, "and me."

Lois nodded. "That's right. You are you, Stanley. That other Stanley might've been the first one, but the second that you woke up on that soccer field back in high school, you were your own person. Your life, your choices, your experiences. Your friends."

A slow smile broke across Stanley's face. "And you g-guys are my friends. You and Herb and Big-D, you really are."

"ME TOOUH," a low, gentle voice offered from behind a nearby tree.

Stanley and Lois both turned in silent shock and watched an unbelievably tall shadow detach from a nearby tree and walk toward them, feet leaving impossibly big prints in the snow.

"HIUH," Kevin the Sasquatch said with a friendly wave.

Stanley gaped openly. Around the time Dallas had learned he was a werewolf, a sick Sasquatch had appeared at his doorstep. The Society had left town and headed north after hearing reports of a giant, mythical, simian somewhere up in Michigan's northern peninsula. When they'd caught its trail, the hunters had left poisoned muffins out to try and catch or kill the beast. The young 'squatch had eaten one of the bad muffins and sought out help. Stanley's friends had fixed him up, and in return, Kevin had helped Lois when she relocated Herb's soul from an old beer can into a new body. That particular event had been more than a little scary and sent Kevin running into the night. No one had seen him since, much to everyone's regret. Lois, Herb, Stanley, and even Dallas had all agreed that Kevin was pretty great.

"And here you are," Stanley breathed. "What in the h-heck are you doing here?"

Kevin pushed a thick digit up a wide nostril and poked around for a bit before responding.

"MUFFINSUH."

It took a little coaxing and some creative interpretation of the 'squatch's one or two-word answers to get more details, but Lois finally put the puzzle together. Campers and hikers often threw treats out for the squirrels and deer that filled the surrounding woods. It was one of Kevin's favorite spots to snag the occasional treat.

Lois shook her head. "But it's winter, Kevin. It's not real likely that hikers would be here in the winter."

"PLAYERS WIN. WINNERS PLAYUH."

The witch shook her head. "You and Stanley, I swear. When will you learn?"

Stanley added his own admonishment. "Stealing from squirrels? That's not n-nice, Kevin. No, sir."

"SQUIRRELS SMALL," he protested. "KEVIN BIG. NEED MUFFINSUH."

"Is that Kevin?" Herb's voice called from the truck's cracked window. "What's he doing here? Good to see you, Kevin," he added. "Just surprised you'd be hanging around, what with all the zombies and stuff. Aren't you scared?"

The Sasquatch shrugged. "SMELLY'S SLOWUH. KEVIN FAST." To demonstrate, he pivoted and stretched his long legs. A moment later, their big-footed friend had vanished.

"We c-can follow your footprints, dummy," Stanley chided as he set out hopping from one large print to the next. "See? You're right... here!" he declared.

But Kevin wasn't. The tracks turned behind a wide oak and simply stopped. Stanley looked up, down, and all around him, but the 'squatch was nowhere to be seen.

"Hey! Where the heck d-did ya go?"

A laugh that sounded like a diesel semi trying to start rumbled from further into the trees, followed by the appearance of a giant hand and shaggy head. Kevin smiled and waved as Stanley sputtered.

"How the heck d-did ya do that?"

"SECRETUH," Kevin answered, a coy grin showing white, wide teeth.

The Sasquatch walked alongside Stanley as they made their way back to Deloris, Stanley's legs working double-time to keep up with Kevin's long strides. They joined Lois next to the truck's cracked-open rear window. After Kevin and Herb traded a few short pleasantries about the weather and the best kinds of muffins, Lois told Kevin why they were hiding out in the woods.

"Dallas is coming back, and we couldn't wait for him in town."

"SMELLIESUH," Kevin agreed sagely.

Lois laughed ruefully. "They are, aren't they? But they're also our friends. We want to help them, but the Society are there, too. They don't want to help. They're just killing as many zombies as they can."

Herb chimed in, his muffled voice working its way out from the truck's interior. "Dallas is gonna kick their asses. Once we run those hunters out of town, we'll find a cure and save everyone. Pretty great, right?"

"If Dallas can find us before the zombies or the hunters do," Lois amended. "We didn't get a chance to tell him where we'd be."

Stanley shook a finger at Kevin. "You shouldn't b-be here, though. Bad Kevin. B-bad. It's dangerous, even if you are qu-quick. And besides, we d-don't got any muffins," he added, and then turned a questioning look on Lois. "Unless you've g-got a muffin spell?"

When Lois shook her head, Stanley reiterated his point. "Well, there you g-go. No muffins. Please, Kevin. You g-gotta get someplace safe."

Kevin's large, brown eyes contemplated Stanley and his friends, his internal struggle clear.

"DALLASUH. HELPUH?" he asked.

When Lois and Stanley nodded enthusiastically and Herb added a quick, "Darn right!" from where he was hunkered down in the shadows, Kevin made an "OK" sign with his thick fingers and thumb.

"OKAYUH. KEVIN GOUH."

Before they could even start to say goodbye and be careful and all the other things they wanted to say, the Sasquatch turned and sprinted into the trees. Even though the trees were bare and there was plenty of space between the trunks, they lost sight of the brown, furry giant almost immediately. A short moment later, a strange, low hooting sounded out from somewhere deep in the woods. It sounded like a child tugging on a tugboat's horn. Stanley, Lois, and Herb had just enough time to start wondering about the unexpected noise when they heard it again. Similar, but not the same, and from much further away.

"K-Kevin, right?" Stanley asked. "That's g-gotta be Kevin."

They had no way of knowing, so they climbed back up inside of Deloris and waited for a desperately needed friend to find them soon.

Chapter 19

T HEY'D BEEN SITTING IN Deloris for hours. The sun had climbed far up into the sky, a faded disc obscured by a high layer of thin clouds, its weak light darkened further by the truck's tinted glass. Even so, Herb groaned and tossed fitfully in the back seat.

"We should go," Lois said. "We'll head north until dark, and then I can try another spirit walk."

"But we might miss Dallas," Stanley objected. "Like two ships in the night. He'd b-be a werewolf ship going south, we'd b-be a pickup truck ship going north. Then you'd astral project, and we'd g-go south, and he'd g-go north. Happens all the time. Ships in the night."

Lois chewed her lip. Stanley surreptitiously picked his nose. Herb moaned and grumbled in the back seat. A half hour passed. Forty-five minutes. An hour.

"We can't stay here," Lois declared. "There could be zombies heading right for us, or worse, the Society, and Dallas's music is terrible."

Stanley couldn't disagree. Not knowing where the zombie horde was heading, or where the Society hunters were was an itch he couldn't scratch. And Dallas's music was terrible. They'd tried a few of the CDs he had in a holder on the visor. *Nickleback* was just too Canadian, and *Neil Sedaka' Greatest Hits* was just too American.

"But Dallas is a really g-good tracker," he reminded Lois. "With that supernatural nose of his? Heck. He c-could find a marshmallow in a mud puddle. He'll find us. Don't you worry."

Lois didn't look convinced, but kept her reservations to herself for another twenty-seven minutes.

"That's it, we're going," she said.

The truck's engine rumbled, the tires crunched on the snow-covered lot, and Dallas burst from the trees and ran straight for the truck. Lois managed to hit the brakes a second before he flopped over Deloris's hood.

"I'm so sorry!" he cried loud enough for Stanley to hear even though the windows were rolled up. "I won't leave you again. Not ever. Did they hurt you? Did those rotten zombies hurt you?"

Lois and Stanley jumped out of the truck, followed a moment later by Herb.

"I t-told ya! What did I say?" Stanley crowed, slapping Dallas's broad shoulders. "B-best tracker ever. Big-D could find a buffalo nickel in a wishing well."

Dallas finally stepped away from Deloris and wrapped Stanley and Herb up in a massive hug.

"You're damn right, Stanley. And I sure did. Track you, I mean. Tracked you all the way."

"NUH UH," Kevin said, strolling into the clearing.

Dallas rounded on the 'squatch and shook a fist. "Of course I did! I'm a wolf. What would you know about it, ya big ape?"

Kevin swatted playfully at Dallas's raised fist. Even though it was gentle, the werewolf's arm whipped to the side.

"SHOWEDUH YOU."

Dallas turned back to his friends with forced nonchalance. "Aww, don't listen to him. He's got muffins for brains."

"CALLED FRIENDSUH. FOUND DALLASUH," Kevin explained, and then tilted his head back and hooted.

The low tug-boat whistle was exactly what they'd heard after Kevin had run off. Just like before, a faint hoot echoed back from a long ways away. Dallas scuffed at the snow with a boot and looked at nothing before finally saying that okay, maybe he'd had a little help.

"But how did you get here so fast?" Herb asked. "I mean, holy crap. You were, um, where were you again?"

Dallas's swagger returned with a vengeance. "Far enough into Canada to smell Santa's poop. As for how? Best damn tracker and a top-tier athlete, Herby," he explained. "Ran the whole way. Only stopped to pee."

Kevin clucked his tongue. "LIAR LIAR, FIRE PANTSUH."

Dallas threw up his hands in disgust. "Could you just not for a minute? Christ on a stick, Kevin! Man's got a reputation to protect."

It took a little coaxing, but Dallas finally confessed that he had been walking, not running, since no one in the werewolf commune owned a car. A Sasquatch had materialized out of the trees, scared the bejeezus out of him, and pointed him in the right direction. The werewolf had hitched a ride and put some long miles behind him before the long-haul trucker turned to head west. He'd only been trudging down the shoulder of the road for a couple of miles when another Sasquatch appeared, scooped him up like a little babe, and carried him at an incredible pace as the crow flies, or Bigfoot runs, or whatever. He didn't know how far they'd gone, but a third Sasquatch showed up, took Dallas like a relay baton, and kept heading south. That happened a few more times before he was finally passed to Kevin about twenty or so miles up. The comparatively little guy carried him the rest of the way.

"And I mean it. Kevin's a runt. Seriously!" Dallas exclaimed. "You gotta see some of his cousins. Big as houses!"

"Oh, that's so cute!" Lois exclaimed. "You should knit them some great big booties to say thanks."

Dallas glowered, but couldn't keep the expression up for long. "Yeah, well. Don't start, okay? They really are a good bunch up there, and old Dallas learned a few unexpected things about himself. Let's not make it a thing."

"My hands are so cold," Lois complained. "Some nice knitted mittens would be just wonderful."

"That's not 'not making it a thing,' Lois," Dallas complained.

While the group fell back into familiar banter, Lois rekindled the fire. Evening was fast approaching and there was a lot to discuss. Since Kevin would never fit inside of Deloris, they resigned themselves to a palaver outside. Stanley and Herb found a few small logs to serve as benches. Kevin and Dallas squatted comfortably in the snow. For a little while, the witch, werewolf, vampire, Sasquatch, and clone of an alien abductee simply enjoyed the warmth of a good fire and the closeness of friends. Eventually, Lois cleared her throat and began filling Dallas in on all that had transpired. She, Herb and Stanley took turns telling the story. They had an attentive audience. Kevin would go wide-eyed during the exciting parts and cower during the scary parts, while Dallas blurted out exclamations like, "The hell, you say," and, "Unbelievable!" and, "Fumble in the red zone, how many Stanleys are there?" When they brought up Aletia, though, Dallas was unusually subdued. He asked how she looked, and if she seemed happy. Lois sputtered at that, but Herb said that from what he could tell, she seemed to be doing fine.

Having never really been in love, Stanley struggled a bit to understand his friend.

I g-guess that's what real love is, he decided. *Someone tries to cut your head off with a sword and you still care.*

"Well," Dallas said when they'd finished their tale, "sounds like things have definitely been on the south side of crazy since I left. The important thing is that everyone's okay."

Stanley thought it was rather amazing how virtually anything Dallas said could send Lois into the stratosphere.

"Everyone's okay?" she repeated. "Were you listening? Did you not hear a single word we've said?"

Herb placed a hand on Lois's arm, but the witch angrily shook it off.

"They're all zombies. Everyone. And the Society is out to slaughter the entire town. Us, too, in case you forgot. How in the hell does that equal 'everyone's okay,' Dallas?"

The werewolf held his hands out. "Whoa, calm down. First, I meant everyone here. You guys and Deloris. You're all okay."

"Your truck," Lois growled.

"Yes," Dallas agreed. "My truck, but she really does prefer to be called Deloris. Now, we're gonna fix this. I skipped town and y'all let things go to hell, but we're gonna fix this."

Herb and Lois protested the notion that any of this was their fault, Dallas retorted that it certainly wasn't his fault, and Stanley basked in the warm glow of having all of his friends back together. After a while, though, the cold realities that faced them pressed back in. Raising his voice, he forced his way into the bickering.

"G-guys! Hey g-guys!" he yelled.

"What?" everyone yelled back in unison.

"We're not g-getting anywhere just arguing. We g-gotta be smart. G-gotta plan. W.W.J.D, right?"

Herb frowned. "What would Jesus do?" he asked, obviously surprised to see Stanley get religion.

"Gosh no, Herby," Stanley scolded. "What would J-Jessica do?"

When the vampire blinked his confusion, Stanley let out a resigned sigh. "Jessica Fletcher. *Murder, She Wrote*? Geez, Herb."

The vampire blushed. "Oh, right. I, ah, I was going to watch it, but. Um. There was the..." he started and then looked to the others for help.

Lois and Dallas shrugged, making it clear he was on his own. Kevin just said, "I LIKE DIFF'RENT STROKESUH."

Stanley shook his head, amazed at his choice of friends.

"I'll t-tell ya what," he started, then made the rare decision to let it go. "D-don't matter. I'll just tell you what that J-Jessica would do. First things first, she'd get some food."

The bickering resumed, but the topic had shifted. Everyone was arguing about whether to try the grocery store or a convenience station, whether Ronnie's was still serving or if they should try Weasel's on the outskirts of town. Finally, Dallas took everyone by surprise when he offered to hunt.

"What? I'm a frickin' wolf, remember?" he challenged when faced with four sets of very skeptical eyes. "And I've been living off the land for the past few months. There aren't any grocery stores in Mammamattawa. Trust me, I checked. So what I'm saying is, if we want food, I can get us food."

Dusk was quickly approaching, which meant deer would be feeding. Dallas explained that he'd just run one down, catch it, and they'd have venison steaks for dinner. Without waiting for further discussion, the werewolf sniffed the air, turned, and jogged off through the ankle deep snow. Lois turned back to her small fire, banking embers around rocks they could use to cook the meat on. Kevin slipped off in search of seeds and nuts. Herb apologized through a long yawn and said he'd be happy to help more once the sun set. After the swaddled vampire had climbed back into Deloris's back seat, that just left Stanley. He wanted to help, too.

"Watercress," he announced, earning a confused look from Lois. "And c-cattails. You can eat 'em, you know. Not the fluffy stuff. No, sir. B-but them stalks, you can eat 'em like uncooked spaghetti. They g-gots the vitamins A, B, even C. They g-gots the potassium and phosphorus. That's real good for your b-bones and teeth and g-gums."

When Lois still looked confused, he raised his chin and straightened his back.

"I'm going to the lake. I'm g-gonna get us some winter forage, yes, sir."

Before Lois could object to his going off alone, Stanley set off through the pines and conifers and wider trunks of maples, their bare limbs crisscrossing above his head. The small lake wasn't far, especially not by rural Wisconsin standards. While not exactly a creature of the woods, like Kevin or Dallas, Stanley still made good time over the frozen ground, and soon the shore was in sight.

The lake was a gentle expanse of white ringed by green and blue spruce and cedar. As he'd hoped, he saw large masses of cattails pushing up through the frozen water at what had to be the shoreline. He had just muttered, "Told ya so," when he saw the deer. It was twenty or thirty yards from where he assumed the bank was, a young two-point buck taking careful steps across the ice.

"Ooooohhhhh," he sighed. "Big D is g-gonna be so mad that I found a d-deer before him."

A low whistle caught his attention, and he looked to his left. A ways down the shoreline, Dallas's crouched silhouette was just visible through the brush. Stanley sagged. Of course, Dallas had found the deer first. He gave a half-hearted wave and instantly realized his mistake when the young buck hopped nervously to the side and raised its head.

Oh crappers, Stanley thought.

He waited without breathing until the deer lost interest and resumed its slow, careful journey across the ice. Crisis averted, Stanley started to think furiously about what to do next. He wasn't too keen on just staying put. It was only around twenty or twenty-five degrees. Bearable if you were dressed appropriately or on the move, but at the moment, Stanley was neither.

C'mon, Dallas, he thought impatiently. *You just get out there and get that deer. Go go go. Aaaand… go! Right now. Go get it, Dallas.*

Whatever else Dallas was, he wasn't psychic. Stanley's friend remained still as stone, waiting for the exact right moment.

Maybe I can help, Stanley decided.

He squinted at the deer and looked sideways at Dallas's hiding spot. He licked a finger and tested the direction of the wind. He quietly scuffed one foot in the snow and tested its traction. With a self-assuring nod, he crouched down like a sprinter and readied himself. On the count of three, he'd take off toward the buck in a wide arc and herd it right to Dallas.

Looks like we got two hunters in the group, and that's a fact, Stanley thought with a grin, and then launched himself forward.

He moved exactly like he thought he wouldn't, with awkward hops and flapping arms, feet slipping on the ice beneath the snow and sending him into a side-to-side lurch. The deer startled and bolted, not toward Dallas at all but toward the far side of the lake. Mortified, Stanley tried to increase his pace while Dallas's surprised and angry yells drove him onward. The buck dwindled in the distance, but still Stanley drove himself onward, desperate to redeem himself.

"Stanley!" Dallas's voice cried. "Stanley, stop!"

"D-don't worry, Big-D!" he panted back, still pumping his legs and lurching in a zigzag after their fleeing dinner. "I'm g-gonna, I'm g-gonna get it," he wheezed.

When the ice cracked, he had just enough time to cry out before plunging into the icy water. His boots turned to cement blocks, his parka became a heavy net, dragging him down. As his lungs bucked and kicked and struggled not to gulp in the surrounding water, he reached and kicked valiantly for the jagged ring of light impossibly far above. Finally, his need to breathe overcame the frayed remnants of his common sense, and ice-cold, silty water flooded his lungs.

Gonna die again, he realized.

We forgot to grab the alarm clock, he realized a half-moment later.

The last of the air in his lungs bubbled out as he tried to say, "Crappers," and everything went dark.

Chapter 20

S TANLEY'S ALARM CLOCK WAS a thing of beauty. A reliable wonder of plastic and circuitry with a blue liquid crystal display. "It's time," it buzzed. "It's that time that you indicated was important. I'm so glad I was able to help wake you at this very important time."

And then it screamed. Or, to be more specific, a small accordion near the alarm clock screamed. Or maybe two small accordions. Stanley couldn't quite tell, but to be fair, he had just woken up.

"Oh, bother," a familiar voice said. "I was certain I'd turned that off. Did one of you turn it back on?"

Another blurt from an accordion sounded from somewhere to Stanley's right.

"No, it's not funny. I swear, you Gerploonkians have the oddest sense of humor."

Stanley finally concentrated on what his just-opened eyes were seeing. It was certainly not his bedroom ceiling. Above him was a slightly curved expanse of smooth yellow lit from beneath with an undulating light. He was stretched out on a low table made of the same material and lit the same way. When he sat up and looked around, he took in a long, narrow room. Tables and counters made of the same strange yellow stuff as the ceiling filled much of the space, each cluttered with strange apparatuses. One wall held a myriad of display screens that shamed Stanley's three-T.V. entertainment center and made him fiercely jealous. The other was lined with cages. Most were occupied by a wide range of Wisconsin rodents. Mice and marmots, pikas and squirrels, voles and prairie dogs all peered at the newcomer with beady little eyes. Many peppered him with chittering that could've been questions, commentary, commands, or some combination of all three. Since Stanley couldn't be sure, he pretended that he couldn't hear them.

When he finished his awed inspection of the room, Stanley settled his attention on an incongruous wooden desk and antique rolling office chair occupied by none other than Stanley Prime. The antique chair seemed to be the only place in the long, narrow room to sit, with the exception of two strangely shaped ottomans directly across the desk's top from the human. Each was round and deep red in color, with three orange, jointed legs and multiple vine-like ropes hanging off its side.

"Wonderful. You're awake," Stanley Prime said, his tone making Stanley question just how wonderful his doppelgänger thought that particular detail was. "You really should be more careful and stop dying so much."

Stanley gaped. "Where the h-heck am I?" he asked, eyes wide with wonder. "Is this it, then? Is this the alien spaceship?"

Prime nodded, made a few notes in a notebook, and rested his pen on the desk's smooth surface.

"Such powers of observation. We're clearly related."

Stanley grinned at the compliment and hurriedly got to his feet. "So where are they, then? Th-the aliens? When d-do I get to meet 'em?

Oh g-gosh, this is exciting. We g-gotta bring 'em into town. Everyone's g-gotta meet 'em. Then they'll know. They'll know the truth."

Prime shook his head. "Expose the Gerploonkians? No. Absolutely not."

"B-but why the heck not? F-first contact, alien relations, intergalactic trade. Maybe they like b-bowling. Maybe they gots the space-aged bowling balls. We g-gotta let people know."

"Hmmm," Prime responded noncommittally. "Well, let's ask them, shall we?"

He turned back to his desk, stood, and leaned forward. "What say you? Would you like to introduce yourselves to humanity again?"

The two ottomans started to shudder and twitch, and the room filled with a cacophony of almost-musical sound.

"Well, there you have it," Prime said with a shrug. "When they first arrived here, the Gerploonkians asked to be taken to humanity's leader. The dolt they approached thought it would be funny to take them to a furniture store instead. The poor Gerploonkians were convinced humans had been trophy hunting their kind and were understandably traumatized. Poor Ploonkooha is still convinced its uncle twice-removed is on display next to a matched loveseat."

Stanley took slow, cautious steps toward the two strange footstools, hands clutched close to his chest.

"You're it, then?" he asked softly. "You're them? The ones that t-took me back in school?"

One ottoman folded a leg and tipped forward in a motion that looked suspiciously like a bow. The other whapped its compatriot with one of its many vine-like appendages and pointed three others at Stanley Prime. There was a brief burst of dueling accordions. When

Stanley turned a confused look to his original self, the other Stanley translated.

"Ploonkooey says yes, it was them, but Ploonkooha says it was, in point of fact, me that was abducted, not you. And they both say it's agreeable to make your acquaintance."

Stanley's mouth stretched in an "O," and he made an awkward bow in return.

"Hi. Um," he started. He was about to say, "I'm Stanley," but he wasn't sure that was right, so instead he hurried to stave off an intergalactic incident.

"That furniture store thing was a rotten prank, and. Um. On b-behalf of humanity, or at least, Wisconsin. Well, okay. Maybe just Trappersville. Or I g-guess just me. On b-behalf of me, I'm real sorry about that."

The little aliens honked what Stanley decided was an acceptance of his apology. Relieved that he'd set things right, he turned back to Prime. "Even so, I mean. Everyone back home p-pretty much thinks I made the whole thing up. Or you. Us. D-don't you want to, I dunno, set 'em all straight?"

"Even if I did," Prime answered in a bored tone, "it is rapidly becoming a moot point. At the current rate, the world's human population will be dead, reanimated or otherwise, in ninety-seven days."

Stanley blinked, then stuck a finger in his ear and wiggled it a bit.

"I d-don't think I heard that last bit right," he apologized. "You said what now?"

In response, Prime pointed at one of the wall's larger displays. One of the Ottomans tapped delicately over to the wall and waved its tentacles in a complicated pattern. In response, the display resolved into a representation of North America. A red blob pulsed near the Wisconsin-Canadian border. The blob stretched and expanded. At the same time, blobs started to appear and expand on other parts of the map. The alien did something to adjust the zoom, and Stanley saw red blobs form all over the globe.

"Air travel," Prime explained. "The most likely scenarios all concur that infected people will end up on planes and hasten the spread. The zombie outbreak won't be constrained by continental boundaries."

Stanley's eyes teared up as he watched the entire globe disappear under a nightmarish blanket of red. Ninety-seven days. A countdown to the end of the human race.

"We g-gotta do something. You're super smart. You and the, um. The Gerploo... The aliens. You c-can help stop this."

The little aliens proceeded to dance in a strange, chaotic pattern around the room, tentacles waving in obvious distress, while Stanley Prime waved a hand dismissively.

"Too late. The Gerploonkian intelligence reports indicate that this particular viral strain originated in Colorado. The D.O.D. and D. A.R.P.A had a secret lab in a stuffed animal factory. They were attempting to develop a virus that could prevent a seriously injured soldier from dying and keep the soldier combat-eligible." Prime's sigh was echoed by soft honks from the aliens. "Humans. Such a waste of intellect. Anyway," he continued, "the outbreak was contained when the building was incinerated. Well, mostly contained. We still aren't certain how the virus was transported to Trappersville, but what's done is done."

Stanley crossed his arms across his bony chest and glared at his clone.

"What's d-done is *not* d-done," he declared. "It j-just don't seem right to let everyone turn into zombies. Those folks in t-town are your neighbors. Your friends. And if there's one thing I know, it's that friends d-don't let friends turn into zombies." Another thought occurred to Stanley. "And you! You're a zombie too, ya know. I mean, one of you is. One of our c-clones. Hey, how'd that happen, d-do you think?"

Prime frowned. "I noticed that, and have been wondering the same thing. It would appear that the infection kills the host before reanimating them. When my clone was infected, he died, thus triggering the cloning device. However, before the original body could be reclaimed, the infection reanimated it. Most unexpected."

"Reclaimed?" Stanley asked.

"Of course. It certainly wouldn't do to have a dead Stanley lying around while a live Stanley was going about his business," Prime sniffed. "Honestly, you're a clone of me. You should be smart enough to put that together on your own."

Stanley ignored the dig and asked how the cloning device worked. Soon, the two twins were elbow deep in charts and schematics and formulas. Stanley Prime even popped the cover off of the alarm clock and showed his clone the various circuits and wires and how they functioned. During the entire hands-on lecture, Stanley was in awe of his progenitor. He'd never imaged someone could be so smart and often said as much. More surprising, though, was the fact that Stanley was keeping up. Hours slipped by as the two men delved into the secrets of energy-matter conversion and recombinant DNA and the dimension-bending principles of teleportation. With each new chart, graph, and formula, Stanley felt long-dormant parts of his brain open up like desert flowers finally tasting rain.

"The scanning function is activated here," Prime explained, pointing at a button on the side of the clock labeled 'Set.' "Once the DNA template has been loaded, the device harvests micro-matter from the surrounding cubic kilometer, folds space-time to a designated point, deposits the micro-matter to serve as a catalyst, compensates for the transfer of energy, generates additional energy which subsequently is converted to matter, and applies the stored architecture of the desired product, in other words, DNA, to complete the reconstruction of the clone. Quite simple, really."

Stanley's eyes nearly popped out of his head, partly due to the staggering amount of smarts he'd just been exposed to, and partly due to an idea that had just taken root deep in his brain. As it grew, it pushed everything else from his mind and started to take shape on his tongue. He readied himself to share his idea, an amazing and wonderful idea, an idea that could save everyone in Trappersville and even the whole world. He took a breath and was promptly interrupted by Stanley Prime.

"Well, this certainly has been enjoyable," the original Stanley said. "Your company has been a most unexpected pleasure. Thank you for that. Now, just give me a moment and we'll make sure you're properly reclaimed."

Reclaimed? Stanley thought with disbelief.

"Re... reclaimed?" he asked, throat gone suddenly dry.

"Of course. It's been on my to-do list, but you know how it is. Busy busy."

The reality of Stanley's situation crashed down around him. He was a clone. An extra just occupying a space until the original wanted to return. With the rest of humanity a mere ninety-seven days away from being nothing more than billions of wandering corpses, there wasn't much use in keeping a place-holder around, so Stanley Prime was going to reclaim the place-holder.

Stanley Prime was going to kill him.

"Oh," Stanley said. "Huh. Th-that's, um. Huh."

Prime patted him amicably on the shoulder. "Don't fret. You've died plenty of times, and let's be honest. Those were in much worse circumstances. This will be quite gentle. Quite painless."

Stanley's mind worked furiously. What would Dallas do? What would Lois do? Or Herb? Columbo? Jessica Fletcher? Veronica Mars? Then he realized something. Something important. Something that changed the very core of who he was. What they would do didn't matter in the slightest. The only thing that mattered is what he, Stanley, would do.

"Sounds g-good, sounds g-good," he managed. "And I sure do appreciate that, yes, sir. B-but do I get, you know. Maybe a last request?"

Prime smiled with forced patience. "Of course. I'd be happy to oblige. What would you like? One last order of cheese curds? Perhaps a Milwaukee's Best? Or both? That could certainly be arranged."

Those all did sound good, real good. Stanley said as much, and Stanley Prime moved to one of the odd tables on the far side of the small room. A small box, open on one side, hummed, and a series of lasers started to crisscross the space inside. With each pass, something appeared to grow up from the table. Stanley recognized a little white and red paper tray and the bottom of an aluminum can. As the little lasers continued to build a tray of curds and can of beer, the smell of deep fried dairy product reached his nose.

Wow, he thought. *I gotta get me one of those. It's even better than Lois's coffee spell.*

For a short moment, he wondered if he could carry the magic food-making box and the alarm clock, but decided against. Instead, he forced himself to whistle nonchalantly and sidled his way toward the plastic clock that had graced his bedside table for years and years. He was sure Stanley Prime wasn't looking. The aliens were tougher to figure, but when he slowly reached a shaking hand toward the clock, they didn't appear to react. Emboldened, he picked it up and gripped it tight.

The animal cages were next. Stanley continued his off-tune whistle and took leisurely steps toward the wall. The closer he got, the more the various rodents chattered in curiosity and distress. After one last subtle glance over his shoulder, he reached out and flipped the latch on the first cage.

The effect was immediate. The squirrel exploded from the cage like a jack-in-the-box. Stanley flipped latch after latch, and the two aliens started to howl in their accordion voices and scamper wildly in every direction. One knocked into Stanley Prime and sent him and the tray of curds he'd just picked up tumbling to the glowing, yellow floor. Stanley flipped open a few more cages for good measure and ran for the end of the room.

"Let m-me out, let m-me out," he cried as he slapped and pulled and pushed and waved.

The entire wall was one smooth expanse of softly glowing yellow. He'd assumed it was the door since there weren't any tables up against it or displays marking its surface. After frantic attempts to make it open, he started to question his assumption. Faced with defeat and impending death,

And I'll bet there's no way he'll let me have them cheese curds now,

Stanley dropped to his knees. "I d-don't want to d-die without c-curds," he sobbed.

Defiant to the end, Stanley punched the wall with his free hand. He felt something depress, something that would've been about knee-height had he been standing, but was about tentacle height for the little ottoman-shaped aliens. A click and whoosh answered. The wall split cleanly down the middle, and the wall swung open just like the doors of a semi-trailer might. Stanley decided the semi-trailer analogy was a good one, since the steel grate of a semi-trailer bumper was directly below the threshold, and he was looking at a bunch of other semi-truck trailers lined up in neat rows in a perfectly normal parking lot.

He didn't have time to consider what he had expected, and had even less time to consider what he was seeing. The myriad of ro-dents chattered madly behind him, the aliens hooted and honked, and Stanley Prime was yelling at them to calm down because Wisconsin rodents thrive on fear. With a quick prayer to Dallas's Great Wolf or whoever else might be listening, Stanley leapt from the opening to the pavement beneath and took off at a run between the rows of parked semi-trucks.

"Hey! Stop!" a voice yelled.

It wasn't Stanley Prime's voice—Prime didn't have an accent or sound like a girl—so Stanley hit the brakes and skidded to a halt. When he looked back, he saw a woman running toward him.

"Aletia!" he cried.

The hunter came to a stop in front of him, shock plain on her face. "Stanley?" she gasped. "Where did you come from?"

In response, he pointed over her shoulder. The woman turned in time to see something that neither she nor Stanley had expected.

Stanley Prime and two agitated footstools shook a fist and a large collection of tentacles from the back of a semi-trailer lit from within by an undulating yellow glow. A plethora of squirrels, mice, pikas, moles, and a really annoyed marmot managed to jump free before the doors of a nondescript semi-trailer swung shut. While Stanley and Aletia rested their jaws on the snowy parking lot's pavement, the semi transformed before their eyes. Little puffs of steam shot out from the seams where the trailer's sides met its roof, and a series of sharp reports sounded out like a string of firecrackers. The trailer's roof and sides fell off and revealed a smooth, oblong shape. Every inch of the strange object that had been concealed inside the trailer was a softly glowing yellow, just like what Stanley had seen on the inside.

The shape floated up from its hiding place, looking for all the world like a yellow submarine hovering about fifteen feet above the ground, tethered by an orange extension cord that snaked its way back to one of the truck stop's outdoor outlets.

"Dios mío," Aletia breathed. "Please tell me that's not what I think it is."

Stanley gulped. "Um. Okay. It's n-not a spaceship."

"Gracias."

"No p-problem."

The craft's steady yellow glow pulsed, each one brighter than the last. After five consecutive pulses, the pattern shifted to ripples that started at the craft's conical front end and raced back to its flat posterior. The ripples increased in speed to the point where the whole parking lot was lit up like a rave. Right when Stanley thought the ripples couldn't possibly move any faster, the extension cord fell free. The alien ship rocketed forward and vanished into the horizon a split-second later. A sonic boom rattled Stanley's teeth, and then all was quiet.

"Was that a spaceship?" a low voice asked from behind him.

Startled, Stanley whipped his head around. The large, bald, and bearded hunter was standing a short ways behind them, eyes still focused on the empty piece of sky that had just held a spaceship.

"Si," Aletia said.

"Cool," the giant rumbled. "Always wanted to see one of those."

Before Stanley could agree, he was suddenly staring at the sharp point of Aletia's blade.

"You were a zombie."

It was a statement, not a question. Even so, Stanley figured he'd better clear up some details before the hunter sliced him up like a summer sausage.

"I am a z-zombie," he started, and realized it was the wrong place to start. Aletia moved the blade closer, and the giant gripped his shoulder with a huge hand.

"No, not like th-that," he sputtered. "One of me is a z-zombie. I'm the other me that's not a z-zombie."

The giant chuckled, low and loud. "And how many of you are there, friend?"

Stanley held up three shaking fingers, and bent them each down as he counted.

"Well, there's the original me, Stanley P-Prime. He's the one that g-got snatched up by aliens back in high school and was inside that spaceship. The one that looked like me, n-not like a footstool. Then there's m-me. I'm a c-clone, but Lois and Herby say that's okay, and that I'm still a real me. And there's a zombie me. We just saw that me for a second, b-but no mistake, it was d-definitely me. And that me's a clone t-too, but it was a c-clone that got bit by a fly that bit a zombie. That t-turned it into a zombie, which means it died and set off the cloner," he explained, holding out the alarm clock, "which made me. Well, me a few me's ago. I've d-died a few times since and keep g-getting cloned. But anyway, that one of me that got bit and d-died and t-turned into a zombie did all that before it c-could be reclaimed, so there wasn't an extra Stanley around."

"I actually almost followed that whole thing," the giant said with quiet wonder. "But you're a little Energizer Bunny when you get going, aren't you?"

Stanley didn't know if that was a question, or a rhetorical question. Since the giant still had a painful grip on his shoulder and Aletia hadn't lowered her blade, he decided it was probably rhetorical. He quivered, terrified at the thought that she'd stick him with the sword and he'd die with the unplugged cloning device clutched in his shaking hand.

"He's always like that," Aletia said, not unkindly. Lowering her blade, she looked at the giant. "He's the one I told you about. Friends with a vampire and a witch and a," she said before her throat caught. "A werewolf. But he's human. Or a clone of a human, or whatever. Let him go, Jonah."

The pressure that had been threatening to snap his clavicle vanished, and Stanley collapsed to his knees.

"Holy c-camoly, you got strong hands, mister."

The giant named Jonah chuckled again and extended one of those strong hands in greeting. Stanley took it and the hunter pulled him to his feet easy as lifting a half-empty pint of beer. During their exchange, a few other people had gathered around. Stanley didn't recognize them, but they were obviously with Aletia and Jonah. With curt instructions to a couple of them to get back on patrol, the giant took Stanley's arm and started walking him across the lot.

The excitement of the past few minutes had blinded Stanley to a surprising revelation. He was at Ronnie's. The truck stop had a parking lot for semis in back. When truckers took a break from the road, they could park in back and rent a private cot inside, or just nap in their truck if they drove one with a sleeper. The semi that had concealed the alien's spaceship was parked at the far corner, completely innocuous.

Good place to hide, Stanley realized. *Gosh, them aliens sure are clever.*

As he, Aletia, and Jonah got closer, Stanley picked up on more details. Ronnie's had changed since he was last there. A number of semi-trucks were circled up like wagons from the old west, forming a protective perimeter, and all the plate-glass windows on the diner and gift shop had been boarded over from within.

"Wow, you g-got this place looking real safe, yes sir," he commented. "B-boy oh boy, it's like the movies. I was watching *Mad Max,* you know, the old one with Mel G-Gibson when he still talked funny. They had p-places like this. No zombies, though. At least, I d-didn't see any in the movie. There might've b-been, though. Sure could've b-been.

But that Max, he was mostly fighting these really wild g-guys. Real bad news. They…"

"Seen it, Stanley," Jonah cut in.

"Oh," he murmured, deflated. No one ever wanted to talk movies with him.

The hunters ushered him through a makeshift gate in the barricade and into the diner. The plate-glass windows facing the front parking lot were covered with heavy sheets of plywood, and the tables groaned under the weight of a wide assortment of weapons and supplies. A mismatched group of people occupied various tables. They were all engaged in cleaning guns, polishing knives, oiling the pulleys on compound bows, wrapping barbed wire around baseball bats, and other odd pastimes. Only one face in the bunch was familiar.

"Hey there, Ronnie!" Stanley said as he waved happily. "G-gosh, they sure did make a mess of your diner."

"Ruined. Absolutely ruined," Ronnie complained. "My life's work. My life's mission. Flushed down the toilet."

If Stanley had expected friendly commiseration, he apparently wasn't going to get it from Ronnie. The truck stop owner buried his head in his hands and started to quietly sob.

"Don't mind him," Jonah said, steering Stanley to an unoccupied booth. After Stanley had slid into one side, the hunter dragged a sturdy chair over and propped his elbows on the edge of the table. "I keep telling him we'll fix everything when the zombie apocalypse is over. He seems to be the glass half-empty type, though."

"When it's over?" Stanley asked excitedly. "You mean you g-guys know how to fix everyone up? I d-din't know there was a cure for zombieitis, but Lois thinks there's g-gotta be. But when I was t-training with Dallas and C-Colton and Randall, they always said there wasn't no way t-to stop a zombie apocalypse. 'J-just smash their heads in.' That's what Randall kept saying."

At the mention of Colton and Randall, Jonah's broad face darkened perceptibly.

"Randall was right. And from what I heard, he was right about a lot of things," the hunter said ominously, "so let me give you some friendly advice."

Jonah's glowering face drew closer and closer to Stanley's. Stanley tried to shrink back, but he was trapped inside the booth.

"Advice is g-good," he stammered. "Everyone needs advice. Especially," he gulped, "especially the f-friendly kind."

The hunter stared at him for a long, tense moment before saying, "Don't mention Randall or Colton again. They're dead because of your monster friends. You really don't want to remind me of that fact."

Stanley tried to swallow. His Adam's apple bobbed convulsively, and his eyes bulged out of their sockets. Finally, after a tremendous amount of effort, he squeaked out an, "Okey d-doke."

Jonah nodded and leaned back. "Now, just so we're clear. There won't be any 'fixing everyone up.' That's not an option. Only option is to put them all out of their misery, and make sure no one gets turned in the process. We've got hunters making their way here from all over the country so we can go on the offensive. When things get bloody, anyone that can use a weapon will. Anyone that can't stays inside and finds some other way to help." He looked skeptically at Stanley. "Can you use a weapon?"

Stanley blanched. "N-no sir. No way. I don't g-got no skills when it comes to the g-guns or the knives or the b-bats or the sling-shots or the b-boomerangs or nun chucks or,"

"Okay. No weapons," Jonah said, holding up a massive palm to stop Stanley's rambling. "So you'll do other stuff."

"Like save everyone," Stanley said.

Jonah looked shocked, the expression completely unsuited to his granite-like features. When Stanley didn't say anything more, he waved a hand at Aletia.

"Tia, get over here."

The hunter made her way across the diner, each step making it clear that she had plenty of places she'd rather be.

"Que pasa?" she asked in a slightly annoyed tone.

"Want to hear something funny?" Jonah asked. When Aletia shrugged, he pointed a thick finger at Stanley and said, "Say that again."

"I, uh. I d-don't got no skills with the g-guns or the,"

"Nope. Not that part. What you said after that part."

Stanley looked from one hunter to the other. Jonah's voice did a fine job of filling the room, and other people were now paying attention. Even Ronnie had stopped his pity party and was looking curiously at Stanley.

"Oh. The other p-part. Well, I was j-just saying that maybe you guys can't save everyone, but I c-can. With this," he said and held out his alarm clock.

Aletia borrowed Jonah's shocked look and then started to laugh. She had a beautiful laugh, rich and full and infectious. Jonah immediately joined her, his laugh a loud rumble that reminded Stanley of a gigantic Santa Claus. In a matter of moments, all the assorted hunters in the diner were laughing heartily, some so hard that tears streamed from their eyes.

"Gracias, Jonah," Aletia said when her peals of laughter finally crested and started to ebb away. "I needed that."

Stanley crossed his arms and hmph'd.

No wonder Lois and Herby and Dallas all don't like these guys. The thought was sour, but he was undeterred.

Turning a cold shoulder on the still-laughing room full of hunters, he set the alarm clock on the table, carefully pried its plastic case open, and started to tinker.

Chapter 21

S TANLEY FIGURED IF HIS friends were going to have a surprise party for him, it would probably be at his house. He decided to take the most direct route, which meant cutting through a long stretch of the Wisconsin woods. The zombie wasn't worried about off-roading it. His tube socks were little more than soaked rags, and his feet were bloody ruins, but they didn't hurt and still worked well enough. Stanley trudged forward, Laura limping contentedly along at his side, and hundreds upon hundreds of his friends lurched and stumbled behind him. He didn't give them much thought. He was too preoccupied with the knowledge that he was soon to be reunited with Dallas and Herb and Lois.

Stanley didn't know how long it took to walk to home. Time didn't really mean much anymore, so when he saw the lights of the familiar windows and a giant, electric blue, chrome-trimmed pickup truck, he didn't really have an opinion about how long he'd been walking. He was just excited to finally be so close to his friends.

Having outpaced the horde, he was the first to arrive at his home. "Suuuuurrr. Priiiissse," he moaned while slapping at the door. "I'mmmmm. Heeeeere."

The door opened, and Stanley's dream came true. His best buddies were there, right there. He opened his mouth as wide as it would go and leaned in.

"Holy shit! You weren't kidding!" he heard Dallas say.

Before his jaws could find anything to bite, strong hands grabbed his shoulders, lifted him off his feet, and swooped him into the room. When Dallas deposited him in his living room, Stanley turned his head and looked for Laura.

"Heeeeeyyyyy," he grumbled when he realized she wasn't there. "Whhhyyyyy?"

"Hooves on a Holstein," Dallas exclaimed. "You really are a fricking zombie. What did you go and do that for, Stanley?"

In response, Stanley stepped forward, bony hands grasping and jaws snapping. He didn't even get close. Dallas grabbed his forehead with a rough hand and held him at arm's length. When Stanley finally stopped waving his arms and chomping his teeth, Dallas let him go.

"No. Bad Stanley," he chided. "No bite Dallas."

"I don't think he can help it," Lois said. "And he can't understand you. In this state, he's just a mindless killing machine."

"Heeeeyyyyy," he moaned again. This wasn't the reunion he'd expected, and he certainly didn't expect his friends to be so mean.

Herb appeared from the laundry room and announced that he'd blocked the back door with the washing machine.

"One out of two ain't bad," he said, hooking a thumb at the zombie. "I really thought the new Stanley clone would be here, though. Oh, gosh. I should probably block that window, huh?"

The vampire pulled a tall bookcase from the far wall and positioned it to block as much of the broken front window as possible. After an appraising look, he dragged the couch over to push up against it. With a shrug that clearly indicated he didn't think the makeshift barricade would do much good, he asked if there was anything else he should do.

"Maybe figure out how we can get past a few hundred zombies?" Lois asked.

The first wave had just reached the house and undead bodies were piling up against the outside. The bookcase Herb had just shoved into place started to rock and shudder.

"Lois?" Dallas asked. "Now'd be a fine time for witchy stuff."

The witch glowered and made some comment about how the Hero of Trappersville had a bad habit of asking everyone else to do stuff.

"What? I'm watching this guy," Dallas said, tilting his head toward the zombie.

As if on cue, Stanley lurched eagerly forward.

"Not so fast, stinky," Dallas said as he easily plucked Stanley up and redeposited him a few feet back.

"Aaaaawwwwww," Stanley moaned. Why wouldn't they let him bite them? He just wanted to be friends again.

"I still can't believe you turned yourself into a zombie," Dallas complained. "Talk about a bonehead move. What the hell were you thinking?"

"Oooooopraaaahhh," Stanley answered.

"Ha! That's funny. You guys hear that? Sounded like he said *Oprah*."

"Oooooopraaaahhh," Stanley repeated.

"See? He did it again! What else can you say? Can you say, 'Daaaal-llaaas?' Or, um. I dunno. 'Beeeeer?'"

"Beeeeeeerrrrr," Stanley said. "Iiinnn. Fffriiidge," he added, waving at the kitchen.

Dallas stared. "Herb? Did you hear that?"

The vampire gulped. "Um, yep. Lois?"

"What?" the witch asked, exasperated. "Working on a spell here. You know, to save us from the horde of zombies outside? But if you really have something more important that staying alive, I'm all ears."

"Stanley talked."

The witch tried to rub the exhaustion from her face, and pulled her long, blond hair back into its ponytail.

"What'd he say? 'Ooooohhhhh,' or, 'Aaaaahhhhh?' Wait, I know. He said, 'Uuuuuuhhhhh.'"

Dallas shook his head. "He said there's beer in the fridge."

"He what?" Lois had time to ask, and then the barricade blocking the window collapsed and zombies started to pull themselves through.

"Basement, quick!" Dallas yelled.

The zombie watched Herb grab Lois and pull her away from her books and candles. Stanley's house had a small basement. The door was set into the wall under the stairs. Swinging it open, Herb pushed his girlfriend inside and quickly followed. Dallas was just a step behind, and managed to slam it shut a second before Stanley caught up with him.

"Heeeeeyyyyy," the zombie moaned loudly as he slapped at the wooden door. "Coooooommme. Oooooonnnn."

"Stanley?" he heard Dallas yell from the other side of the door. "If that's really you, and you can really understand me, let's get a few things straight."

Stanley relented and let his hands fall to his sides. More and more of his friends were piling inside and making quite the commotion, so he leaned up against the door to hear better.

"I'd really like to help you, but you're making it tough, buddy," the werewolf said. "I'm not real inclined to help people that keep trying to bite me."

"Frieeennds," Stanley pleaded.

"That's right, we're friends. And friends don't bite friends."

"Moooorrre fffrieeends," he explained. Why couldn't Dallas understand? If they would just let him bite them, they wouldn't be in any danger. They'd be friends with everyone.

The wooden door creaked under the strain of more and more pressing bodies. Stanley heard the noise and smiled. Just a little bit longer, and everything would work out fine. Just a little bit longer, and they'd all be friends again.

Chapter 22

HE HAD IT. A week ago, he would've never believed that he could figure out how to reprogram a cloning alarm clock. But truth be told, reprogramming the device really wasn't much harder than programming a universal remote. Everyone said that was really hard, but for Stanley, it was second-nature. A perk of being the clone of a super smart Stanley, he reckoned.

He thought back on what he'd learned in the alien ship and peered at the little clock from multiple angles.

That there's what scans the DNA. And that little bit there, with the funny wires, that's what generates the matter-conversion whatnot and the recombinant stuff. I can set the storage here, and matter-capture parameters here, and target efficiency constraints here...

It was elegantly simple. Everything his progenitor had explained clicked into place like Linkin Logs in his brain. He just needed a little piece of DNA to scan, like a hair or even a bit of spit, and he could set the clock to clone that person.

Bouncing with excitement, he started to clamor for attention, anyone's attention. Unfortunately, after their earlier laughing fit at his expense, everyone had settled into completely ignoring him. Pairs and trios of Society hunters readied weapons, rechecked the boards securing the windows, and tried to convince each other that everything would be fine, just fine. Jonah was cleaning some guns with the other hunter Stanley had seen earlier. The rough-looking one in dark jeans and leather jacket that had shot him with a crossbow. Just looking in his general direction made Stanley nervous, so he stopped trying to get their attention and instead focused on reassembling the clock.

While Stanley had fiddled with the alarm clock, Aletia had been in and out of the diner. More hunters had been arriving, one and two at a time. Apparently, Aletia had put out a coast-to-coast call. As hunters got the message, they'd dropped what they were doing and bee-lined for Trappersville. When they arrived, Aletia would greet them and ex-plain that they were going out in teams to keep the zombies contained. The plan was apparently to try to keep the horde from spreading by picking off ones around the fringe. Once enough hunters responded to the call, they'd attack en masse and wipe them all out.

"They d-don't need to do all that," Stanley complained to himself. "I c-can save everyone. Why won't anyone listen?"

After snapping the last couple of plastic clips into place, he con-templated the little alarm clock. It was strange to think how the little contraption had made such an immeasurable impact on his life. He was still wondering at the strangeness of it all when Aletia walked back into the diner and called for everyone's attention. Unlike Stanley, she got it.

"We've found them. The ones we've been searching for are holed up inside a house. I need a team to head out with me. Who's up?"

Jonah raised a hand, along with a couple of other hunters. The dangerous guy shook his head.

"Someone's gotta keep this place in line, I reckon," he said. "Since I'm second in command, that someone should be me."

Aletia gave a curt nod, but the biker wasn't done.

"And when you're dead, I'm in charge."

The temperature dropped about fifteen degrees. When Stanley finally dared to exhale, he was surprised his breath didn't come out in a white cloud.

"Sure, Dempsey," Aletia said, her words edged in ice. "You can be in charge over my dead body."

The man named Dempsey nodded. "Okay, then. That's all settled."

After the hunter spoke, he turned his eyes on Stanley. It wasn't a friendly look, and Stanley responded by shooting a hand straight up into the air.

"T-Tia! Hey T-Tia. I'm going with you. Wherever you're going. I want to g-go."

Jonah shook his head, but Aletia's brow furrowed in thought.

"We could use him," she announced. When Jonah groaned loudly, she added, "Bait."

Stanley didn't know what she meant by that, but Jonah shrugged and raised himself up to his feet. His giant club was resting against a wall. After retrieving it, he turned sideways to fit through the door and headed outside.

"Come on," Aletia commanded. The two other hunters quickly grabbed their weapons and followed Jonah into the gathering night.

"Y tu," she said, looking at Stanley and tilting her head. "Vámonos. We've got a truck."

Stanley shoved the alarm clock in his parka's pocket and ran outside. The truck Aletia had mentioned was a beat-up SUV. The couple that had raised their hands inside took the front seats. Jonah had pulled open the back doors and sat easily with his legs hanging over the rear bumper, his massive club balanced across his thighs. Stanley gave him a wide berth before climbing into the SUV's backseat.

"Where we g-going?" he asked as Aletia slid into the seat next to him.

"It's reunion time," she answered with a cold grin.

Stanley didn't have to wonder what she meant by that for long. After heading back down the highway toward town, the SUV took a familiar turn.

"My house?" he asked, confused. "Why the h-heck are we going to my house?"

No one answered, but they didn't need to. The reason became clear when they got close. Even with a mob of undead surrounding the house, Deloris was impossible to miss.

After Stanley died in the lake, his friends had apparently come to find him. There was no way for them to know that Stanley Prime had stolen the alarm clock, so they'd gone to his house. Stanley couldn't believe his luck. While he, Lois, and Herb hadn't cooked up much of a plan, what little plan they did have involved Dallas beating the crap out of the Society so Lois could work on finding a cure for the zombies. Now, the Society was going right to Dallas. Even better, Stanley could save Lois the trouble of figuring out a cure.

"Boy, oh b-boy, are you guys gonna be sorry," he whispered excitedly.

Aletia didn't respond. She either hadn't heard him or had no interest in what he'd said. Instead, she leaned forward and placed an arm on the driver's shoulder.

"We need to get into that house," she said as the driver parked a safe distance away from the outer edge of the zombies. "Luke, Julia, you two are going to be the distraction. Use the truck to draw as many of them away as possible. Once they thin out a bit, Jonah and I will smash our way inside."

"What about me?" Stanley asked.

"Stay close, but not so close that I smash your head," Jonah advised.

It seemed like a good plan. Stanley had just hopped clear of the SUV when it took off and started blaring its horn and flashing its high beams. As Aletia hoped, many of the zombies started to peel away and follow the new distraction.

"Now!" Aletia hissed. She freed her long blade and ran forward. Jonah followed, veering off just far enough to ensure his club had plenty of room to swing.

Stanley couldn't believe that two people could create so much gore. Each swing of Jonah's club produced a tidal wave of destroyed flesh. Aletia's blade darted and danced, curtains of blood following its bright flashes. Stanley's unfortunate undead neighbors were felled like stalks of corn before a combine. Rather than having to worry about squeezing between grasping hands and biting teeth, Stanley only had to worry about not slipping on the blood-soaked snow. It was like walking down a gruesome red carpet to his front door.

"You," Aletia said as she grabbed him and thrust him over the threshold. "Start yelling for your friends."

He didn't need Aletia's stern coaxing. After being shoved through the door, he was face-to-face with a group of twenty or so zombies. As the ones nearest him took notice, they moaned and stretched toward him. Screaming was the only rational response.

"Oh c-crappers! Help help help help! Lois? Herb? Anyone, help!" he cried as he tried to back away.

Unfortunately, Aletia was directly behind him and not inclined to let him leave. She held the back of his coat like a Spartan warrior clutching a shield. As the zombies encroached, she jabbed her blade over Stanley's shoulder and impaled one right between the eyes.

Stanley's screaming finally had the desired effect. The door to his little home's basement burst open, and a ready-for-anything Dallas burst out. More specifically, a ready-for-anything-except-seeing-his-ex-girlfriend Dallas burst out.

"Tia!" he exclaimed, slugging a hungry zombie and tossing it to the floor. "How... I mean, you look," he managed before another zombie lurched toward him. After kicking out its legs, he continued. "Wow. You look good. So, um, how've you been?"

The blade flashed uncomfortably close to Stanley's cheek, stabbed another zombie in the eyeball, and quickly pulled back.

"Fine," the hunter replied coolly. After yanking Stanley to the side so she could kick another zombie, she dragged him back in front of her and added, "Y tu? You seem to be doing pretty well for a dead werewolf."

Dallas danced around two grasping sets of bloody hands, grabbed Stanley's T.V. tray and swung it in a wide arc. The zombies that had dared get too close were knocked aside, and the T.V tray shattered into splintered chunks of woods.

"Not dead yet, babe. Old Dallas, he's a hard one to kill."

Aletia stabbed another zombie and shoved Stanley forward, closing the distance between herself and her former lover.

"Hard is good. Makes things more fun," she retorted.

"And old Dallas, he still likes to have fun," the werewolf quipped while pulling another zombie into a headlock, punching it twice in the face, dropping it to the carpet, and taking another step closer to Stanley and Aletia.

"Too much fun can be dangerous," Aletia cautioned as she pushed Stanley away from a chomping mouth and brought her blade around in a sharp arc. The spray of blood splattered across Dallas as he closed the final distance between them.

"Damn right, it can. But that's what makes it fun."

They came together like storm and sea, their passion roiling the world around them. Dallas's arms wrapped around Aletia's back as her hands fiercely grabbed the back of his neck. Their lips came together in a kiss so powerful Stanley was convinced they were both going to lose a few teeth. It was a breathtakingly violent reunion. Stanley was completely captivated by the moment, so much so that he didn't see the impending disaster coming until it was too late.

Zombie Stanley lunged for Dallas, slipped, and fell mouth-first onto Aletia's shoulder. Stanley watched his undead double's jaws clamp down hard. He heard the hunter scream. He saw Dallas cry out in shocked disbelief. A moment later, Lois and Herb came running through the basement door. Herb grabbed the zombie's shoulders and pulled. His supernatural strength dislodged his zombie friend's mouth from the hunter's shoulder and sent the undead Stanley careening across the room. Lois grabbed Dallas and asked if he was okay, had he been bit, was he okay? Dallas roughly brushed her aside and gathered Aletia up in his arms.

"Everything alright in there?" a loud voice called from just outside the front door.

In the commotion, Stanley had completely forgotten about the other hunter. He ran to the door and saw that Jonah was engaged in keeping a large group of zombies at bay with his club.

"It's Aletia," he cried out. "She's b-been bit!"

Jonah cursed and shifted from defense to offense. The zombies that hadn't been drawn off by the other hunters in the SUV were quickly reduced to a pile of crushed and mangled bodies. Panting, the giant shoved Stanley aside and ran inside the house.

"Get away from her!" he yelled, his voice loud enough to rattle the remaining shards of glass in the windows.

Dallas had helped Aletia lay down amid the dead undead and cradled her head in his lap. He turned flat eyes up at the massive man looming a few feet away.

"Not a chance, buddy," he growled.

"It's alright... Jonah," Aletia said in a weak voice. "It's alright."

Jonah shook his head angrily. "No. It's not. We need to get you back to camp. Say the word, and I'll kill all of these assholes."

Aletia looked up at Jonah and shook her head. Even that small gesture obviously caused her tremendous pain, but she still managed it.

"This is it, Jonah. Mi fin se acerca," she said before gasping. "Mierda, that hurts!"

"What can I do?" Dallas asked. "Lois, what can we do?"

Lois clutched Herb's arm, eyes darting from Dallas and Aletia to Jonah and back. Aletia noticed the other woman's hesitation and let out a harsh laugh.

"That's right, puta. Not much. The change happens fast." Looking back at Dallas, she continued. "You either let me die or you kill me. But if you let me die, you'll still have to kill me."

Dallas violently shook his head. "Herb? Lois? C'mon. There has to be something we can do."

Lois turned her eyes away, shame and regret darkening her countenance. "I'm sorry, Dallas."

"It'll be a kindness," Jonah said quietly. "But it should be me. One of her own, not one of you."

The inflection on his last word made it clear what the hunter thought of the werewolf, witch, and vampire. He stepped forward and slipped a sturdy bowie knife from a sheath hooked to his belt.

"Stand aside," he advised, but stopped when the dying woman raised a hand.

"No, Jonah. It's... it's okay. I want it to be him." A pained groan interrupted her words, and her beautiful face contorted. When the spasm passed, she gasped, "Please, Dallas. Please."

Jonah was incredulous. Stanley watched him struggle with a maelstrom of emotion. His free hand clenched and unclenched with impotent rage. Cords stood out on his neck and his broad shoulders bunched. When Dallas held his hand out for the knife, an unexpected sob broke from Jonah's throat. He contemplated the blade, indecision clear in his eyes.

"It'll be a kindness," Dallas said.

Something in the werewolf's voice reached the hunter, and Jonah responded by holding out the knife. Dallas took it carefully by the blade, rested it gently on the floor, and picked it back up by the handle.

"I don't want to do this," he said, voice catching. "There has to be another way."

Aletia raised a hand to his cheek and held it there for a moment. She sighed a long, weary sigh and her arm dropped lifelessly to the floor.

"Now," Jonah said.

"But I c-can save her," Stanley said.

"Now," Jonah repeated. "Before she turns,"

Stanley tried to step closer, but was blocked by Jonah's massive arm. "I c-can," he protested. "You g-gotta believe me."

No one was listening. All eyes were on Dallas as he turned Aletia's head to its side. He took a long, deep breath, exhaled, and shoved the bowie knife's long blade into the back of her neck and up into her brain.

"Huuuunnngry," zombie Stanley announced, rocking eagerly from foot to foot across the room.

Lois and Herb startled, and Jonah moved to attack. Dallas jumped to his feet and planted himself firmly between the hunter and the undead version of his friend.

"No, not him," Dallas commanded, his tone brooking no argument. "You killed enough people today. You ain't killing him."

As he spoke, Herb stepped up to his side and bared his fangs. Lois moved to his other side and raised her hands. A crackling ball of hot, white energy formed and hovered like a small sun between her palms. Stanley moved next to Lois and raised his small fists.

"J-just go," he told Jonah. "Go back to Ronnie's. We c-can all fight later."

Jonah sized them up. "What about Aletia?" he asked.

Dallas stood straighter and nodded his head. "We'll bury her. Someplace beautiful. Someplace she would've liked."

"Huuunnngry," the zombie behind them complained.

"If you're still in there, buddy, now would be a really good time to shut up," Dallas advised over his shoulder.

The zombie's shoulders slumped. "Ooohhh. Kaaaaayyyy," he said.

A horn sounded from outside. The other hunters had circled back. Jonah gave the vampire, witch, werewolf, alien clone, and zombie a final long look, turned his back, and stomped outside. Stanley and his friends waited in tense silence until they heard the SUV's engine fade in to the distance.

Something snapped in Dallas. He rounded on the only remaining upright zombie in the room.

"What in the damn hell is your problem?" he screamed. "Why did you do that? Why would you do that?"

The zombie shuffled from foot to foot. His teeth clicked as he opened and shut his mouth. His bloodshot eyes moved from Dallas to Herb to Lois, and finally to his twin. When Stanley and his undead double's eyes met, Stanley saw something wholly unexpected. A look of sad confusion.

"I, I th-think we need to go, Dallas," Stanley said quietly.

"We have to bring him with," Lois pleaded. "We have to help him."

Dallas stooped and gathered the dead woman into his arms. Standing again, he cradled her as gently as he could to his chest. Blood seeped from the deep wound in the back of her skull and spread in a wet, growing stain across the front of his coat.

"No. We don't," he said. Without another word, he walked out of the house. A moment later, Deloris's engine rumbled.

Shaken, Lois and Herb followed, leaving Stanley alone with his undead clone. He looked over the house they had each called home. Broken bodies littered the floor. The furniture was covered in blood. Tables had been upended and smashed. His beloved televisions were ruined. Exhausted and empty, he tried to find a piece of his life that hadn't been lost. When he found it, a small sob worked its way from his constricted chest.

The glass still had the coaster from Steinknockers duct taped to the top. It rested on its side in the corner of the room, miraculously untouched. Inside, a strange little horse fly roamed its confines and twitched its desiccated wings. Stanley tried to borrow Dallas's rage, his righteous indignation, but it didn't fit. He wasn't a victim. He'd done this to himself. Literally.

"You and me, we sure d-did make a mess of things, d-didn't we," he said.

"Yaaaaaahhhhh," the zombie agreed.

"D-do you even know you're a clone? That you and me, we're kinda like brothers?"

"Nnnnaaaaaaahhhh," the zombie replied after a moment, slowly shaking its head.

Deloris's horn blared from outside. Stanley heard Herb yell that there were more zombies coming. With a final, sad look at his unfortunate twin, he squatted down next to the stain of Aletia's blood on his living room carpet. It took a moment to find what he'd hoped would be there. When he did spot the long, dark hair, hope fluttered deep in his chest.

"I'll fix this," he promised the other Stanley as he tore a page from a nearby book and folded the hair up inside. "B-but what am I g-gonna do about you?"

Stanley ran to join his friends, his question hanging unanswered between the dead and the undead reminders of a foolish decision gone horribly awry.

Chapter 23

D ALLAS DROVE WITHOUT DIRECTION. His eyes were continually pulled to the rearview mirror, as if waiting to see Aletia pop up from the truck's bed and wave that everything was okay, she was fine, and it had all been one big misunderstanding. Lois and Herb held each other in the back seat, neither one able to speak. Stanley rode shotgun and stared out the window at a night made darker by all they had lost.

A small roadside motel appeared on the horizon. A cone of light cast by a single pole showed a vacant lot, but the office lights were on. Dallas pulled up in front and put Deloris in park. With a gruff command that everyone should stay in the truck, he went and pulled on the door. It didn't budge, so he peered in a window and then gave the door a mighty kick. A moment later, he returned with a room key.

"No one's there," he said in a flat monotone. "Living or dead or both."

"They probably ran off," Lois reasoned. "But we should still be careful."

"Whatever," Dallas replied.

The room Dallas had selected was at the far end of the row. He and Herb went in first to make sure it was safe, then waved Lois and Stanley inside. Two full-sized beds with floral-print bedspreads occupied most of the space. While everyone shed their bloodied coats and slipped off their boots, Dallas went back to Deloris and retrieved Aletia's body. After carrying her back into the room, he laid her gently on one of the beds.

Herb and Lois exchanged a look. The vampire slipped his boots back on and headed outside. When he returned, he held up another key and hooked a thumb at the adjacent room. Lois gathered up her coat and told Stanley to come along.

"Oh, um. If it's all the same, I'm g-gonna stay here for a b-bit," he said. "Just, you know. G-gonna make sure Big D is okay."

The witch and vampire nodded their understanding and left him alone with his werewolf friend and the dead woman on the bed.

"You don't need to be here, Stanley," Dallas said. "I appreciate it and all, but I'm fine. You go on."

Stanley ignored his friend and instead went to the table between the two beds. A cheap excuse for an alarm clock rested on the tabletop's wood veneer, its red digital digits proclaiming that it wasn't quite midnight. Stanley slid the table back so he could reach the clock's plug and yanked the cord from the wall.

"Look, Stanley, whatever you're doing, I'm sure you think it's important. But I gotta be honest. Now ain't really the best time for, well, whatever it is you're doing. I just want to be alone, alright?"

"Nobody, not nobody wants to be alone, Dallas," Stanley responded absently. "That just isn't how it is."

He retrieved his coat and pulled his alarm clock from one pocket and a folded piece of paper from the other. Returning to the table, he leaned over and fought with the outlet until the plug was situated the right way and pressed it firmly into the slots. His alarm clock blinked twelve o'clock until Stanley pressed the hour-button and started the blue digits on a slow climb. After a few moments, the numbers reached twelve o'clock again, and the little 'p.m.' indicator lit up.

"Shoot. I didn't ch-check the time. What time is it D-Dallas?" he asked.

Dallas shrugged, irritation plain in the gesture.

"Oh, okay. P-probably won't matter if it's not exact. J-just one more sec."

Stanley set the time to eleven fifty-seven p.m. Next, he unfolded a little scrap of paper, held it near the clock, and pressed down on a small button on the side. He counted quietly to five and released the button. That task finished, he pressed down the alarm button until a blue twelve o'clock started to blink again and the 'p.m.' indicator went dark. Still holding the alarm button, he pressed down the hour button and held it until the clock had cycled all the way through twenty-four hours. Finally, he turned the clock and pointed its digital display toward the empty bed.

"Okey doke," he said, trying to sound more confident than he felt.

At the same time, Dallas's patience ran out. "Stanley, I really need you to leave, buddy. I gotta have some words with the Great Wolf, and I'd rather do that in private, you know? Just, for crap's sake, just let me alone for a bit, would ya?"

Instead of leaving, Stanley moved to the armchair in the corner of the room and settled into its worn and cigarette-burned upholstery.

"I'm not gonna ask again," Dallas warned, voice raw with emotion.

Stanley finally looked at his friend. "You've known me for how long now?"

The werewolf looked confused. "Gosh, I dunno. Fifteen, twenty years? More? High school, I guess."

Stanley nodded. "And in all them years, you always thought I was m-me, right?"

"Of course I thought you were you. Look, Lois and Herby told me all about the first you, and you being a clone or whatever. But that don't matter. You're Stanley. My buddy. My pal. Always have been, always will be. And that's why I'm asking you, as a friend, just to give a guy a little space."

"Space," Stanley agreed. "That's where that c-came from."

He pointed across the room to his little alarm clock. It truly was a thing of beauty. A reliable wonder of plastic and circuitry with a blue liquid crystal display. Just when Dallas turned to look at it, the digital display flipped to midnight. Stanley heard the buzz, and instantly imagined the helpful little clock was talking to him, just like any other morning.

"It's time," it buzzed. "It's that time that you indicated was important. I'm so glad I was able to help wake you at this very important time."

Stanley wished he could come up with a truly wonderful way to thank his alarm clock. This time more than ever. As the electronic beep filled the motel room, a shadow formed above the empty bed. It stretched and ballooned and started to spark with an inner light, looking like a tiny little thundercloud lit from within by brief flashes of lightning. The shapelessness began to take on shape. A split formed in the strange cloud near the foot of the bed and worked its way up, separating into two parallel lengths of churning, flickering smoke. Near the top of the bed, the dark cloud pulsed and pushed two more lengths out to either side. The ethereal substance quickened, the change making it look more like a heavy gel. Its vague shape accentuated, and more concrete details started to appear. Black boots with dark laces. Black leggings covering lean, muscled thighs. Hips rounded and stomach flattened and breasts swelled. Fingers splayed, and finally, the features of a face shaped and formed.

The entire shape was still a uniform, dark grey. Little flashes of light still pulsed from within, and with each flash, new details began to emerge. Colors and textures painted themselves across the golem. Individual strands of hair separated. Skin deepened to a rich brown. Lips reddened.

Her chest rose with a breath, her eyes opened, and a satisfied yawn stretched her mouth wide. Aletia pushed herself up with her arms, yawned again, and then realized she was not alone.

"Dallas?" she gasped. "Stanley? What are you doing here?"

Dallas hadn't moved. From the moment the alarm clock had started to beep, he'd been transfixed, staring at the newly forming woman. When Aletia spoke, it broke the spell. A hand reached out and clumsily pressed the snooze bar before reaching for her.

"You're back," he whispered, unbelieving. "You're actually back."

"Back from where?" she asked, confused, and then she saw her dead body lying in repose on the other bed.

"What the…" she managed before being shocked to silence.

Stanley was really curious to see what happened next, since it had been his fate more than a few times. Stanley Prime had talked about the dead body being reclaimed. He finally had a chance to see what exactly that meant and leaned forward with impatient interest.

His curiosity was satisfied a moment later, although what hap-pened wasn't terribly exciting. It was a bit like watching the creation of Aletia in reverse. Color drained away from her lifeless body and clothes until everything was reduced to the same smoky grey. Details started to melt away, reducing the body to a nondescript mannequin. The melting and softening continued until what was on the bed was only vaguely person-shaped. The gel-like substance thinned into something more closely resembling a cloud. It shrank slowly down to a small, roiling ball and then finally dissipated completely. Where a dead body had been, there was now only a bed. Body, clothes, and even the bloodstains on the covers had all been reclaimed.

"Whoah," he exclaimed. "That was d-different."

Dallas and Aletia turned abruptly to look at him, as if they'd just realized he was there.

"What just happened?" Aletia asked.

Dallas spoke before Stanley had a chance. "What do you remem-ber?" he asked carefully.

Aletia talked about being at Ronnie's diner and learning that his pickup truck had been spotted. She remembered riding over there with Jonah, Stanley, and a couple of other hunters. She remembered fighting her way into the house and using Stanley as a shield.

"Oh, um. Lo siento, Stanley," she said with a self-conscious frown.

She remembered seeing Dallas. She remembered their reunion and... And...

"And you were bit," Dallas finished for her quietly. "By another Stanley. A zombie one, not this one. Do you remember that?"

Aletia's dark eyes widened in remembered fear, and her hands cov-ered her mouth. A small, "Si," escaped her lips.

"I *t-told* you I could save everyone," Stanley said, unable to keep quiet any longer. "I t-told you and Jonah and everyone else in the d-diner, and you all laughed at me. Not so f-funny now, is it? No, sir."

A fist hammered on the door. Aletia and Stanley startled, but Dallas told them to relax. He could smell that it was just Herb and Lois. He twisted the door's handle, and the vampire and witch burst into the room.

"I heard!" Herb said. "Sorry, I um. I wasn't listening. Not really. But you know, my ears are real good, and it was pretty quiet in our room since Lois had fallen asleep, and these little hotels, I swear the walls are like tissue paper… but anyway, I heard! Holy crapola, Stanley. How in the heck did you do that?"

Stanley beamed. "Wasn't so hard," he said modestly. "Prime showed me a b-bunch of stuff. It made a lot of sense, and then I f-fiddled with the clock, and now it'll clone anybody, and even get their clothes on right, not backward like it d-did to me back in high school. I'm not so sure how it knows what clothes to p-put on, but it does. Pretty g-great, don'cha think?"

"Anybody?" Lois said, finally comprehending just what Stanley had in mind.

"Everybody," he replied, earning a delighted laugh from Lois and a whoop from Herb.

Aletia rose up from the bed and studied Lois, Herb, Stanley, and, finally, Dallas. Her brow furrowed, and she chewed her lip. Her fingers pulled nervously at the hem of her coat. Finally, she spoke.

"You were telling the truth. At the cabin. You don't want to hurt people. You aren't… You aren't evil. And you," she added, pointing at Stanley. "You think that little thing will really work on everyone?"

Stanley nodded. "Yep," he said. "D-don't see why not."

The hunter nodded. "Then we need to get back to the truck stop. Right now."

Chapter 24

DALLAS LET UP ON the accelerator, and Stanley peered through the windshield.

"G-gosh, Aletia. Your friends have been b-busy," he observed.

When he'd left a matter of hours earlier, the truck stop, diner and gift emporium had a loose ring of semi-trucks around the building, and its windows were boarded up and reinforced. Now it looked like a post-apocalyptic fortress. The gaps between and beneath the semis were filled with wooden pallets, old tires, fifty-five gallon drums, and other truck stop detritus. Spikes and poles jutted haphazardly from the junk, making the ring look like a steampunk porcupine. Flood lamps were positioned at regular intervals. They bathed the surrounding parking lot with a harsh light and ensured that anything bigger than a field mouse would be easily seen by the Society sentries that prowled the tops of the semi-trailers. There were no zombies at the moment, but the entire place radiated a sense of grim readiness.

Even though Dallas had stopped a long distance from the barricades, he was sure Deloris's headlights had been seen.

"All them folks up there, it's a sure bet they saw us coming," he complained.

"No problema," Aletia said. "Just approach slowly. They're smart enough to know zombies don't drive."

"Or if they d-do," Stanley added, "they probably don't do it well."

Dallas did as instructed and idled forward. He had just reached the edge of the circle of light when a sharp report was followed by the terrifying sound of a bullet hitting metal.

"They shot Deloris!" he screamed. "Holy shit, they shot my baby!"

Aletia placed a steading hand on his shoulder. "Relax. Everyone knows your truck. It was a warning shot. They don't know I'm back, so they're just trying to figure out what you're doing here."

"Well, get out there and tell them to stop shooting," he complained. "Assholes could've hit the radiator. Those are expensive to replace."

Aletia climbed down from the truck and raised her hands above her head. In a clear voice, she called out to the sentries.

"It's Aletia! Don't shoot. It's me!"

"The hell it is," a woman's voice shot back. "Aletia's dead. Whatever you are, you ain't her."

"Monique, I swear it's me. You've been hunting with us for three years, ever since your mom got snatched by a lake monster in Vermont. You keep a picture of her in a locket, and you had a cat named Mr. Stinkers."

Stanley squinted against the bright glare of the flood lamps. He could see a woman's silhouette and saw other shapes gathering around her. Aletia needed to convince them quick, or there'd be a lot more guns pointed in their direction real soon.

"Get Jonah," Aletia called out. "We're not armed," she added, and then turned back to look over her shoulder. "Are we?"

Dallas poked his head out of the driver's side window. "Nope. Unless you count these guns," he added, flexing a bicep.

"We're not armed," Aletia repeated.

Voices from the trailer tops called out. A few moments later, a chunk of corrugated steel that had been propped up between the end of the trailer and the next semi's cab was lifted and swung to the side. Jonah appeared, carrying the giant chunk of steel like it weighed no more than a beer can. After he set it aside, he took a few steps into the light.

"Aletia?" he called out. "Come forward, but just you. Your friends stay put. If that truck even moves an inch, we'll put every bullet we have into it."

"Entiendo," she replied and took slow, measured steps into the light.

"That's far enough," another voice called out.

Stanley squinted harder, but couldn't make out the person that just spoke.

"Herb?" he asked. "C-can you see who all's up there?"

Herb obliged, his supernaturally keen eyes scanning the scene before them. "The giant one. A woman and a few men are still up top on the trailers. The guy that just spoke? Hang on a sec. Yeah, yep. It's him. It's the guy that shot you with a crossbow back at Dallas's house.

"D-Dempsey," Stanley said. "Oh boy. That one's bad news. Real b-bad news, yes, sir."

Lois shushed them and continued to listen to the exchange just outside of the truck.

"You're dead," Dempsey said, matter-of-fact.

"Si, I was," Aletia agreed. "But there's some next-level shit happening here. The people in that truck aren't our enemies. They saved me."

"The people in that truck aren't people," Dempsey corrected. "By my count, you've got a werewolf, a vampire, and a witch in there. And if the rumors are true, an alien."

"A clone m-made by aliens," Stanley shouted out his window in a helpful voice. "The aliens, they l-look like footstools."

Dempsey moved closer, his ever-present crossbow trained on Aletia's heart. "Whatever. Point is, they don't exactly qualify as people, now do they? I think we can safely put them in the 'not people' category. And last time I checked, the Society was in the business of killing not-people."

"Dempsey, we don't have time for this," Aletia complained. "Let us in. I swear, they won't hurt anyone. More than that, they can help us *save* everyone."

Dempsey shook his head. "I don't think so. I mean, if I thought you were Aletia, I'd maybe give it some thought. But," he said, turning to Jonah. "Some zombie nipped her, and the werewolf there shoved a knife into her skull, right?"

Jonah looked conflicted. "Yeah, that's right," he said. "So what are you?"

Aletia pushed a tired hand through her hair. "I'm me. It's not a long story, but I'd rather tell it inside. It's freezing out here."

"Tough," Dempsey said. "Talk."

Aletia haltingly started to explain what she remembered. As she spoke, Dallas, Lois, Herb, and Stanley slowly exited the truck and clumped up around her. As promised, it was a short story. When she finished, Dempsey looked at Jonah.

"Whadaya think, big guy? You think our Aletia was rescued by the werewolf that stabbed her in the head and reincarnated by some geek's clone with an alien alarm clock?"

Jonah turned his palms up and shrugged. "I don't know, Dempsey. We've seen weirder shit."

"Yeah, but this shit still stinks."

Aletia growled. "Okay, fine. My papa was bit by a werewolf and ate my mom. I cut his head off with a gas-powered hedge trimmer. In the fight, he bit my boyfriend, so I killed him with the hedge trimmer, too. Colton found me, brought me in, and I've been hunting ever since. I met these people last fall when we came to investigate reports of a vampire. Yes, we fought. Yes, they killed Randall and Colton. But it's not what I thought. They aren't what I thought they were. If you'd just give them a chance, you'd understand."

Taking a few bold steps forward, she stared directly at Dempsey. "And no matter what you think about all of that, the scrawny one really does have a way to save everyone. All the people in town. Actually make them human again. I'm proof of that. But they can't do it alone. They need our help. We have to work together."

Dempsey laughed a mirthless laugh. "You know as well as I do there ain't no cure for zombies except a bullet in the brainpan. Hell, even the place this started at didn't have a way to cure them. They torched the whole building, killed everyone inside."

"He's talking about that p-place in Colorado, isn't he?" Stanley said. "Prime talked about that place."

Lois, Herb, and Dallas all started to ask questions at once, until Aletia shushed them.

"We discovered the source," she said in a low voice. "This started in some secret government research facility in Colorado. I guess it was contained, but there weren't any survivors."

Except a horse fly, Stanley thought.

Dallas huffed. "No good government sons of bitches. If we get out of this, I'm never paying taxes again."

"Trouble is, Trappersville is a lot harder to deal with," Aletia continued. "Most of the zombies seem to be staying together, but there are always strays. We've just been waiting for more hunters to get here so we can go on the offensive."

"And kill everyone," Lois said. "Wow. And people say we're the monsters."

"Give me a break," Aletia sighed. "I'm trying, aren't I?" She returned her attention to Dempsey. "What can I do to convince you that I'm telling the truth?"

Dempsey smiled a wicked smile. "Maybe we just need to kill you again and see this amazing alien alarm clock in action, huh?"

Aletia said something, and Dempsey said something, and Lois yelled something, and Jonah yelled something back. Dallas put his fists up, and guns that had momentarily relaxed were pointed at them again. In the midst of it all, Stanley realized Dempsey was right. Only one thing would prove they were telling the truth.

"Herb. Hey, Herby!" he said. When he had the vampire's attention, he looked him steadily in the eyes. "Take this, find an outlet. Maybe, I d-dunno. Maybe by one of them nice cots Ronnie's got for rent inside. Set the alarm, and I'll see you in a b-bit."

Before the vampire could react, Stanley slapped the alarm clock in his hand and took off at a run toward Dempsey. As he'd hoped, the hunter was ready. The crossbow raised up, a twang split the air. There was the briefest moment of bright pain, and then all went dark.

237

Chapter 25

HE WAS RIGHT BACK where he'd started: alone and hungry and more than a little confused.

No, not alone. Stanley saw a body stir and heard a gurgling moan. It was Laura. The stripper looked like an over-tenderized hunk of steak. Her face was mottled with dark purple and blue bruises. One eye refused to open, and her jaw had been dislocated. As she pushed herself awkwardly to her feet, he saw that the fingers of one hand had been crushed, and her other arm dangled uselessly. The rest of her body looked just as battered. Something had gashed her bare stomach. One stubborn stiletto heel still clung to a foot, but the heel itself had snapped off long ago. The other foot looked like it had been run over by a lawn mower.

Stanley stumbled forward, arms outstretched, and pulled Laura into a stiff embrace.

"Hiiiiiii," he moaned.

"Hiiiiiii," she moaned back.

Taking her mangled hand in his own, he led her past the carved up and crushed bodies of their friends and through the still-open front door. Outside, a few undead still meandered aimlessly among the remains of the fallen. As Stanley and Laura shuffled past, the stragglers turned and followed. The once-mighty group of friends had been splintered, but was slowly reforming.

Chapter 26

S TANLEY'S ALARM CLOCK WAS a thing of beauty. A reliable wonder of plastic and circuitry with a blue liquid crystal display. "It's time," it buzzed. "It's that time that you indicated was important. I'm so glad I was able to help wake you at this very important time."

Stanley sat up and pressed the snooze bar. He was a little disoriented, a condition that wasn't helped by being suddenly tackled.

"You're back!" Herb yelled. "See? He's back! We told you it worked."

Trying to disentangle himself from the vampire's embrace, Stanley managed to ask who was back, and why the heck was Herb in his bedroom. But he wasn't in his bedroom. Beneath him, a small folding cot strained under the combined weight of the two men. A little wall-mounted shelf held a lamp and familiar alarm clock, and a luggage rack was buried under a pile of winter coats. Besides that, the compact room didn't have any furniture, much less space for it.

Guess that's why everyone is standing so close, he reasoned. Herb, Dallas, Lois, and even Aletia—wherever the heck she'd come from—were practically shoulder-to-shoulder.

"You're back, buddy," he heard Dallas say. "And let me be the first to tell you that what you did was incredibly stupid. Like, picking up chicks at the V.D. clinic stupid."

Stanley tried to figure out just what the heck was going on. There were memories, but they bumped and collided against one another and refused to line up. He was standing in a bright pool of light. He remembered that much.

"Did I g-get abducted by aliens again?" he asked.

No one answered him. Instead, they all piled up against the small room's only door and started to pound on it. Cries of, 'It worked,' and, 'Let us out,' were answered by a muffled, 'Calm the hell down and step back.' The group obliged as best they could, bunching up near the end of the room opposite the door.

A crack of light formed and widened. The door swung open and revealed the largest man Stanley had ever seen. He instantly thought of Kevin, his Sasquatch friend, and with that thought, a floodgate opened up and a wave of memories poured into his conscious mind.

"Whoah," he exclaimed. "D-Dallas, you were right. That was st-stupid of me."

"But effective," Jonah replied. "You've proven your point. The little clock works, so it stands to reason that you really did save Aletia. But," he added, looking at Dallas. "Would you be so keen to make nice if Aletia wasn't hot? Would you have saved Randall if you could've? Or Colton?"

Aletia put a hand on Dallas's chest and answered instead. "He tried, Jonah. I didn't want to believe it, but they really didn't want to hurt anyone. They just want to live their lives."

Jonah frowned. "Goes against everything the Society stands for, teaming up with you. What do you think, Dempsey? The clock worked."

The smaller-than-Jonah, but no less intimidating, man leaned in.

"One test doesn't prove a theory," he grumbled. "I say we kill 'em all and try again."

Jonah turned a grim smile on his companion. "Or we could kill you. Would *that* test meet your exacting standards?"

Rather than responding to Jonah, Dempsey leveled a hard stare at Stanley. "Works on anyone? You're sure? One hundred percent sure?"

Stanley bobbed his head.

"And when that one wolfs out," Dempsey continued, pointing at Dallas, "he's not gonna go wild and try to kill the rest of us?"

"Scout's honor," Dallas said while Stanley shook his head.

Dempsey moved in front of Herb. He pushed up a sleeve and held his bare arm out.

"Thirsty?"

"Yes," Herb replied tiredly. "But you're not my type."

"Who is?" Dempsey asked.

"Her," Herb said, hooking a thumb at Lois. "Look, I know what you're getting at, but I really don't like biting other people so much. It's a lot harder than you'd think, and honestly, it's kind-of a rotten thing to do to someone. I'm good with my girl or blood from a blood bank."

The hunter moved fast. One second, he was holding his arm out in front of the vampire. The next, he had Lois in a choke hold with a knife pressed up against her neck. Dallas bunched up his shoulders and Herb bared his fangs with a hiss, but neither one moved.

"I'll say it one more time," Lois said. "We really, truly, honestly, with cherries and fun little sprinkles on top, don't want to fight with you."

The hunter released Lois and turned back to Jonah.

"Let's call it a win-win," he decided. "I'm going to kill a bunch of zombies. If the little geek can bring everyone back to life, yippee. If not, I still get to kill a bunch of zombies, plus these freaks if they do anything I don't like."

With that, Jonah stepped aside and swept an arm out. The group spilled into a narrow hallway that led past a number of small rent-by-the-hour cots and made their way back to the attached diner. Everyone settled in around a table to make a plan: Sconnies on one side, Society hunters on the other, and a thick slab of tension in between.

"So," Aletia finally asked. "How do we do this?"

The plan took shape. It wasn't fancy. It wasn't clever. It was straightforward and clean. Lure the zombies in, trap them, kill them all, and then clone them. Luring would be easy. Aletia would send out hunters to act as bait and lead the zombies to a designated point. Once they had as many of the undead as possible in one large group, they'd start leading them to the trap.

To everyone's surprise, Dallas volunteered Deloris.

"What?" he asked. "You want to make sure they get back here, right? Ain't nothing can stop my girl. Besides, I won't be able to drive her. Full moon," he explained in response to their confused looks. "So while your hunters lead them back, I'll work the edges of the horde and make sure no zombies wander off."

"No," Aletia objected. "It's too dangerous. What if you get bit?"

"No biggy," Dempsey said, earning darks look from around the table.

Dallas surprised the group again by agreeing with Dempsey. "He's right. When I'm wolfed out, I'm damn hard to kill. I heal super-fast. So one, I won't get bit, and two, if I get bit, I'll heal, not die, right?"

Despite the surly hunter's remark, none of the Society had any experience with werewolves getting bitten by a zombie. It was doubly hard to know what would happen since the zombie virus was man made and not supernatural. But Dallas's logic seemed reasonable, which was especially surprising considering its source. Aletia laced her fingers in his and gave a worried nod. With that, the matter was settled.

"I have an idea for the trap," Jonah said. "We take some of those semis we've got circling the place and move them out to the main road. We'll make a wedge, lure the zombies in, and bottleneck them. There aren't many of us, but we'll all head up on top of the trailers with every gun we have. They'll be undead fish in a barrel. We just need to make sure they don't break free."

Lois raised a hand. "I think I can help with that," she said. When Jonah asked how, she leaned over and rubbed her fingers on the diner's worn linoleum floor. Sitting back up, she brought her fingers up to her lips, whispered some strange words, and started to weave her hands in an intricate pattern.

"Hell no!" Dempsey yelled. "No spells!"

He reached for his crossbow, but Aletia grabbed his arm.

"A little trust goes a long ways," she advised.

Dempsey pulled his arm free and Dallas shifted his weight, but both men stopped when Lois looked up at Jonah and said, "Come here, big boy."

The man was standing across the table from Lois. When Lois made her request, his eyes widened in embarrassment. He looked quickly around the table and then asked, "Why?"

Lois smiled. "Come here and I'll tell you," she said playfully.

Jonah took one last look around, shrugged, and stepped forward. At least, he tried to. The leg he intended to move was stuck firmly to the floor. The unexpected development almost cost him his balance, and he waved his arms in wide circles to reclaim it.

"Impressive," he said with a smile. "Ill-advised, though. Let's all agree that surprises are hereby banned to prevent someone's untimely demise."

Lois grinned back. "Agreed. Now, about that spell…"

After releasing Jonah, the group reviewed the plan and went about making preparations. A short time later, Aletia called them all back to the diner.

"All set?" she asked the small group that was about to risk their lives to save the world. When everyone nodded, she held a hand out. One after another, everyone placed their hand in the center of the circle. When the last palm touched the pile, Aletia smiled a tight smile.

"Hear me," she said quietly. "We are the light that keeps shadows at bay. When darkness gathers, we must not fade. Bright, we burn to light the way and never let our brethren stray. Warriors are we with shining blades. When darkness gathers, we will not fade."

The hands separated, and everyone moved to fulfill their part of the plan. Two pairs of hunters took off, intent on making a wide sweep around the sprawling town. Their goal would be to draw as many zombies as possible back toward the main highway that led to Ronnie's. The first pair puttered off in an old Ford Escort. The second pair roared off in Deloris, with Dallas yelling after them that if anything happened to his truck, a giant horde of zombies would be the least of their concerns. Aletia started double-checking the clips of a large pile of guns, Jonah and Dempsey readied themselves for the task of moving the semi's into position, Lois stretched her fingers and flipped through her spell books, and Herb practiced his vampirey equivalent of Kung Fu.

That just left Stanley.

"What the heck am I supposed t-to do?" he asked. "Everyone's d-doing so much stuff. This whole mess is my fault. I n-need to help."

Lois looked up from the book she'd been studying, and Herb's shining eyes turned his way. Dallas abandoned his task of helping Jonah and Dempsey figure out which keys went with which trucks and rejoined his friends.

"You have the most important job of all," Lois said seriously, Herb nodding in agreement.

When Stanley continued to look glum, Dallas slapped his friend on the back. "Clone patrol, little buddy. Once we get 'em into the trap, we'll be bringing back body bits. All our neighbors. All our friends. It's up to you, Stanley. You're gonna run your little wonder clock and bring them back to life. You're going to save the entire town."

A slow smile broke across Stanley's face. "G-gosh, Dallas. That'll make me the Hero of Trappersville, don't ya think?"

Dallas stammered about people getting too big for their britches, and Lois and Herb shared a laugh. The moment of good humor didn't last long, though. Aletia joined their circle and announced that Jonah and Dempsey were going to start moving trucks, and that the moon was about to rise.

"Time to see if we can make this work," she said. "Because if it doesn't, we're probably all going to die."

Chapter 27

*F*OOD! THOUGHT STANLEY. *FINALLY. I'm hungry.*

There were two meals. A middle-aged couple had screeched up in an old Ford hatchback, honked and flashed their headlights, and then started to idle away. Stanley and Laura turned, and the rest of their friends followed, shuffling across the snowy asphalt in pursuit of the slowly receding taillights. Every so often, the car's passenger would lean out of the window, point at her head, and yell things like, "Tasty!" or "Fresh from the noggin!"

Why can't they just stop, then? Stanley grumbled. Being teased like that was infuriating.

"Aaaaallll. Mmmooooosst," Laura moaned, her dislocated jaw turning the words into mush.

"Yaaaaahhhhh," Stanley agreed, giving her crushed fingers a gentle squeeze.

It was a little strange, the car rolling slowly in front of them. They never got closer, but the car never pulled away either. Strange, but not enough to distract him from the important part. Food was so close, only a few yards away. He just needed a little stroke of luck. A flat tire. A busted radiator. A broken axle. Just one little mishap and he'd be able to feast.

Shame there's only two in there, he thought. *Not much to go around.*

As if created by his wistful thought, a second vehicle approached from an intersecting road, trailed by its own collection of zombies. Stanley recognized the truck instantly and watched Deloris pull in alongside the small Ford and match its speed. The two vehicles continued their slow crawl through town and onto Highway Fifty-Five. The two hordes of zombies merged and followed, feet shuffling, hands grasping, throats moaning, and teeth chomping. When a glow appeared in the distance, Stanley smiled. Ronnie's Famous Truck Stop, Grill, and Gift Emporium lit up the horizon like a beacon. The little car and giant truck were definitely going that direction. It was, Stanley realized, perfect. How many times had he shared a meal with his friends at the local truck stop's diner? Ronnie's was a symbol of coming together after traveling vast distances. What better place to finally eat his friends than the place they always went to eat? Fixing his gaze on the chrome testicles hanging from Deloris's trailer hitch, Stanley moved steadily and eagerly forward.

At last, the zombie horde was in the home stretch. Each dragging step brought them closer to the car, to Deloris, to the diner and its reunion dinner. They were so close. If Stanley had been able to feel his face, he was sure he would have felt the warm glow of Ronnie's well-lit sign. His undead friends around him crowded closer, pressing up more firmly against his shoulders and back, their desire to feed feeding his own. He glanced left and right and noticed that semi-trucks had been parked along either side of the road. They made a narrowing chute that emptied into Ronnie's parking lot.

That's so nice, he thought. *Making sure we all get to Ronnie's.*

Suddenly, the Ford pulled ahead and sped off toward the narrow gap between the furthermost semi cabs. Stanley watched its taillights disappear as it made a sharp turn out of sight. Disgruntled, he tried to move his wooden legs more quickly and catch Deloris. The big truck still rolled at a snail's pace, with Stanley, Laura, and the leading edge of zombies just a few yards behind. It threaded the space at the end of the chute and stopped.

This is it! Stanley thought excitedly.

He reached the bumper of the truck and was pressed up hard against it by the mass of undead bodies behind him. He tried to squirm to the side so he could get to the driver's side door, but wasn't able to move. The press of undead flesh against him made moving impossible. He was trying to puzzle out how to get around the truck when a familiar voice called out from above.

"Gestrum nostuul, drothken zoll! Ground beneath, under shoe, hold you fast like sticky glue!"

Lois! he realized. Craning his neck, he peered up and saw her standing high atop one of the semi-trailers.

The witch had her arms splayed wide, her black jacket billowing in an unfelt wind. Herb stood to her side, his fangs glinting and eyes shining. Stanley tried to turn their direction, but something had grabbed onto his feet. He twisted left and right, but neither foot lifted from the asphalt below. Laura mimicked his twisting, but she wasn't able to move either. And while multitudes of bodies still pressed in all around them, they were all clearly stuck in place.

"Heeeeeeeyyyyy," he complained loudly, hoping Lois or Herb would hear, but neither one looked his way.

He was about to call for them again when the gunshots started. Lots and lots of gun shots. Stanley twisted from side to side. No matter what direction he managed to face, the sight was the same. His undead friends were literally losing their minds. Skulls shattered and bodies fell awkwardly, feet still magically glued to the pavement. Some bent at the knees and flopped backward. Others slumped forward, the weight of their bodies snapping bones in their ankles. It was horrible.

Stanley called again for Herb and Lois, imploring them to stop, to just stop. They didn't understand. They weren't in danger. Stanley just wanted them all to be friends. At least, that's what he meant to say, but all that came out was a long strand of shapeless vowels. He turned to Laura, intending to ask her to lend her voice to his, and watched what was left of her beautiful face get blown away by a high-caliber shell.

"Naaaaaaaahhhhh!" he yelled, and Lois heard him.

The witch's eyes widened, and she hopped down from the semi-trailer to the cab's roof before Herb could stop her. Another jump, and she was in Deloris's bed.

"Stanley!" she yelled over the gunshots. "Hang on!"

By this point, Herb had rejoined her. Stanley looked up at his friends, teeth bared in a fierce smile, and stretched his hands toward them. Lois and Herb were clearly arguing, but that was okay. Soon, they wouldn't argue ever again.

Something Lois said finally won Herb over. He gripped her arm and anchored her while she leaned over the gate and reached for Stanley's grasping hands. It was tricky for him to get a grip since there were so many other reaching, grasping hands all around him. Lois had to bat them aside while trying to grab him at the same time. Their fingers brushed, and then he had her. She started to pull, stretching his arm to its limit, but his feet didn't lift off the pavement.

"Crap!" she yelled. "The spell!"

Stanley felt the witch try to release his hand. He felt the pressure lighten, felt her fingers go lax. She was trying to leave him. They were going to leave him again. He clutched harder and brought his other hand up to grab her wrist. He just needed to get one little bite in. One bite, and she'd be his friend again. Then she could bite Herb, and Herb could bite Dallas, and they'd all be friends forever.

Lois's foot slipped. The vampire's grip twisted just enough, and Lois was falling into Stanley's waiting embrace. He wrapped her up in a fierce hug and bit down hard. Her scream was echoed from above by Herb, but soon it dissolved into the hundreds and hundreds of moans filling the air around him.

Something was pummeling him. The blows rained down, battering him from all sides. It was Herb. The vampire had leapt down among the undead and was swinging his fists so fast they were just blurred shapes trying to beat him back. Stanley recoiled from the onslaught and took a step back. The spell was broken, and the zombies surged. Herb was beset by zombie after zombie and fought against a sea of grasping hands and biting teeth. He managed to get an arm around the fallen witch and lift her to her feet, but it was a short-lived victory. Even with his incredible speed and strength, the crush of zombies was too much.

Released from their magical restraints, the zombies were free to press and push and shuffle and shove. They strained against the confines of their cage and reached for the humans perched precariously above on the trailer tops. Their surging rocked the trailers, and people began to fall screaming to the ground. As each one fell, the surrounding undead piled forward, eager to feast.

Stanley started to shoulder his way toward one of the fallen humans when a loud roar sounded from far behind him. He turned in time to see a giant hairy monster arc through the night sky and land in the midst of the zombies. Clawed paws lashed out and sent pieces of undead in every direction as the werewolf snarled and slashed its way forward. Dallas almost made it to where the vampire and witch had fallen, but there were too many zombies for even him to fight through. Stanley saw the werewolf drop to its knees and finally disappear beneath a large pile of undead.

Shots still rang out from all around, but fewer than before, and they continued to dwindle. When the combined strength of the horde finally managed to overturn one of the trailers, the trap failed. Zombies spilled forth like flour from a split sack and filled the parking lot. Stanley and the others pushed through the breach and followed the hastily retreating hunters as they fought their way back to the diner. Stanley knew that this was it. This was the end. It was only a matter of time before the fighting would be done and everyone—everyone—would be friends again.

He felt a pressure on his shoulder pull him to a stop. Turning, he saw that the hand that had stopped him wasn't a hand at all, but a large, clawed paw.

"Hhhhaaaaaaa," the tall, hairy, undead beast moaned, its oddly spaced and bloodshot eyes staring down a gore-covered snout.

"Hhheeeeeyyy," Stanley answered with a smile.

"Uuuuurrrrrr," Dallas growled, pointing over Stanley's shoulder.

Stanley made a slow pivot and immediately saw what Dallas was looking at. The vampire and witch had regained their feet and were wobbling toward them. They forced their broken and twisted bodies forward, shoulder to shoulder, with the rest of the undead. Lois leaned against Herb, one leg so twisted it could barely support her weight. When Stanley and Dallas closed the distance, she moved one hand in the approximation of a wave while holding the vampire's waist with the other. The vampire-turned-zombie opened his mouth in a wide, one-fanged smile. The other had broken off, probably at the same time that something ripped off most of that side of his face. Stanley pulled them into a hug and held them until the reunited friends were caught up in the swell of shuffling bodies around them and pushed forward. As one, they piled up against the barricaded windows of the diner, slapping their bloody palms and chomping their bloody teeth, hungry for the handful of humans that had taken shelter inside.

For the first time since he'd woken up after the fly bite, Stanley felt a genuine warmth inside his cold, stiff body. He didn't know if zombies could cry, and certainly couldn't feel his face well enough to know for certain, but he decided there were happy tears rolling down his undead cheeks.

Chapter 28

"**C**RAPPERS. C-CRAP CRAP CRAP," Stanley muttered, teetering on the verge of hysteria. "C-crap."

Only Aletia, Jonah, and Stanley had survived. All the other hunters were part of the undead mob, either actively beating at the walls and windows or filling the bellies of those trying to force their way inside.

Aletia grabbed Stanley's shoulders and shook him hard. "Keep it together. We'll get through this."

"How?" he wailed. "We're d-doomed."

The sounds from outside underscored the statement, lending his words a dark certainty. The windows rattled behind their plywood reinforcements, and wave after wave of moans broke over the diner like storm-tossed waves over a sinking boat. Stanley paced frantically between the booths and tables. He'd seen his friends fall, and if that wasn't bad enough, had seen them rise again. Being surrounded by zombies was bad. Add a zombie vampire and zombie werewolf to the mix, and things were definitely worse. He wasn't sure about the zombie witch. Spells were probably tough to cast when all Lois could do was stagger around a moan a lot, but who knew? It had been a strange weekend.

"How the heck are they z-zombies?" Stanley asked. "Is that supposed to happen?"

Neither Aletia nor Jonah had an answer for that. They were out of their depth and said as much.

"Oh b-boy, this is bad. So, so b-bad," Stanley muttered, hysteria eroding his fragile self-control.

"Jonah? What do you think?" Aletia asked. "Can we get out of here?"

The large hunter had been peering through a slit between the plywood sheets and reinforcing two-by-fours. He stepped back from his inspection of the hell outside the diner and shook his head.

"I think Stanley may be right," he opined. "I think we're screwed. We thinned the herd before the trap failed, but there are still way too many zombies out there to fight our way through."

"Mierda," Aletia swore. "We can wait it out. More hunters should be on their way."

Jonah shook his head sadly. "If, and that's a big if, anyone gets here before the zombies break in, they're going to have the same problem. If we can't fight our way out, how can we expect them to fight their way in?"

"C-call the Army. The National G-Guard," Stanley suggested. "They got the tanks and the j-jets and really big guns. They can save us," Stanley pleaded.

This time, it was Aletia, shaking her head. "Can't risk it. The more people that come here, the more people are going to get bit and turned. It'll only make things worse."

"Worse," Stanley repeated, shocked. "I d-don't think things could g-get much worse. Oh, crappers. Gotta knock on wood. Don't want to j-jinx us."

Stanley scurried over to a large sheet of plywood spanning one of the diner's plate-glass windows. He gave it a quick knock and then staggered back as the window it was covering shattered and the masses outside smashed up against the wooden board. The plywood creaked, bowed, and snapped, and undead bodies fell face-first into the diner booths lining the wall.

"It g-got worse!" he screamed. "It j-just got a whole lot worse!"

Large hands grabbed him and lifted him away from the growing pile of undead.

"Run!" Jonah screamed. "Grab the alarm clock and run! You have to stay safe!"

The hunter had retrieved his long, heavy club and started to swing. Bodies flew and heads exploded, but the zombies were climbing in faster than he could smash them. Aletia leapt to his side, her blade flashing. Stanley clutched his little plastic alarm clock to his chest and took clumsy steps backward through the diner. When his back hit the countertop, he quickly rolled over it and continued to retreat, pushing his way through the swinging door to the kitchen. Frantic, Stanley ran back and forth between the walk-in cooler and the flattop grill while hungry, inhuman moans boiled the air and made it difficult to breath. There was no escape. The front of the diner was filling up with undead. The back door that led from the kitchen to the back lot rattled and shook under the onslaught of more zombies. There was nowhere to hide. Nowhere to run. Nowhere to go.

Except up.

When he saw the iron ladder in the corner, he did the only thing a man trapped by a zombie horde in a diner kitchen could do. He scaled its rungs toward the ceiling. Stanley had just reached the small access panel at the top when the first zombie lumbered through the swinging door. He screamed and shoved at the panel, terror giving him a strength he'd never known he had. The panel lifted, and a blast of winter air washed over Stanley's tear-streaked face. A moment later, he was on the diner's roof and slamming the access panel shut behind him. A rising wind buffeted him as he ran across the snow-covered rooftop and peered out over the edge.

Zombies. Lots and lots of zombies. He made a slow trek around the diner roof's perimeter, shocked at the sheer number of living dead below. For a small town, Trappersville had made a surprisingly big zombie horde. They pressed against every side of the building. The diner, gift emporium, even the long, low building that housed the rent-by-the-hour cots and showers were all completely surrounded. Ronnie's was an island in an undead sea, and Stanley was its castaway, clinging to a life that was no longer to be measured in years, but in minutes.

"My goodness, this certainly does appear to be the end, doesn't it?" a voice said behind him.

Stanley yelped and spun around. A few feet away, Stanley Prime stood in his colorless single suit, a look of resigned sadness on his face.

"I admire your determination. You've certainly made me proud of myself. However, I do think this has gone far enough. Now, I'll take that," he said, pointing at the alarm clock Stanley still clutched in his trembling hand, "and I'll be on my way."

Stanley was mortified. He glared at his progenitor, a temper he didn't know he had rising to a boil.

"No, you will not," he said. "No sir. These are your friends, your neighbors. Even if you h-haven't been living with them, they've been living with you. You c-can't just let them all go on like this. Especially when we g-gots a way to save them. Every single one."

When Prime raised a skeptical eyebrow, Stanley explained the plan they'd concocted with the Society and how it went horribly wrong when Lois fell to her death and the spell holding the zombies was broken.

"But if we c-can just kill 'em all, we can still save them," he begged. "Maybe your alien friends c-can help. Maybe they c-can, I don't know, fly back and forth with a ray g-gun and zap 'em all."

Prime bowed his head, sadness plain on his narrow, angular face. "The Gerploonkians are here on a science expedition. Researching and cataloguing indigenous life forms. They aren't fighters. They don't have any weapons. If they encounter trouble, they hide. I'm sorry, Stanley. The good people of Trappersville are lost. Every last zombie would need to be killed to stop the spread of the infection. It would take an army to kill them all, and we simply don't have an army."

Stanley Prime was right. There were too many zombies for just the two of them to handle. But there didn't need to just be two of them.

"Can this thing make more of us?" he asked, holding up the clock.

Stanley Prime's eyes widened at the suggestion, and he slowly nodded his head.

"Any limits on how m-many?" Stanley asked.

"... No," Prime answered slowly. "At least, not that I'm aware of. There's certainly never been a need to test that particular scenario."

Stanley hmph'd. "Well, we're g-gonna test it now."

He cast about until he found was he was looking for, an outlet near the rooftop HVAC unit. After plugging in the clock, he popped its plastic cover off and started to poke around its innards.

"Okay, now we j-just need to do... that," he said, "and that. And if this here wire goes over there..."

Stanley Prime leaned in, curiosity piqued. "Actually, it would be better to rerun the black wire, so it creates a loop with the scanner," he offered. "And here, you'll need this to solder the new circuit bridge," he added, passing Stanley a futuristic, pen-shaped tool.

Stanley zapped the suggested circuits, popped the plastic cover back on, set the time, and finally, the alarm.

"One Stanley army c-coming up," he said with a hearty thumbs' up. "Best army ever, and that's a fact."

The twins waited without breathing, the world around them forgotten. For a long moment, all that existed was the little plastic alarm clock. A reliable wonder of plastic and circuitry with a blue liquid crystal display that had woken Stanley every single day since high school, even if he'd been dead.

"It's time," it buzzed.

"It's time," it buzzed.

"It's time," it buzzed.

"It's time," it buzzed.

Stanley after Stanley formed, stood, and joined the growing ranks of their brethren. At first, Stanley rushed frantically back and forth, helping his new clones climb out of their confusion and understand the plan. Once enough Stanleys knew what was going on, they took over orientation for the newly made clones. The first Stanley clone assumed command of the growing army and marched back and forth like a general, yelling encouraging words and readying his troops for the battle to come. As the crowd of Stanleys continued to swell, more of the Stanley started their own stirring speeches, and soon the rooftop was full of stuttering bravado. Prime stood in the middle of it all, awed by how courageous he was. An hour passed, then two. The diner's rooftop wasn't big enough to hold them all, so Stanley after Stanley climbed on to the gift emporium's adjacent roof, and then to the roof over the wing housing the cots and showers. When the sun finally rose, painting the cold grey sky with warm oranges and yellows, there were a thousand and more Stanleys pressed shoulder to shoulder over the entire truck stop. Their stuttering created a din so loud that Prime had to yell to be heard.

"Do you think there are enough of us?" he asked his first clone.

"I sure hope so," the clone yelled back, echoed almost immediately by hundreds more saying the exact same words. "But k-keep 'em coming j-just in case."

Prime chewed his lip nervously. "This is going to be very hard to explain to the Gerploonkians. They were concerned about two of you running around. Now? Oh dear, what will I do with all of these me's?"

The first Stanley clone slapped Prime on the slippery fabric stretched across his back, and ten or more Stanleys repeated the gesture, knocking the man about like a piñata.

"Maybe we c-can start our own bowling league," he suggested.

"Leagues," dozens of nearby Stanleys amended. "Yes sir, we g-gots enough for lots of bowling leagues."

The first clone climbed up on top of the HVAC unit and surveyed his army. A thousand identical faces looked up, eager for what he was about to say next.

"We only g-got one shot at this," he said.

"Only one shot," the thousand Stanleys agreed.

"So let's g-go save our town!"

"Save the t-town!" they all cried.

Stanley after Stanley ran for the rooftop's edge and flung themselves down like rock stars diving into a sea of fans to surf the crowd. Unlike rock stars, when they landed among the zombies, they whacked heads and grabbed throats and poked eyes. The Stanleys picked up rocks and bricks and swung them spastically at anything that moaned or tried to bite them. When one of the Stanleys retrieved a gun, zipping bullets added to the mayhem, but also furthered their cause. Stanley might've been a terrible shot, but there was so much to hit that simple odds were in his favor. Many of the Stanleys fell quickly. Some were chewed to death by the horde of zombies. Others were accidentally felled by their nearby, flailing clones. Only numbers were on their side, but they had lots and lots of numbers. There were two or three Stanleys for each zombie, and slowly the tide turned in their favor.

"I might b-be worth less than a wet fart in a fight," the first clone said to Prime as the battle for Trappersville unfolded beneath them in the truck stop's parking lot, "but when there's lots of wet farts, b-boy oh boy, you'd better watch out."

It was a sloppy, gory, bloody, crazed battle. Zombie after zombie went down beneath the zealous Stanleys and stayed down. After an hour or so, the only Sconnies left standing were the exhausted and ragged clones, their matching velour shirts soaked in the blood of victory. A cheer went up, and Stanley heard his voice holler out from hundreds of throats.

It was done. He'd saved the day, saved the whole town. Heaving a huge sigh of relief, he pulled Stanley Prime into a warm embrace.

"We d-did it!" he sobbed, relief and exhaustion pouring out in a fresh wave of tears.

Prime patted his clone's back and slowly extricated himself from the other Stanley's embrace.

"You, Stanley. Not me. You did this. I've been so blind, only ever thinking of you as a temporary thing, something to be used for my convenience. But you are so much more." The original's eyes misted up as he considered his glitchy copy. "You, my good sir, are a hero. A genuine hero."

A smile split the first clone's face and was matched by the faces of the hundreds of surviving clones.

"I sure am the Hero of T-Trappersville," he announced.

"No, I am," another Stanley said.

"I am," a third protested.

"No way. If there's a hero here, it's d-definitely me," said a fourth.

As hundreds upon hundreds of Stanleys bickered over who best deserved the prestigious title, the first clone winked at Prime.

"Dallas is g-gonna be so jealous."

The Final Chapter

WHERE DO MONSTERS GO when they just want to live their lives?

"Strike! Holy c-camoly, I g-got a strike!" Stanley squealed. "You g-guys saw that, right? You saw it!"

Laura clapped and whistled, and a second Stanley slapped him on the back.

"Sure d-did. That makes two this month!" the second Stanley said. "Boy oh boy, we should b-bring back another c-clone and have our own t-team. We'll give those King P-Pins a run for their money, yes sir."

While Laura planted wet kisses on first one, then the other Stanley, Dallas guffawed. "Fat chance, double-douche. Even if me and Herby replaced you with a drunken badger, the King Pins would still kick your identical asses."

The vampire lifted his arm from Lois's shoulders and gave Dallas a fist-bump as the werewolf strode past. Dallas reached the ball return, picked up his familiar ball, rolled a seven-ten split, and cursed.

"Awww, don't pout," Aletia said. "It makes you look like el niño mimado." When Dallas glowered, she translated. "Spoiled child, mi amor."

The Stanleys settled onto two brightly colored, molded plastic chairs, one on either side of their girlfriend.

"How do you think they're doing, all the other Stanleys?" Laura asked. "You think they're having fun?"

"You bet'cha," the Stanleys said in unison. "The things they're seeing, the stuff they're learning? Wow. It sure must be exciting. But it's b-better being with you."

Laura batted her eyelashes, causing her two boyfriends to blush, and returned her attention to the lane. Dallas had nicked the seven and grumbled his way back to Aletia's side. The hunter playfully poked his ribs while Herb and Lois told him not to feel too bad. Bowling was, after all, a tough game.

The group had made bowling a regular pastime, a chance to settle into their second lease on life and reflect back on the past few months. After Stanley and Stanley Prime had saved the town, they'd spent a full week bringing everyone back to life, one clone at a time. It had been a long, gruesome process that required getting bits of blood or hair or skin from the hundreds and hundreds of dead bodies that littered the parking lot around Ronnie's truck stop. But many hands made might light work. The Stanleys made a bucket brigade of sorts, passing bits of each friend and neighbor up the line to where Stanley Prime waited with the alarm clock. He would scan the DNA, set the alarm, and another Sconnie would wake up gasping and shocked to be alive.

Some of the reunions were truly beautiful. Herb and Lois. Dallas and Aletia. Even Dempsey sniffled a bit and complained that he had an eyelash in his eye when Jonah was brought back. Other reunions were a bit acrimonious, like when Stanley cloned the town's florist, Betty Johannsen and her husband, Kyle. No one knew that Betty didn't really want Kyle back. It had taken three Stanleys to prevent her from killing her husband again, and two more to do some impromptu marriage counseling afterward. For the most part, though, cloning the folks from Trappersville settled into a familiar pattern. People woke up confused, then became terrified by all the Stanleys hovering around them, then reverted to confusion as memories slowly resurfaced, then went right back to being terrified again when they realized they'd been flesh-eating, undead monsters, then finally were overjoyed to realize the nightmare was over.

After the Stanleys had revived the people that had died at Ronnie's, they set out all over the surrounding town to round up everyone else. In some cases, they were accompanied by a revived resident that knew where to find their family or loved ones. Other times, they had to slowly comb the woods or go room by room through house after house. It was a slow process, but infinitely rewarding. Each time they found a finger or a bit of an ear or a piece of a foot, they'd bring it back to the truck stop where Stanley Prime would check to see if it had already been cloned. If not, he'd set the alarm and another neighbor would wake up to their second life.

One of the Stanleys even made a surreptitious trip into the woods outside of Cecil's restaurant, where a decrepit little cabin leaned tiredly in a small clearing. It took a bit of digging to find the grave, but later that afternoon, Fancy Dan ran out of Ronnie's wearing his authentic Domenico Dolce reproduction shirt. Dallas was there, which made for an awkward reunion. The werewolf apologized for eating Dan. Dan apologized for anything and everything he had ever done or might ever do that might upset Dallas. The two men shook hands and agreed that they should probably see as little of each other as possible.

Once the Stanleys had cloned everyone they could find, they set themselves to more humble tasks. A great many homes and buildings had been damaged by the horde. Every project to replace a door or window, mend a broken fence, or right an overturned car had at least two or three extra sets of identical and willing hands. Thanks to the Stanleys, the transformation from horror movie set to sleepy northern Wisconsin town was accomplished far quicker than anyone would have imagined. And during their work, the most amazing thing had happened. No one argued, no one bickered. Everyone was nice to everyone, including Stanley, and not just Midwestern nice. They were genuinely nice, the kind of nice you can only be if you've been turned into a zombie and then saved by the local *Jeopardy* fanatic.

Another surprise was when Kevin reappeared. Four of the Stanleys and Deputy Farman were helping to repair the Get'n'Gobble and get it restocked. They were in the middle of wheeling in cartons of muffins when a large, furry head appeared around the far corner of the building. The Stanleys all immediately started trying to shoo him away, afraid someone would see. Despite their efforts, Farman saw the giant beast and gasped.

"Is that what I think it is?" the sheriff's deputy asked the gathered Stanleys.

"Nope, uh, d-definitely not," two of them replied, while the other two said, "Yeppers. That there's a Sasquatch. His name's K-Kevin."

While the Stanleys glared at each other and asked each other why in the heck they would say that, the deputy walked cautiously over to the large ape-like monster.

"HIYUH," Kevin said politely. "GOT MUFFINSUH?"

Farman opened a package, drew one out with trembling fingers, and held it up. The Sasquatch plucked it gently from his hand, pulled at the paper wrapping, and popped it in his mouth.

"THANKSUH," he said with a wide smile.

One of the Stanleys peeled off from the argument and begged the deputy not to arrest him, but Farman just shushed him.

"Stanley, there's something you have to understand. I've been a monster. Heck, we all have. And when I was, I didn't want to hurt people, not really. Not in a mean way. I guess I was just acting according to my nature. I imagine the same is true for that big fella, and, if what I hear is true, for your friends Herb and Dallas."

Stanley stared into Farman's eyes, looking for a trick or trap, but what he saw was nothing of the sort.

"D-do you think other folks feel the same way?" he asked. "I mean, you think they'll b-be okay with Herby and Dallas and, um, well..." he trailed off.

"All the others," another Stanley chimed in. "Heck, there's all sorts of monsters in the Midwest. And I'll b-bet they'd love to know they can c-come up here and just be, you know, themselves."

Farman had called the sheriff. The sheriff had called the mayor. A town meeting was held, there was a vote, and it was near unanimous. Not a single person in town could claim they hadn't walked a mile in the shoes of a monster, and they all agreed that just being different wasn't any reason not to be welcome. If monsters wanted a place to vacation, or even settle down, Trappersville would greet them with open arms. No eating people, of course, but that went without saying (although the mayor said it anyway, just in case).

Even the Society had agreed to give Trappersville a wide berth. After Aletia, Jonah, Dempsey, and the others had been consulted, they agreed that maybe just killing monsters wasn't the best way to keep folks safe. Maybe, just maybe, it was worth taking the time to learn if a monster was really all that bad. If not, the Society knew of a certain Wisconsin town that was worth a visit.

"And I think my hunting days are done," Aletia had added. "I like this town. I might just stick around."

Dallas had grinned like an idiot and was about to say something stupid when Aletia silenced him with a passionate kiss.

Winter slowly released its grip on the northwoods, and as the snow melted away, the town healed. When all the dust had settled and life was about as close as it would get to being back to normal, there was only one issue left.

"What are we going to do with all of you Stanleys?"

Lois had asked the question one night at Steins. The bar was packed, and about two-thirds of the patrons were identical.

"It does make things a little cumbersome," Stanley Prime had agreed. "Do they get one listing in the phone book, or a few hundred? During elections, do they all have to agree on a candidate, or can they cast their own votes? And what about the census?"

The surrounding Stanleys had argued and bickered about their options, but fell quiet when Prime raised his voice above the din.

"I have a proposition," he had announced. "The Gerploonkians have offered to help. They have countless research teams all over the galaxy and are always looking for lab assistants. Would any of you like to go with them? Visit new worlds, discover new life forms, and solve all the mysteries of the Milky Way?"

Hand after hand, each with identical fingerprints, raised up into the air. After the final count, only two Stanleys wanted to stay, the clone of the one that had been a zombie, and the one that had come up with the plan to save the town. Laura had been ecstatic. She had taken quite a shine to Stanley and proclaimed that two boyfriends were manageable. Two hundred plus boyfriends... not so much.

Over the following week, Stanley after Stanley was teleported up to the yellow spacecraft, and from there sent off to who knows where. When the final one was readying himself to go, he had solemnly shaken his remaining clones' hands.

"You send us recordings of *Jeopardy* and *Judge Judy,* and we'll send p-postcards," he said.

There was a flash of light, and he was gone. In the following months, postcards would magically appear on Stanley's dining room table with the most unexpected selfies. In return, he'd leave a fresh VHS tape in the same spot, and it would be gone the next day.

"Penny for your thoughts?" Laura asked StanOne while StanTwo was bowling.

The clone took a moment to look around the bowling alley. It sure had changed. A witch and vampire bowled with a werewolf and monster hunter. A few lanes down, Fancy Dan was trying to teach Kevin how to roll a hook. Back in the karaoke bar, the faint voice of a siren named Rebecca floated past the saloon-style doors, bringing verses of Fleetwood Mac's *You Can Go Your Own Way* to his ears, and a troll was helping Slow Johnson, the bowling alley's owner, spray shoes with disinfectant. A satyr walked by, complaining that none of the shoes fit his hooves, while his companion, a beautiful pixie, flittered by his ear and scolded him for making excuses for a rotten game. Back in the bar, a goblin was helping Rhonda wash glasses, and two other vampires, a young college couple up for the weekend from Madison, were taking turns putting the whammy on Jimmy Tibeaudeax and making him do all manner of embarrassing things.

"Oh, you know," Stanley said. "Just thinking about how interesting Trappersville is these d-days."

"You bet'cha," another voice agreed.

StanOne turned and saw Herb's old neighbor, Jerry.

"Hey there, Jerry! P-Pam and the girls having fun?" he asked, pointing down the lanes to where Jerry's wife and daughters were squaring off against a gnome named Rufus and two wood sprites whose names no one could pronounce.

"Heck yeah," Jerry said. "Wish I could stay. Can't, though. I have a sales trip tomorrow. Heading up to Massachusetts for a few days. I have to pack and get some samples together."

"Oh, that's a shame," Stanley commiserated.

Jerry nodded. "It's funny. I used to crave putting as many miles between me and Trappersville as I could. Now, though?" The paper salesman shrugged. "Well, it's definitely more interesting around here. But it should still be a nice trip. I'm staying in a town called Innsmouth. They're supposed to have great seafood. Maybe I'll bring back a can of sardines or something."

While the Stanleys and their friends waved, the paper salesman headed toward the door, briefcase swinging at his side.

· · · · · ● · ● · · · ·

AUTHOR'S NOTE

Thank you for reading **Monsters in the Midwest**! I hope you enjoyed your time with Herb, Dallas, Stanley, Lois, and all the rest. Ratings and reviews are always welcome. If you have friends that would enjoy a trip to Trappersville, Wisconsin, I hope you'll show them the way.

Want some more? Check out **Bjorn Again**, a Monsters in the Midwest short story!

· · · · ● · ● · · · ·

If you like paranormal comedy, sign up for my once-a-month newsletter, **The Paranomedy Pint**, and get a FREE short story! Each month, I share a great book to read, a fun show to watch, a tasty drink to drink, and a little paranormal weirdness, too.

· · · · ● · ● · · ·

THE END

Did you have fun?

I HAD A HECK of a good time writing this book. If you enjoyed reading it, I hope you'll take a moment to share a rating or even a review! Ratings and reviews for authors are like tips for bartenders. We love 'em. They also help others who stumble across the book decide if they should give it a try.

Use these QR codes to easily post a review on your preferred site(s):

Amazon

Goodreads

BookBub

Peace, Love, and Zombies

Why are zombies so fond of other zombies?

It's a question that has plagued—pun intended—me for years. Every zombie that I see in the movies or on T.V. looks like terrible company. Seriously. Who would want to spend time with a zombie? The smell. The moaning. Bits of, well, everything eventually rotting and falling off. Gross. Just gross. And yet, zombies love other zombies. Why?

Sometimes, all it takes is a question. You look at something you've been seeing since forever in a slightly different way, and the world shifts. I asked myself why zombies were always hanging with other zombies, and I realized an eloquently simple answer: zombie hordes are judgement free zones. Are you tall or short? Skinny as a bean pole or round as a barrel? A college professor or a grade school kitchen cook? From Wisconsin or not from Wisconsin? Doesn't matter. If you're undead, you're in the club.

Awesome, right? For millennia, humanity has strived for world peace and repeatedly missed the mark. There's always something that inevitably becomes *us* versus *them*. Wouldn't it be nice to set all that aside? To shamble along secure in the knowledge that everyone accepts you just the way you are? Yeah, I think that's zombies, and I think those zombies are pretty cool. When deciding what monster to turn Stanley in to, I had plenty of options, but only one made sense. Stanley likes everyone, and Stanley wants everyone to like each other. Stanley was destined to become a zombie.

Don't get me wrong. I'm glad that he fine folks of Trappersville, Wisconsin got to go back to being their regular old selves and living their regular old lives. I'm glad they'll continue to have their bake sales and bowling tourneys and benders and bar fights. Hopefully, they've learned a thing or two, though. Maybe they'll be a bit slower to anger, a bit quicker to forgive. Maybe they'll realize that, deep down, we have much more in common than we realize. That we're not so different after all.

Maybe the rest of us will learn that lesson, too. We can if we try. It won't be easy, but it's worth it.

And if you want to speed things up a bit, just hold out your arm the next time a fly is buzzing around.

A Bit About Scott

People say you should write what you know. That's damned good advice, so Scott writes about ordinary Midwesterners making an extraordinary mess of things. Hey, if the flannel fits...

Oh, one more thing. "Ordinary" totally includes vampires, werewolves, zombies, witches, shapeshifters, aliens and more!

Find Scott on:

www.swbauthorblog.wordpress.com

www.facebook.com/swbuthor

www.instagram.com/swbauthor

www.goodreads.com/swbauthor

www.bookbub.com/authors/scott-burtness

... and in bars and bowling alleys up in the Midwest.

FREE Short Story

Beer-Fueled Urban Fantasy by Scott Burtness

THE MISADVENTURES OF A PARANORMAL
POST-RELATIONSHIP PERSONAL EFFECTS
REPOSSESSION SPECIALIST

An Oracle Walks into a Bar

A Scarecrow Wins an Award

A Siren Sings Her Heart Out

MONSTERS IN THE MIDWEST

Wisconsin Vamp

Northwoods Wolfman

Undead Cheesehead

Monsters in the Midwest: The Complete Trilogy

Bjørn Again: A Monsters in the Midwest short story

ODDS 'n' ENDS

A is for All the Monsters We Can't Stand: A Hilarious Mon-
ster-Themed Coloring Book for Grownups

Story and poems by Scott Burtness | Illustrations by Harold Torres